DAUGHTERS OF KERALA

Twenty-Five Short Stories by
Award-Winning Authors

Translated from the Malayalam
by Achamma C. Chandersekaran

Introduction by
R. E. Asher

Daughters of Kerala: Twenty-Five Short Stories by Award-Winning Authors

Published by Hats Off Books®
610 East Delano Street, Suite 104
Tucson, Arizona 85705 U.S.A.
www.hatsoffbooks.com

Publisher's Cataloging-in-Publication
(Provided by Quality Books, Inc.)

Daughters of Kerala : 25 short stories by award-winning
   authors / translated from the Malayalam by Achamma C.
   Chandersekaran ; introduction by R.E. Asher.
      p. cm.
      LCCN 2004111000
      ISBN-10 1-58736-377-1
      ISBN-13 978-1-58736-377-1

      1. Short stories, Malayalam--Translations into
   English. 2. Women--India--Kerala--Fiction.
   3. Malayalam fiction--20th century--Translations into
   English.   I. Chandersekaran, Achamma C. (Achamma
   Coilparampil) II. Asher, R. E.

PL4718.82.E52D38 2004   894'.81230108071
                     QBI04-200369

rev201102

To honor and remember my beloved mother,
the first, and for many years the only, woman in our village
to hold a job outside the home. She taught primary school.

CONTENTS

Foreword...vii
Preface xi
Preface to Second Edition..xiii

In the Shroud, Lalithambika Antharjanam (1931)................................. 1
Underling, K. Saraswathyamma (1945) 11
Female Intellect, K. Saraswathyamma (1948) 21
The Devil's Jacket, Karoor (1959)..29
A Rented House, Sachidanandan (1960) 35
The Daughter of Man, Lalithambika Antharjanam (1962) 48
Wooden Dolls, Karoor (1963)...54
The Dawn of Enlightenment, M. P. Sahib (1969)................................62
The Lullaby of Dreams, Martin Eresseril (1974)................................ 68
Rosemary, K. L. Mohana Varma (1988)... 78
Sandalwood for the Funeral Pyre, Madhavikutty (1991)....................85
Fraction, Gracy (1993) 90
Arya Reborn, Chandramathy (1993)..92
When a Star Is Falling, Gracy (1993)..100
When Big Trees Fall, N. S. Madhavan (1993) 102
Baby Doll, Gracy (1993) 114
Amma, Johnny Plathottam (1994) 117
Nerchakkottan, Moidu Vanimel (1995) 121
The Lies My Mother Told Me, Ashita (1996) 126
One Still Picture Cannot Capture a Life's Story,
    Gita Hiranyan (1997) 130
Ghare Baire, Gita Hiranyan (1998) 143
A Rest House for Travelers, Sara Thomas (1998) 151
The Riddles in Life, Asha Krishnan (1999)...................................... 167
A Love Story, N. S. Madhavan (2000) 177
A Dream from Israel, Sarah Thomas (2001) 189

About the Authors 201

FOREWORD

Two aspects of the beginnings of prose fiction in Malayalam are perhaps significant in the context of this collection. Firstly, the earliest Malayalam novel to merit being considered a classic, O. Chandu Menon's *Indulekha* (1889), has a well-educated, intelligent, witty, and self-assured young woman as its clearly central character. She is well grounded in Sanskrit, English, and music, and is portrayed as being worthy of admiration for her "mental attainments and amiability of character." Second, the first novel set in Kerala to be published in Malayalam was written by a woman. It is true that the author, a Mrs. Collins, wife of an English missionary stationed in Kottayam, was not a Malayalee, and the posthumously published version of her story (1878) was a translation from English. Yet these two factors were an indication of the way that prose fiction was to develop in Malayalam, with female authors making a major contribution and with fascinating female characters being created by both male and female writers. Both works also anticipate future trends in Malayalam prose fiction by containing elements of social criticism.

The history of the short story in southwest India, at a little over a century in duration, is almost as long as that of the novel. From its earliest years, women have made a significant contribution to its development. An important element in this is the fact that for as long as information on the subject has been available, the level of literacy in Kerala has been the highest in the subcontinent, and even at a time when girls in all sections of society were not routinely given an education, the percentage who could read and write was relatively high in comparison with any other region in South Asia. Even in the late nineteenth century, Indulekha's intellectual attainments were quite believable. Since the birth of the Malayalam short story, it is estimated that between two and three thousand stories by women authors have been published.

It would therefore have been possible to produce an anthology selected from these alone. Happily, this has not been done in this collection, for this would provide a very incomplete picture of the women and girls who populate Malayalam fiction. To restrict the choice on the basis of a theme, however, was a laudable inspiration, for in this way each story contributes to the understanding and appreciation of all the others. In terms of the time span of the dates of appearance of the stories, they cover some 70 years. The range of experience of the score of authors was gained over an even longer period, for their years of birth fall in every decade from the 1890s to the 1970s.

The chosen theme, that of the girls and women of Kerala during the twentieth century, not only gives unity to the volume, but also allows much variety. Taken together, the 25 stories in the collection could almost form a historical document showing what it could mean to be a daughter of Kerala at different times over the last hundred years, for it must be allowed that there is much truth and many truths in the best fiction, however imaginative.

Though the authors do not necessarily set their stories in their own communities, the reader is reminded, both by the names of the authors and by the events they relate, that Kerala has long been the home of three major religions, each substantially represented among the population. There is a recollection, too, of the former Jewish community in Cochin.

Kerala, linguistically the most homogeneous of all Indian states, is the home of the majority of the world's speakers of Malayalam, but Malayalees, perhaps because of their strong educational background, have had a tendency to disperse in hard times in search of a better living, and we read in this book of Malayalee women elsewhere in India—in Bombay and Calcutta, for example, with one member of a Christian order heading a convent in Meerut, to the south of Delhi. A feature of the late twentieth century is illustrated by husbands employed in the Gulf States.

Not infrequently a writer will draw attention to disadvantages suffered by female members of society, a feature that, unsurprisingly, tends to be more common in stories by women writers. Sometimes an author will speak directly to the reader, sometimes she will express criticism of social norms through the mouth of one of her characters, and sometimes the development of the plot will indicate a need for reform. The nature of the abuses signaled will often depend on the period when a story was written. In the first half of the last century, we find a man taking as many as four wives, the fourth inevitably being much younger than her husband. In the second half of the century, there is a recurrent theme of the effects of a husband's neglect of his wife, whether by his having a job in faraway places, or by his being too preoccupied with his interests or career to find time either for his spouse or his family. In all periods there are depictions of the ways in which a man can take selfish advantage of a woman.

It is clear from this that a full appreciation of these stories demands a certain historical perspective, in that neither the description of conditions that prevailed at the time of writing nor the opinions expressed or implied by the authors are necessarily applicable to the present day. This is, of course, true in the case of another recurrent theme in the book: that of the education of women, which for good reason remained of interest to creative writers throughout the period covered, despite the relatively favorable position enjoyed by women in Kerala. In the cases where this theme is taken up, we find two principal strands. One is that of the real need for a woman to have the benefit of schooling—illustrated by the story of a Muslim woman who makes sure that her daughter can read, with a view to avoiding the hazards she herself has experienced, of having a male take hold of her hand when a signature or thumbprint is needed by the postman. The other strand is an argument about the prevalent attitude that education is more of an adornment as far as a woman is concerned, and at most a passport to marriage or a means of earning a living, rather than a way of ensuring her real independence or developing her true potential as a human being.

While prose fiction in Malayalam has almost from the start had an element of social criticism, sometimes spasmodic, sometimes quite dominant, this is far from being a universal characteristic of the short story. This collection therefore contains, along with stories of a campaigning sort, examples both of straightforward well-told narratives and of studies of human behavior and psychology. The various categories are not, of course, mutually exclusive. The young woman who is forced to become a man's fourth wife, for instance—a situation that the writer clearly finds unacceptable—is shown as suffering from the guilt of having loved another man before her marriage. Love that is not returned or love that, for social reasons, cannot be fulfilled is indeed a recurrent topic that allows for many variations.

Some of the problems of human relationships have as their setting the upper reaches of society; others are among the less privileged. The potential problems associated with socially unequal relationships, too, are touched on, often in the context of the more fortunately placed asserting their superiority.

Linked with some of this range of themes are studies of intellectual underdevelopment or mental derangement. As an indication of the variety that all this implies, the stories are presented on a loose thematic basis. Some readers will reflect on whether this corresponds to their own classification, for the multifaceted character of several of the stories means that other arrangements might be feasible. Other readers will be content to savor each story separately. Either way, they should gain a clear impression of all that being a daughter of Kerala might mean. They will also see something of the universality of human feelings and behavior, whatever one's origins.

The pages that follow contain examples of the work of authors whose writings have already achieved the status of modern classics in Malayalam, such as Karoor Nilakanta Pillai and Lalithambika Antharjanam. Some of the great names of twentieth-century Malayalam prose fiction are nevertheless absent from this collection, among them Vaikom Muhammed Basheer (1908–1994), Thakazhi Sivasankara Pillai (1912–1999), O. V. Vijayan (b. 1931), and M. T. Vasudevan Nair (b. 1933)—and two who are mentioned in one of the stories, P. Kesava Dev (1904–1983) and S. K. Pottekkat (1913–1982), all of whom have contributed significantly to the development of the short story. This, however, is not to be seen as a disadvantage, for it helps to show even more clearly Kerala's great wealth of talent in the field of short fiction and the richness of modern Malayalam literature. This book will, I believe, whet the reader's appetite.

At the personal level, I am happy to have been granted this opportunity of being associated in a small way with this very worthwhile project of a daughter of Kerala whom I have known for half of my lifetime.

R. E. Asher
June 10, 2004

PREFACE

Reading Malayalam literature, after a lapse of many years to prepare a presentation for the Second World Malayalam Conference held in Washington, D.C. in 1985, made me appreciate the beauty of the language and the thematic variations.

People who do not read Malayalam can recognize this beauty, at least partially, only through translation. The translation work Dr. R. E. Asher and I did for the UNESCO Program of Representative Works, of three novellas by the late Vaikom Muhammad Basheer, published under the title *Me Grandad 'ad an Elephant*, was well received in India and elsewhere. That was an incentive for me to undertake this project. Malayalam writers and Kerala culture have to pass through translation before they can be presented to the world. That is what this book is about.

This volume contains 25 stories about women in many different situations, within a time span of 70 years. The earlier stories reflect the many difficulties women faced. Times have changed and today some of those stories seem unreal. Stories written in the 1980s and 1990s show how women struggle to get out of the constraints society has kept them under and reach their potential. They are all touching stories. I hope you enjoy reading them as much as I enjoyed translating them.

There are many people who helped me bring this book out. Some of the names have to be mentioned—Advocate Jacob Arakal, who did most of the legwork for me in Kerala, Dr. R. E. Asher, who has kindly written the foreword, Mr. Kenneth C. Mahieu, who spent many hours reading the stories and commenting on them, Ms. Savitha Pal, who provided the beautifully designed book cover, Dr. M. G. Sasibhushan, Sreemathy Sugathakumari, my son Ashok Chander, my friend Shirley Bornstein, and Mr. Mathew Cheepinkal. I could not have accomplished this without the help and encouragement of my husband, C. S. Chandersekaran. I thank them all for their help and support.

Achamma Coilparampil Chandersekaran
June 10, 2004

Map of Kerala

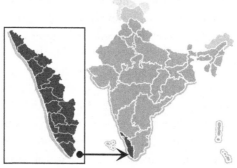

Preface to Second Edition

Reading some of the comments by reviewers of *Daughters of Kerala*, I realized that the stories presented in chronological order will make it easier to observe the "cultural evolution" and "progression of women" mentioned in the reviews. Dr. MV Pillai remarked, "This literary feat illustrates the cultural evolution of a populace, elegantly presented with finesse"; Gita Bhatia said, "The stories depict the progression of women from burdensome and rigid social mores to a more open society that exerts different pressures." Dr. Braj Kachru remarked, "The collection provides a **touching chronicle of the contexts of women's experiences, frustrations, and struggles in the changing social order of that exciting part of India.**"

Other than the order in which the stories are presented there is no change in this edition from the original. I present this edition with the hope that readers will better appreciate the evolution of women's life in Kerala.

Achamma Coilparampil Chandersekaran
November 2, 2010

IN THE SHROUD
Lalithambika Antharjanam

The new fabric was very thick. There was not the slightest hint through the thick material what kind of a figure it covered—young, old, ugly, charming, or slender. Underneath, it was sleeping peacefully on a bed of dry grass. The surrounding pitch darkness was given a change in hue by an oil lamp burning nearby.

The silence was deafening. However sad one might have felt, no one disturbed the quietness even by a sigh.

She did not see the world when she was alive. She did not like the din and clamor. However loud her heartbeats were, they were muffled so as not to be heard. That being the case, why were we troubling her with this show of kindness that was not requested, in these last moments?

Peace, tranquility, relief.

Whatever she did not enjoy in life, she has now. But cruelty could not make her cry anymore. Rebuke would not hurt her. Authority would not suffocate her. Peace and liberation from all problems. Sleep, my sister. For the first time, sleep peacefully!

In the next room, some people were whispering. Sighs, which didn't really come from the heart, could be heard. A custom they had to follow. In life she did not hear one kind word. Now they were trying to praise her. "Pappy is lucky. She died when she still had the thali[1] on."

The sound of a tree being cut down could be heard. They had already finished digging for the funeral pyre. Everyone was trying to get things done for the cremation, as if a big burden had been lifted, similar to the sense of quietness in a house when a girl's wedding was over.

Why was I the only one feeling so upset? Who was this woman to me, she who has died and been set free? She was no one, just a neighbor, an acquaintance. I think we were distant relatives also. Was it only the family ties that will relate two people? How about the relationship of one who got to know the inner secrets of another? If that forms a relationship,

---

1 The wedding chain or string tied around the neck of the bride by the bridegroom. A widow is supposed to break it off.

there was no one who was a closer relative of her than I. But who knows that except the two of us, and now just me?

She fully opened her tender heart to me. She showed me the deep cuts, burns, and wounds, and the sweet but painful memories that were hiding in them that no one else knew. My dear sister, you must pardon me. I do not have your permission to reveal them. But, just let me remember that painful history that came through the numerous emotions of your broken heart. It will not, in any way, hurt your soul—it will only raise it to a pure and sacred environment.

Women's hearts have great secrets that even the funeral fire cannot bring to light.

Under the rules of religion, community, and even fate, they live a life where they cry without tears and live without breathing. Like a volcano that does not emit smoke, the explosions are within.

A simple-minded, half-crazy girl! Who knew there was a revolt working within her? As a result of that she died so young. Pappy had not seen her 25th birthday.

She had been ushered into the kitchen yard in the middle of the monsoon season. There had been no decorations or boisterous noise to welcome her; not even the traditional lit oil lamp. When the old Namputhiri[2] who had gone to Thirunavai came back with a fourth wife, all that greeted her were three angry faces, in addition to the music provided by rain, thunder, and lighting.

Selfishness is natural to every human being—man or woman, young or old, everyone submits to it. So the women cannot be blamed. The older women naturally were scared because the new wife was pretty and young. Is there any reason to think that this 60-year-old man would not surrender to the new bride?

Somehow, things went just the opposite. Pappy did not pay any attention to her husband. She did not take care of him or even go near him. If he called her she would not say a word. He scolded her, advised her, and even punished her—with no results. People started whispering, "She is an awful girl. He may be old and ugly. But he is her husband, her god for this life. Then why doesn't she love him and worship him? Why doesn't she compete for his affection?"

Thousands of questions waited for her answers. But Pappy spoke to no one. She didn't want to find out anything from anyone either. At daybreak, she took her bath and then went into the kitchen and toiled there till midnight. She did not comb her hair nor put the caste mark on

---

2   A member of the Kerala Brahmin community.

her forehead. No one saw her smile. Was this any way for a new bride to act?

The older wives complained to one another indignantly, "She is such a useless woman. Don't know where he found her."

She could easily have gotten her way with her husband and paid back the other wives. But Pappy did not want to do that. She detested his looks, voice, and nearness.

Sometimes she stood for a long time with a far-away look, as if dreaming about something that was lost and could not be found. Other times, she just sat there with the cooking spoon in her hand, lost in thought.

On bright, starry nights, she sat by the jasmine bed in the front yard looking at the stars, sobbing as if her heart was breaking. Why did she cry? Who knows? It seemed that her life was in an imaginary world, far away from her surroundings. No one knew if there was someone to join her there.

Word spread that the new bride of the illam[3] was crazy. In the beginning, I thought so too. But I remember that day, that memorable day she opened the curtain and showed me the clear, pitiful picture of a great secret. Since then, I have thought about it many times, and will always. She was carrying a heavy burden by herself. It was a conflict between yearning and customs, a clash between emotions and principles—the eternal conflict between right and wrong in a woman's heart. She did not fail, but she did not succeed either. That battle made her a mad woman. No, the mad world misunderstood her, made her silent and apathetic. It pushed her out of life itself. That day, without realizing it, she put part of that burden on my shoulders. Now that unbearable weight is completely on my shoulders. She has left the nest and flown, free from everything, into eternity.

What a night it was! Sivaratri,[4] the holy night when peaceful and sacred emotions are sown into the hearts of Siva devotees. People who fast that day get together in temples or homes and stay awake, singing hymns, reciting prayers, and gossiping.

That night, the meeting of the Antharjanam[5] Society was in her illam. Usually, I had no interest in such societies. But for appearance's sake I had no choice but to attend.

---

3   House of a Namputhiri.

4   Siva's night, in commemoration of Lord Siva subduing the destructive arrow launched by Lord Vishnu in his dispute with Lord Brahma. It is believed that those who stay awake and pray through the night will join Lord Siva after death.

5   Namputhiri women.

Also, from their unending conversations I could pick up information on several broken relationships in the women's quarters.

The conversations went on late into the night. The night was peaceful. I looked out and saw nature standing like a woman all covered in a shroud of pitch darkness. The cold wind blew with the strong smell of the kuvala[6] flower. From the temple came the sound of fire works and the conch. In the tumult of the temple festival, people cried out, "Hara! Hara! Mahadeva![7]"

As if in response to that came the tired voice of a woman who had been fasting the whole day:

"I was born a human into this world
In the midst of a sea of suffering
O Lord, get me out of this hell!"

What a depressing song! I must have heard this song a thousand times. There is nothing new in that. But on this darkest of nights, it had a special power and added meaning as it came from a starving, tortured woman. For how many generations have women sung this song, but to what end?

I hummed the song, changing the words to "We will get out of this hell" and walked around in the yard, deep in thought. Suddenly I heard a cry and looked around. In the dim light of the night, I saw a woman sitting by the jasmine bed with her head bowed. I realized that it was her–that crazy young woman who never smiled nor spoke. Some inner voice made me walk towards her.

She was in her dream world, deep in thought. Some intense disappointment must have affected her deeply. I felt sorry for her and wondered if she was really crazy. That disappointment must have made her go crazy.

"Pappy," putting my hand on her shoulder, I called her tenderly. She startled at this unexpected touch and got up quickly.

"Who are you? Oh, you, Edathy![8] I didn't expect you at all."

She was surprised. I had not spoken to her before. No one had.

"Why did you come here in this pitch dark, all by yourself?" she asked.

"Why are you sitting here in this pitch dark, all by yourself?" I didn't let her get away with her question.

---

6   A sacred medicinal tree.

7   Siva.

8   Elder sister.

"Me? I ... this is my usual practice. Today ..." She was lost for words. "I like to sit by myself."

"Well, it is my usual practice to wipe away tears if I see anyone cry-ing."

"Who are we to try to take away someone's pain? Everyone has to endure whatever is destined for her."

"That is our misunderstanding," I said. "We forget that destiny is what we make of it ourselves. We can change and rewrite it. Talk to me about your sorrow, however big it may be. Pappy, any problem is reduced when you share it with someone."

She lifted her face suspiciously and looked at me, quietly checking to see if I liked her or she could trust me.

That face was beautiful, though it was flushed, her eyes were red, and her hair unkempt.

"Pappy," I called her with excitement. "Would you tell me the truth? You are not crazy, are you?"

"No, I am not crazy," she confirmed, "I have never been crazy."

"Then why do you act like one before others?"

"I don't know. Why do others treat me like that?"

"That is because you cry all the time, and you don't love your hus-band."

"Husband? Oh, husband." She shuddered again. "Who is my husband?"

"The man you married, with fire as the witness. Isn't that the custom in our community?"

Pappy didn't say anything for a long time. I could feel that some deep mental anguish was making her tremble. A sigh came out as if some storm inside was slowly released. Slowly I caressed her back and said, "Don't cry, Pappy. If you don't like it, I won't ask you anything. I won't even stay here. But you shouldn't cry."

"It is not like that, Edathy. I want to talk about it. I will talk about it." She had made up her mind and continued, "Isn't it sinful for a woman who has touched a man to become the wife of another man? Isn't it immoral?"

I was taken aback. What a question! No one has heard of a Nam-puthiri girl asking such a question ever before. Wasn't it a sin for a virgin who had not only seen, but also touched a man, to become the wife of another? Isn't she breaking moral codes? Sacred hymns, customs, and priests will undoubtedly declare her, along with him, outcasts. I didn't have a response. Her long wait was futile. Then she said, "That's what I said, Edathy. That is my fate, my destiny! I will tell you that story." She sighed again.

Like today, it was a Sivarathri. At illam both my mother and I were fasting. My father went to the temple and Apfan[9] went to his wife's house. It was a big festival day at the Siva temple and even the neighbors were there. Amma[10] was inside on her knees, reciting prayers, staying awake. From the kitchen, you could hear the servant reciting her prayers. It was very hot inside and I opened the door and came out to the yard because I couldn't sleep. Through the banana trees and the coconut palms, I could see the light of the fireworks and illumination and hear the indistinct voices of the crowd at the temple.

I sat at one end of the jasmine bed and looked towards the temple, as we used to do when we were young. Don't ask me whom I mean by "we." If you examine the dreams of unmarried girls, they themselves will be scared. Some vague wishes, body shapes, and expectations! I was deep in thought about all these. Suddenly, I heard footsteps behind me. I got up frightened, as I did when you came today. It must be Achhan[11] or Amma, I thought. I turned around, ready to be scolded. Surprise! It was someone else. Even in darkness we recognize some people. It was a man. A man I knew.

I think he was also embarrassed at the unexpected meeting. For a moment our eyes met. I was about to run inside, scared, but my legs froze. After being silent for a short while, he called me, "Pappy!"

Oh, that voice! I have never heard anyone calling me like that in all my life! Such an affectionate tone, a call from the heart! "Pappy, you have forgotten me, haven't you? You are angry at me."

What could I say? I forgot? How could I forget my Kunjettan? My playmate? My father's nephew? We grew up together, playing together. We went to school together. Those days we used to even pinch and beat each other. I had no complaints, because I have heard Amma say, "Kuttan[12] is going to marry Pappy." A wife has to put up with the husband's beatings. It was a pleasure. Those good old days passed. After oathuchollal,[13] he went somewhere far for higher studies. I attained puberty and was closed up in the kitchen. We were seeing each other for the first time in five years.

During the day, when Achhan said, "Pappy, make some coffee for Kuttan,"

---

9   Father's younger brother.

10   Mother.

11   Father.

12   Pet name for a boy.

13   Ceremony for a boy indicating puberty.

I forgot that I was tired from fasting. How long I stood there forgetting myself, looking at the man I waited so long to see! After being apart for five long years, he was asking me unkindly, "Have you forgotten me?" I couldn't control my tears!

"Who is the one who forgot?"

The emotional tone of my question showed him that I was upset. If he wanted, he could have come every now and then. He is a man. Men can do whatever they want, they can go wherever they want.

Coming closer to me, he continued with a sweet smile, "How can I forget you? It is easier to forget myself. No, Pappy, we do not have the strength to forget each other and we never will."

"Then, for so long..." I burst into tears. He couldn't bear it. He might have thought that I would fall down, anyway, he held me up. It might be because I was shaking that he caressed me. But, Edathy, I could not push him away. I was powerless.

Leaning on him, I cried to my heart content for a long while. Some teardrops fell on my head too.

Edathy, sometimes we forget ourselves. When he lifted my face I didn't object. How many stars were looking down at us from above? The heaven and earth were witnesses. That face bent down to mine. We kissed.

When we were little, we have kissed without fear. Realizing the circumstances, I struggled out of his hold and ran into the house. A meeting between a Namputhiri girl who has attained puberty and a young man was unimaginable. If someone found out, anything could happen. My God! My fear made my heart beat fast and my body shudder. Was Amma awake?

In the prayer room, the lamps were burning dimly. Through the flowers I had used to adorn the picture of Parvathi Devi,[14] I could see the holy statue of Siva. Doesn't he know what is going on?

Like a child who had done wrong, trembling with fear, I bowed down before the deity and prayed: "Forgive me dear Lord, for what I did. Please don't let anyone find out!" I don't know how long I stayed that way. I knew it was morning only when Amma came and woke me up.

Kunjettan left early in the morning. I haven't seen him after that and no one ever found out about our meeting. But that incident, that moment! I live only for that memory. That memory consoles me and makes me act crazy.

---

14 Siva's consort.

She stopped talking.

Two bees flew from inside the jasmine bush, buzzing. A few flowers fell in the light wind. On a dead tree nearby, a pair of birds was having an argument.

"After that day, he didn't come back and no one proposed you as a bride for him, right?" I asked.

"No, Edathy, there was no opportunity for that. That is what I said, it is my fate.

After that day, I didn't hear anything about him for a long time. One day I heard Achhan telling someone, "That accursed Kuttan has cut his kudummy,[15] eats with all castes, and has joined the Congress Party. Now he is in jail." Then I realized why he had not come. Would Achhan marry me to one who is driven out of the community?

Many proposals came for me, but the amount of dowry and the status of the family didn't match. I was scared all the time. If I am given away to someone else, how will I look at his face? How will I hold his hand? Before that happens, oh, God, take my life away!

To add to my misfortune, suddenly, Achhan died. Apfan had no time for us after taking care of things at his wife's house. All of Amma's tears and pleadings about my marriage didn't do any good. I had the hope that when he came out of jail, he would think of me. I was ready to give up everything and elope with him, if only we could meet. But, what can I say? One day, Apfan went to Thirunavai but came back unexpectedly at midnight. There was an old man with him whom we considered a guest. At daybreak, when Amma came with the ring and henna, the truth came out. I had no way out. I didn't have time to run away or commit suicide.

So it happened, the marriage took place with out any challenge. They burned my tender heart, all its hopes and the dead body of my life in that smoking fire before which we were sitting. But I didn't cry, didn't say a word. I didn't even sigh, but sat there like granite and went through the short ceremony. When the old man took my hand with his skinny hand Apfan boasted, "Who can find a groom for 500 rupees these days, except me?"

But I was not defiled. The old man was not as strong as I. This pretence of being crazy saved me. Still, try as I might, I cannot get that night and that man out of my mind! Isn't it a sin for a married woman to think of another man? Isn't it being unfaithful?

---

15   Tuft of hair denoting caste.

Like a lawyer looking anxiously at the judge after pleading his case, she looked at me. What could I say?

"Morality is man's rule, dear, always and everywhere. We don't have the right to question that. But, if thinking about that incident, even that man, will cool your wounded heart, it is not wrong. But I don't think it is right for you to stay here, considering the situation. Go back to your house. Just forget about this marriage. Do as you like."

The morning star shone through the cloudy sky in the east. Somewhere far away, a cock crowed. People coming from the temple were talking and laughing along the pathway nearby. It was getting to be daybreak. We got up.

Before long, Pappy went to her mother's house. I was happy to hear that she became all right there and was doing well. Let her wounded heart find some peace at least that way!

Five or six years went by. As far as I was concerned, they were demanding years. In a woman's life, the time between the age of 16 and 30 is most important. During that period, it is her responsibility to cooperate with nature in the creation and nurturing of the future generation. In that busy life, I had forgotten about Pappy and her sad life.

One evening, I was in my room busy writing when the servant girl came to the door and said, "Pappy Kunjathal[16] has come back. She is very sick. It would be nice if you go and visit her."

I was surprised. She had come back after a long time. What was the reason for coming back after so long, in this condition? I wondered. I learned that Pappy's ailment was a peculiar one. She did not eat anything or take any medicine. She didn't even get up from bed. She was adamant, "I just want to die, and die in my house." So she was brought here, though she was just skin and bones, in a rowboat. Why was she anxious to come back to the house she had given up forever, at the end of her life?

Pappy was lying in a dark room. Outside the room some women were talking softly, "At the most she will live till tonight; not beyond that, for sure."

Wiping tears from my eyes, I sat on her bed, took her skinny, long hand and placed it to my chest. I called her softly, "Pappy!"

She opened her eyes and gave me a pitiful look. "Edathy!" she said. Her voice cracked. We both cried—like two sisters.

16 A term to show respect.

"Your illness is not too bad, Pappy. You will get better in a few days." I tried to pacify her.

"You are right, Edathy! It will be over soon. I came back to see you all before that, one last time," she said unflinchingly. "I am not sorry. Isn't it better to die and then live rather than live and die inch by inch?"

We had something very important to talk about. But I didn't have the nerve to ask her, nor she to start. After being silent for a few minutes, she continued in great distress, "I saw him again—that Congress Party worker, that community leader, that man I waited for so long. He did the required penance to get back in the community and married Apfan's daughter. Every night, they walk in the front garden. They sing and laugh. What love and happiness! I couldn't accept that, Edathy. I won't die there. This is my home. My husband is here, isn't he?"

Who is her husband?

She said that she had fallen at the feet of the old man and tearfully asked for forgiveness, "Forgive me all my wrongdoing. Give me happiness at least in my next life." He also burst out crying.

That way, her soul attained unimaginable peace and tranquility.

Don't touch that shroud. Don't look that way or disturb her even with a sigh. Let that poor girl sleep peacefully, undisturbed!

UNDERLING
K. Saraswathyamma

Paruamma sat still, unaware that the rice had boiled over and put out the fire. On her right hung a screen made of palm leaves. If she turned her head and looked through the large hole in the screen, she could see what was happening in the house across the street. Paruamma knew everything in the house: the number of rooms, where the kitchen was located, and how the bathroom was designed. Once in a while, when someone cames to stay there, Paruamma's thoughts went back to her youth. Then she couldn't think of anything else but that.

Today there is big commotion in that house. The Commissioner of Devaswam,[1] who is on tour, is staying there, along with his two daughters.

Those working there have divided up the chores to please the commissioner in every way. The duty that falls on Paruamma as charwoman employed to clean the temple was...

Paruamma still shudders whenever she remembers what happened that morning long ago.

For the past two days, Paruamma's daughter, Lakshmikutty, had tidied up the temple and yard instead of her mother because of the mother's severe arthritis. This morning her mother had gotten up only at ten.

She was sitting in the sun rubbing her knee when Srikaryakar showed up. With no introduction, he told her the purpose of his visit.

Paruamma was tongue-tied for a while. It was the commissioner's demand, and if they didn't comply? No one questioned whether the demand was fair or not. Sri wasn't stupid enough to say that it was his idea to please the commissioner.

Seeing Paruamma's silence, Sri said, "You mustn't think too much about it this time. The commissioner's good will is not a small thing. Many favors can come out of it. The driver said that wherever he goes he gets his wish. If that is so and we don't comply, think of the consequences.

---

1   Temple property.

Someone will tell him that you were the one who prevented it. You won't be able to bear what happens after that."

Paruamma slowly found her voice. "Suppose Lakshmikutty were your sister?"

He was furious. He screamed with arrogance, "Is that bastard like my sister?" That response made Paruamma realize that she could not coax him into changing his mind.

When Sri realized that she was conceding, he said calmly, "I will send Lakshmikutty home early. After worshipping in the temple, the commissioner will leave his daughters there and come home alone. Then I will come and get Lakshmikutty. At that time if you raise any uproar..."

He took precautions against possible attempt by Paruamma to get out of this. He said in a tone that was meant to scare her; "You should remember who you will be displeasing–the commissioner. He can easily get the police to charge you with something. If that happens, the girl will be in a pitiful situation. Men will pass her from one to another. This is better than that any day. It will be good for her future also."

Paruamma kept quiet when she realized that her words were of no use. Sri left as if all necessary arrangements had been made.

After that Paruamma didn't know what peace of mind was. Did this happen on an Ashtamirohini[2] Day, when she could not even think straight? Why did she have to a find a solution to this problem on this day? She lived the rest of the year looking forward to this day. For the last 18 years on this day she had celebrated the anniversary of an incident that happened when she was 17. Her mind drifted to the time when she was young.

Until Dr. Krishna Pillai came to that area, there had been no one who could treat people bitten by snakes. The drawing master in the local middle school took an oblong board, drew a hooded snake in the top left corner, and wrote: "Snake Bites Treated Here." That was hung in front of the doctor's house and was like a certificate the locals had given him in appreciation of his skill in treating snake poison. Good fortune was on his side, and he became famous.

In his family life also the doctor was very fortunate. His wife was a good-natured woman admired by everyone who knew her. However, before long she left this world, leaving behind her three-year-old daughter with the tearful doctor and many other mourners.

The locals gave the doctor's second wife the nickname "snake." It seemed that all the poison the doctor had taken out of his patients had

---

2 Lord Krishna's birthday.

taken her form. Under her, a house that had been quiet and peaceful became a place for frequent screams, fights, and fasting. Six or seven years later, the doctor contracted typhoid and left this world to join his first wife. His only concern was for his daughter, Parukutty.

Life under her stepmother made Parukutty realize that it is not the consequences of the parents' deeds or the result of one's own deeds that determine happiness or sorrow in life, but something unexplainable. Although life became extremely difficult for her, Parukutty never contemplated escape through suicide. At first she became upset when her stepmother scolded her, but she learned to be detached when treated cruelly. Finally she could put up with anything–even momentary pleasures. That was the only way she could live and her body could grow.

Five or six years after her father died, Parukutty's stepmother bought a piece of property opposite to her house and built a house there. The stepmother's brother came to help, and he moved into the house. From then on, Parukutty had more than one person to torment her. When the house was completed, it was rented out. A judge and his family moved in.

On her 17th birthday she did not get anything to eat, and by sundown she was exhausted. She sat on the veranda at the back and started crying, thinking of her father.

The children from next door were at the wall, clamoring, "Look here, look here!" Hearing that, she turned that way and saw the children's grandmother standing behind them. The kind old lady said, "Don't cry. Get up and come here. I will give you what you need."

Yes, the old woman gave Parukutty whatever she needed. Food was for her immediate physical need. She also needed love and affection, and she received them. Another person might have said that the realization of her wishes might bring undesirable results. But Parukutty's thinking was that to a hungry person even poisonous food is better than no food at all.

In that house there were the judge, his wife, three children, the judge's brother (who was a lawyer), and Amma, the judge's mother, along with three servants. Amma was born poor, but married a rich man. That is why she was kind to the poor, especially those who had once lived well.

Parukutty's job was to take care of the children. Once in a while she had to wash some clothes and clean the house. Collecting flowers or Amma's pooja[3] in the morning and evening was one of her favorite

---

3 Ceremonial prayers.

tasks. She would spend the whole day at that house but returned to her house to sleep, suffering rebuke from her stepmother and her brother. They complained that she brought disgrace to the family by working in somebody's house. But the pleasant memories of the day surrounded her like a cloak, and the arrows of their cruel words could not penetrate it. Light had come into Parukutty's dark life.

Unfortunately the judge was transferred, and he and his family left for the new place along with the servants. The lawyer's practice was bringing him a good income, so he decided to stay back, and Amma said that she would also stay. Amma told Parukutty that she would take care of her and her son, the lawyer. They were better cared for than before by a thankful Parukutty.

On Ashtamirohini day, the lawyer came home from the office, had tea, and prepared to go for a walk. He encountered Parukutty on the staircase. She had just bathed, and was dressed in a fresh mundu,[4] a light blue blouse, and a half sari: her long hair was casually tied at the end.

She had a plate full of flowers—hibiscus, jasmine, thulasi,[5] sankhu-pushpam,[6] anthimandaaram,[7] and pavizhamalli[8]—she had gathered for Amma's pooja. The youthfulness and natural beauty of the 17-year-old attracted him.

She walked along one side respectfully, looking down. Uncomfortable saying something to her, he finally asked, "Where is Amma?"

She stopped going up the steps, turned around, and said, "Amma is taking a bath."

He went back up two steps and stood by her. Looking into the plate full of flowers he asked, "Why do you need so many flowers today? Is it a special day?"

She looked up at his face and said, "Today is Ashtamirohini. Amma may say even this much is not sufficient."

Both the fragrance from the flowers and her beauty had caught his attention. "Do you know whom you worship on Ashtamirohini day?" he asked.

She was surprised and happy at the young master's attention. She said, "Yes, I know. Today is the birthday of Sri Krishna. I have gathered these flowers to pay homage to him."

---

4   A lower garment, consisting of a length of cloth.

5   Basil.

6   Butterfly pea.

7   A flower that blooms at dusk.

8   A flower resembling coral.

Gopalan[9] Nair moved a bit closer and said, "Then do the pooja. I am his namesake. So you can offer the pooja to me. I like flowers a lot."

Parukutty couldn't move and stood there bewildered. Was it a joke? If Amma saw them together like that, there would be trouble. She said, "You can take whatever flowers you want. I have to go and get things ready for Amma's pooja."

"I deal with bundles of papers, what do I know about flowers?" Her puzzled look amused him. "Why don't you select one for me?"

She wished to get away from there before Amma saw them. Her youthfulness might have wished just the opposite. She took some jasmine flowers and pavizhamalli and gave them to him. "Here, you can have these." He reached out not for the flowers but for the hand that held them. She panicked. She also experienced an unfamiliar excitement, and in the confusion the plate fell down. He thought he heard his mother's footsteps and said, "Amma is coming. Gather all the flowers and go to the pooja room."

Because it was Ashtamirohini day, the pooja was long. In the past, once she entered the pooja room her thoughts were only about Sri Krishna playing the flute. But that day, instead of Sri Krishna, she could only think of the smiling face of Krishna's namesake. She now knew the thrill of a man's touch, and when she prostrated before Sri Krishna's picture, that unselfish girl could only pray, "Oh Bhagavan![10] please make him a great man. Let me be of help to him and not cause any problems for him."

Sri Krishna heard her prayer in an unexpected way. Amma received a telegram saying that her oldest grandson was seriously ill, and that she should come immediately. She had to leave for the judge's house before dawn.

She got ready quickly. When it was time to leave, she called Parukutty and said, "I am not sure when I can come back. Until I get back, you should take care of Gopi and not let him starve. He doesn't like to eat anyone's cooking but mine. But he is satisfied with your cooking. Finish the day's work, give him dinner early, have your dinner, and go home. Nobody will say anything about your doing that. You must do everything to his liking."

Whatever she might have meant by that last sentence, Parukutty satisfied her patron's order to the letter. She fulfilled Gopalan Nair's every wish with a sense of self-sacrifice. The results of that selfless act ...

9   A synonym for Krishna.

10   God.

She had no one with whom to share those results. She didn't wish for anyone either. Amma had said that she would come back as soon as possible. When she didn't return even after a month, Parukutty was frightened. She was concerned that she might become an obstacle to the wealth and fame the lawyer was to have achieved by marrying a suitable girl. More so, she did not want to seem ungrateful to the kind woman who took her in, by snatching her beloved son. Even when she was enjoying the love life with Gopalan Nair, she continued to think practically. She realized that their love scenes would not be the preview of a married life. But even after he went away, she would have the memories to thrive on.

Because of the lawyer's cleverness, no one was aware of the life they had together. Before others they were the master and servant, at other times lovers.

That blissful dream did not last very long. One day Gopalan Nair asked her, "What will you do after I leave?"

That question shook her. She stood silently for a while and said, "I will work and earn a living."

"For people who will come and live in this house as I did?"

Parukutty looked hard at him. She realized what he meant. Her strong protest to his allusion was reflected in her look. The self-respect of a poor woman! She said, "Those who want to work can somehow find a way to earn a living. No woman in my family has sold her body to make a living."

The response of this 17-year-old put him to shame. But her pledge not to live with another man pleased his selfish mind. He said with love, "I will get you a job to earn a living as a charwoman at the Sri Krishna temple here. I have only to ask the Devaswam Commissioner. Otherwise I will ask Amma to talk to him. It is his daughter that Amma and my brother have chosen for me. The order for your job will come before my marriage. I will leave only after giving you enough money to live until then."

In that manner Gopalan Nair said goodbye to that place and his work as a lawyer. Parukutty, who never used to think about things that had no solutions, was sobbing for days. That sight touched Gopalan Nair's heart deeply. At the time of his leave taking, she stood with a grateful heart full of loving memories and eyes full of tears. He wiped those tears lovingly and left her life with tears in his own eyes.

Gopalan Nair kept his word, and the news of her new position came in the mail. After four months, his generosity came out in another way too. "Taking care of the lawyer, my daughter has become a mother." Her stepmother repeated that observation often, but Parukutty paid no attention to that. She loved her baby more as a memorial to a life she loved than as a part of herself.

After that, 18 Ashtamirohinis went by, bringing old memories to Parukutty. Every year she would forget the Thiru Onam[11] and, without realizing it, would think about Ashtamirohini. On that sacred day at dusk during the lighting of lamps, everyone came to worship at the Krishna temple to ask Him for favors they needed. From one woman who forgot her needs but joined her skinny hands together would He hear an unselfish prayer. She had only that one prayer—if the progenitor of her fatherless daughter is alive bless him in every way; if he is dead, may he be taken to heaven!

Even this morning, Paruamma woke up with those memories, and from her heart came the same prayer. But Sri's visit changed all that.

Paruamma didn't understand many things. Why is this grief happening on the anniversary of the first day of her love life? Is this a punishment from God?

Paruamma thought further about the experiences she'd had in that house. One day, a new world full of happiness opened unexpectedly before her. But very quickly the owner of that world closed it up and continued his life's journey. But whatever she had experienced had not been forgotten. What about her daughter's situation? Let alone the scandal that would fade in time. Why should she destroy her virginity to satisfy the fancy of some man for just one night, even if he is an emperor? There will be no remembrances in the act that will satisfy the girl, and there is no love relationship that will protect the mind from other thoughts. Paruamma saw before her a life bled by the memories that will be forgotten only after death.

Suddenly a new thought came to her mind. In her imagination she saw her daughter's bleeding body. She saw grief and pain in that also. But that would be only for a moment. What happens after that? Will a murderer go unpunished? The policemen with red caps, hands in iron cuffs, the stone room in the dark jail, the judge, the court with lawyers in long black coats—Paruamma saw all these and more in her mind. But she had developed an ability to take any kind of suffering while she had lived with her stepmother.

Lakshmikutty, after taking her bath and with her long hair just tied casually at the end, went to her mother with a plate full of flowers. She woke

11 Kerala state festival.

her mother from her dream world and said, "I finished cleaning up the temple and courtyard before going for my bath. Mr. Sri said that I don't have to go back there again today. Amma, the commissioner had come to the temple with his daughters. We have not seen such beautiful girls ever. They don't look anything like the father. Their clothes and jewelry were so shiny that I couldn't look at them. Mr. Sri asked me to put flowers on their hair. Amma, I was standing so close to the commissioner when I was putting flowers on their hair."

Paruamma stared at her daughter, realizing why Sri asked her to put flowers on the girls' hair. She could visualize that scene. Poor girl! Until now she didn't have to wonder what kind of life was destined for anyone born as a girl in a poor helpless family. She said, "Hurry up with the flower garland. It is time to light the lamps."

Lakshmikutty went to do her mother's bidding without changing her damp clothes. Paruamma took the pot of rice and put it in the rope shelf. She went outside and looked at the house across the street.

It is time for the lamps to be lit at the temple. In that house, the two girls, dressed to the nines, are putting the last touches to their makeup. How lucky they are to be in such a prosperous family! As her daughter guessed, they must be just like their mother. Lakshmikutty's father must have such a family, with all imaginable comforts. Paruamma faced the temple, closed her eyes and, with her hands joined in prayer, offered the memories of her life 18 years ago to God.

Lakshmikutty was decorating the picture of Sri Krishna, kept against the wall besmeared with cow dung. The clarinet sounding from the temple, announcing prayer time, could be heard in the distance. It created waves of devotion and love in her also.

Paruamma stood behind her daughter with folded hands, looking at her getting ready for the pooja. But her mind was not on prayer. She heard footsteps and saw the lean shadow of Sri. Suddenly, Lakshmikutty, who was arranging the garland on the picture of Krishna, collapsed with a loud scream she couldn't finish.

The small yard of the hut was full of people in no time.

Paruamma was standing with folded hands before the glass-framed picture of Krishna, whose incarnation was to uphold virtue and morality, and to uplift the poor. She was not aware of what was going on around her. Even the bleeding body of her daughter didn't touch her heart. The only picture in her mind was the image of Krishna's namesake, as he was 18 years ago.

People parted, saying "Commissioner, Commissioner" as he strode onto the scene. He asked in an authoritative voice, "What happened here?"

That voice brought Paruamma back from her prayer. She recognized it. Standing where she was, she just turned her head.

The commissioner got on to the veranda, taking care not to hit the low doorframe. A gaslight was brought in and it made things visible. People who had gathered there praised the sympathetic nature of the commissioner. Pointing to the bloody body on the floor, he asked, "Who did this?"

Paruamma bowed before the picture of Krishna and turned towards him. She saw that the lean handsome body had become ugly and puffed up with the arrogance of his high position. In her natural voice she said, "I did it."

"Why?"

"Death and jail are better than going astray and living an immoral life."

Her expression, manner, and voice shook his heart. He sensed that he somehow was the reason for this horrible event. Without showing any signs of agitation, the commissioner asked, "How are you related?"

He thought he saw a fleeting smile on Paruamma's face. He was indignant that she was smiling regardless of his position. Then she said, "It is my daughter who is lying here. About 20 years ago, there lived a fine lady next door. Her name was Lakshmikuttyamma. Because of my devotion to that family, I gave my daughter that name."

The commissioner thought back to his youth. From among the many unclear faces of women, the face of a 17-year-old girl slowly became clear. With no need for force, she offered herself. Without thinking of the dishonor she brought on herself, she let him have his way—Parukutty! In the beginning, for no reason at all, she would come to mind quite often. Slowly it faded out.

The commissioner stared at the woman standing in front of him. He felt that he must have guessed wrong. That hair! How could it get so short and skimpy? How could that face become so ugly? What happened to the beauty and strength of that young girl who had proudly proclaimed her determination to live a moral life?

Suddenly, the commissioner's eyes went to the girl who was covered with blood. Had the mother transferred her beauty and good health to the daughter? He was shaken. If he remembered well, this was the girl the manager had showed him. "Who is she to me?" he wondered.

He controlled his voice to stop it from cracking, "What is your name?"

Bending down to rub her swollen knee, Paruamma said in a calm voice, "My name is Paruamma. People used to call me Parukutty. Now people know me only as 'Paruamma, the charwoman of the temple.

FEMALE INTELLECT
(WOMEN HAVE A MIND TOO)
K. Saraswathyamma

She attracted some and alienated many. One group opined, "She is a self-willed girl who listens to no one. It is because of the way she was brought up, pampered to no end." Meanwhile, another group said, "What courage and guts! This is how children should grow up. It is wrong to say that pampered children will grow up to be worthless."

Until she completed middle school, Vilasini went to a school for boys and girls. A majority of the students were boys and therefore girls in general were shy and nervous. They couldn't even stand up and answer questions. Sometimes the teacher used to say: "You should kindly do one thing: I will set aside one period for you to be shy and cover your face. Then you will not waste time during class. Stupid kids! Look at Vilasini and learn from her."

Vilasini wondered why her classmates were acting shy. She would jump up as soon as the teacher asked a question and give an answer. She was determined to be first in the class.

It was traditional for the boys and girls to elect their representatives as co-chairs of the Student Association. But typically the boy did everything, and the girl was there only for formality. However, when it was Vilasini's turn, things turned around. She was indispensable for giving speeches, reading poetry, and for debates. When the school anniversary was to be celebrated, Vilasini opted out, saying that there was going to be a wedding at her house. But the headmaster said, "Even if you are not there, the wedding will take place without a hitch. But here things won't go as well. Your co-chair doesn't know a thing about receiving the presiding guest and reading the report. Leave him in a corner. We are counting on you, Vilasini. You will one day become a competent lawyer!"

When she completed middle school and joined an all-girls high school, Vilasini felt out of place. First the girls didn't like her because she liked to get wet in the rain, climb trees, and laugh out loud. But those who got to know her came to like her. When the exams were over and the results were out, the teachers' disregard changed to fondness.

But Vilasini realized that there was something wrong in girls' schools. Men teachers would like girls who studied well, but, in general, lady teachers had different criteria. They looked first at the position held by the girl's father, how well she dressed, and how pretty she was. Smartness and the ability to study well were secondary. The girls behaved the same way. They liked and cared more for teachers who were pretty and dressed well. Women who could teach well and did teach well were liked only by a few girls like Vilasini.

She realized that even in school, intellect didn't count too much among women. Slowly she got into the dressed-up group. Still, her carelessness in dressing up was always evident.

When she completed high school, Vilasini could not continue her education because of financial difficulties. Many of her teachers, especially the middle school headmaster, felt bad about the situation. Vilasini came out first in her graduating class, although she rarely read the books and instead made kites with pages from her notebooks, got out of extra classes, and played around like a mischievous girl. Seeing her marks in the final exams, her math teacher said, "I have never seen a girl so smart. But she is not destined to make use of it."

For the next two years Vilasini stayed home. While her guardians were bargaining about a husband for her, she read whatever books she could get hold of. The third year, she joined a typewriting institute.

Vilasini was surprised to see that the lack of teamwork among boys and girls in middle school had reached a kind of hostility as they grew up to be young men and women. She also saw the secret efforts to attract one another in spite of it. There were only a few students who were paying attention solely to studies. Among the young women Vilasini and Annapoorna were the only two, and they became good friends with a few smart young men.

When Vilasini heard how that friendship with men was being interpreted, she was surprised and pained. Annapoorna escaped the slander because she was married. Vilasini consoled herself, saying that there was something wrong with people's way of thinking.

To the few friends who came to her to get the truth, Vilasini said, "I can only say that there is no truth in all these stories. I don't know what else to say. My friendship with them can be interpreted only as with smart students who are interested in what they are studying. At the most you can say I like them as individuals. But I have not felt the love a woman feels for a man with any man, inside this institute or outside, so far."

The sincerity in her voice could not be doubted. Still, one girl asked, "It may be true in everyone else's case, but how about Vyomakesan Nair? I have seen you many times talking to him without realizing the passing of time."

"So what? The more you realize how smart a person is, isn't it natural to like him more? What I don't get is why people cannot understand that there can be an intellectual attraction."

While she was studying at the institute, Vilasini had a new experience. The principal had given her special permission to practice on the typewriter on holidays, as the exam was getting closer. Their teacher/student relationship was strong and deep-rooted. On a holiday, as Vilasini was concentrating on practicing her typing, the principal came and stood behind her, watching. He said, "This is not for you, Vilasini. It is sad when smart girls come to learn typing. Why aren't you going to college?"

"Financial difficulties," Vilasini said with a sad smile and continued with her work. He moved forward, put his hand on the typewriter, and said, "Suppose someone will gladly spend the money. Would you agree to that?"

His voice was cracking with excitement. Vilasini turned her head and looked at him. Everyone considered him as part of the machines because his words and actions were so dispassionate. Now Vilasini stared at his face full of emotions, and left.

But the next day they both acted naturally, as if nothing unusual had happened. The day before, her silent anger had made him uncomfortable, but today he behaved as usual.

A week before the examination, they had a social gathering. Many of them spoke, bidding goodbye, and one of them referred to Vilasini as "a woman with manly qualities." Everyone thought that she was being ridiculed. The principal's lack of emotion vanished for a minute when he looked at the speaker, as if to call him "a fool who believes in the superficial."

That day, after the party, when cigarettes were distributed among the students, Vilasini held out her hand. As a joke someone put a packet of cigarette and a box of matches in her hand. As Vilasini was trying to smoke a cigarette (using a Muslim girl who smoked beedi[1] at home as a role model) her colleagues were arguing about her.

Annapoorna said, "This Lasi is a great pretender. There is something wrong in using the word 'manliness' because I have not seen as much fem-

---

1 Cheap smoke made of fragments of tobacco wrapped in a leaf.

ininity as she has in anyone else. Why does she give the wrong impression to others?"

In response to that, Vilasini blew cigarette smoke on to Annapoorna's face. The others made fun of Annapoorna, saying, "Look at femininity coming out as smoke!"

At that juncture, one of the male students brought some flowers for the women. As her friends were selecting flowers they liked, Vilasini said, "I don't want flowers. If you give me one of the garlands kept in the office room, I will take it."

"I will give you the garland," the male student said, "But not now. My wish is to give it to you at an auspicious time!"

"You better forget that wish, as it is not going to come true." So saying, she got up and walked away.

Seeing the young man also leave, one of the young women said, "See how bravely she answered him! Someone else would have kept quiet with embarrassment."

"Why should one be embarrassed?" Vilasini turned around and asked in a scornful tone. "He forgot that this is a school. I am not standing in the bridal chamber with him to feel shy."

After everything was over that day, Vilasini was walking home alone when the young man caught up with her and said, "I apologize for joking like that. It went too far. But I was not joking. I was serious in expressing my wish."

"It is OK as a joke," Vilasini said while walking, "but please don't add insult to injury."

When the results were out, Vyomakesan went to congratulate her. While discussing future plans, he proposed to her. She responded lightly, as if it was a joke and there was nothing to think about: "Everything will be the same for me. Please remember one thing, your expression of affection should not go beyond what it is today. We will always be friends just as we are today."

Vyomakesan said goodbye and left. A month later he wrote a letter to Vilasini, declaring his brotherly love for her. She read that and smiled, relieved. Then she wrote him in response, "Ours is not a brother-sister love because it reflects the distinction between male and female. Our relationship is a friendship grown out of attraction of two intelligent people for each other."

Several months later, all her friends talked to Vilasini about Vyomakesan's marriage when they saw her. Annapoorna talked to her confidentially, "I never thought that he would do this to you, Lasi. I never thought that he would hurt you like this. He betrayed you, didn't he?"

Vilasini just laughed and said, "What betrayal?" and nothing more. She didn't want to take the trouble of explaining to others that theirs was not the relationship of two hearts but of two minds, because no one seemed to understand it.

Before long, Vilasini got a job as a typist in an office. Because there were no other women in the office, a place was set up for her in the manager's office.

He was a bachelor in his thirties with the attitude and looks of one in his fifties. No one knew for sure if he was angry at women or just indifferent to them. But everyone was sure that Vilasini would suffer under him. The manager didn't like the fact that he had to share his office with her.

But the way Vilasini behaved towards him made him realize that he was wrong in thinking that every woman is a pest that takes away a man's freedom. She did her work with diligence and enthusiasm like any man, and she was open in saying what she wanted to say. He hadn't expected such behavior from a woman.

One day he made her type a letter saying it was for a friend. There was a part in it where a man who disliked women was remorseful about it and proposed to the young lady. She typed the letter, gave it to him, and went out for lunch. When she returned, the letter was on her desk—with the request for the girl's hand underlined twice. Vilasini pretended she didn't understand anything and put it back on his desk.

At that point, she thought about her behavior towards him to figure out if she had done anything to give him the wrong impression. She had not felt anything more for him than camaraderie with a colleague, nor had she acted in any other way. She had only behaved like a man would to another man. Of course, physically she was different. Still, why do these men have a one-track mind? Is it because of natural instinct or society's tradition?

The next morning when she got to the office, the letter was back on her desk with the pertinent part underlined in red and the typewritten letters gone over in hand writing to make it solid. She took the letter and went to his office and asked very seriously, "It seems you made me type this for nothing. Shall I tear it up?"

He just looked at her in silence. But he didn't touch her heart at all. She just admired his ability to speak so eloquently with just a look.

He felt that mentally she was ridiculing the weakness of his heart, as she didn't even have a kind word for him. When his pain was clear on his face, she changed her serious look to a smile as she tore up the letter and went back to her desk.

That afternoon one of her friends visited Vilasini. Saramma told her love story in a low tone with a sad face and weary eyes. She said that she was going to sacrifice her life for love, an act that has been celebrated from the beginning of the universe. She added that she had gone beyond religion and caste. He was not very old. The fact that he had a wife and children only intensified her feeling for him. He was ready to take even reckless steps for her. For example, he said that he was ready to run away from home if he could forget things and there was someone to love.

Vilasini said, "He knows that you will love him more for saying that. When he proclaims what should be done quietly, there is pleasure in it. How did all this start?"

"The Lord made me start it," Saramma said with a sigh. "He became acquainted with my father recently. One day when he gave me something, accidentally our hands touched each other. He told me that he was sorry to have tainted my hands with his touch because he was a great sinner. After that he told me all about the miseries of his married life. It was a sad story, enough to make anyone cry."

"When you should have scorned him, you showed sympathy. Is it true that he is leading an immoral life?" Vilasini asked.

"He was like that," Saramma said, tears falling freely from her eyes. "But if he mends his ways because of me, why can't I sacrifice my life for that? God alone knows how they are treating me at home. They have me under house arrest. Still, the other day we met at the beach without anyone knowing. He said that he would gladly give up his life if I ask him to."

"Then why don't you ask him to jump in the ocean?"

"Oh, my God!" Saramma imagined her lover thrashing his arms and legs in the ocean and that thought broke her heart. Still, her feminine curiosity, an inseparable part of every woman, took over, and she asked, "Had he jumped into the ocean at my suggestion, what would that show?"

"That he can swim in the ocean!"

Saramma sat there stupefied. Vilasini said, "I don't like to jump hastily into action based on emotion, rather than thinking about responsibilities and acting wisely. I can't help blaming your parents either. This is the result of not doing their part in helping you meet the needs of your body and mind at your age."

"I ... I ..." Saramma lost her self control. "What are you hinting, Vilasini?"

"Whether you like what I said or not, I am not ready to take it back because it is true."

What Vilasini said turned out to be true. Saramma's parents found a groom for her without paying attention to her likes or dislikes and got her married. Two or three weeks after her marriage, when Vilasini visited

Saramma she could only talk about her husband and nothing else. Vilasini smiled, but said nothing.

Many more of her friends went to Vilasini for advice regarding their love life. They all had enormous faith in her ability to think objectively and come to a decision with courage. But in one thing she didn't satisfy anyone. When someone spoke about lasting love that was almost divine, Vilasini marveled at the statement and said, "That I don't understand at all. For a love that is eternal and almost divine, what is the need for this mortal body and an earthly marriage? Is limitation the goal of expansion? Isn't love that is so great, even if it is not returned, in itself satisfying?"

Nobody understood what she was driving at. She realized that people didn't understand her view. In the end, to those who approached her for help in this matter she said, "What is needed in this matter is not somebody else's decision. One should have the determination to accept whatever comes her way and leave the decision to one's heart and instincts. That is all I have to say. One thing you should remember: a lover can enjoy the love of any kind of man. But being a wife is a responsible job. In this life of struggle for existence, children cannot be brought up with just love."

Vilasini had a friend who had similar views: Vijayalakshmi. She also came out first in her class although she didn't pay much attention to books. She was just a very smart girl. However, Vilasini was just one step ahead in intelligence and knowledge.

In the beginning Vijayalakshmi found married life enjoyable, but very soon she was tired of it. In the eyes of the ordinary people she was a lucky wife and mother. But an unexplainable dissatisfaction started to bother her.

One day she told Vilasini, "There is the word 'ennui' in the English language. I am experiencing the meaning of it. I feel a kind of weariness all the time. It is not of the body but of the mind. The gold medal I got when I graduated first in my class was useful in grinding the children's medicines. But the brain that enabled me to get that medal is going rusty. For men the brain is useful to the end, to earn a living and to get ahead in life. Bur for a woman who is born to be a parasite, being too intelligent is a curse."

"Can't you help your husband in some way?" Vilasini asked.

"Help my husband!" Vijayalakshmi said sarcastically. "A wife gets that much respect? A wife is only for the husband to come home early at night and not to waste his salary. What else is a wife for?"

Vilasini kept quiet for some time and then asked, "If that is so..."

"What if that is so?" Vijayalakshmi said in a helpless voice. "My daughter's experience will be the same. Tradition, circumstances, societal customs, and nature's secrets have gotten together and the woman's brain has to surrender before all these. Maybe, Vilasini, you also will have to experience this. But listen to what I say: this surrender won't last too long. You should ensure that when the brain raises its head, the area of its activity will not be empty. I mean that you should be very careful in choosing a life-mate."

Vilasini just laughed as if it was not important but said nothing. Vijayalakshmi said, "Don't laugh. This is not a laughing matter. Women are entangled in the house, society, and customs. Men are not so. Therefore, as an individual, a sharp intellect that helps men to rise up and grow is not only unnecessary but also a nuisance to women—not only to themselves but also to others."

"May be if the woman is born in a culturally high society…"

"She can be born anywhere. But the belief that women do not need and don't have an intellect has taken hold. How much intelligence does one need to manage the household, gossip, and get dressed up? An intelligent woman is not the rule, but an exception."

"Meaning?" Vilasini asked laughing. "Does it mean she should put up with scandalous stories?"

"Yes," Vijayalakshmi was angry that Vilasini took it as a joke when she was talking in all seriousness. "You are well experienced in putting up with scandals, aren't you?"

THE DEVIL'S JACKET
Karoor

Kuttappan woke up, moved the gunny bag he had used as a blanket, and got up from the mat. He lifted the palm leaf screen and stepped out into the yard. His chin began to tremble in the cold weather, and he returned to the hut. "This cold will freeze even blood. I don't want to get up for some time," he said.

His mother looked at her ten-year-old son with sadness.

"This won't do. I have to get up," he said and rose once again.

"Wait till the fog clears. If you get a fever and become bed ridden..."

"I won't get any fever, Amma.[1] I can't bear this cold. My plan to buy an undershirt is not working out."

"What can be done? With the money you spend on my medicines you could have bought many undershirts. My fate is to put my son in hardship even at this tender age." Her voice cracked before she could complete the sentence.

She is always sick and cannot go out anywhere. When Kuttappan brings some palm leaves she plaits them, and when he brings thazha[2] she weaves mats. Her whole body aches when she sits for a while. Then she stops. Kuttappan has to take the plaited palm leaves and mats to sell them. For the past four or five days, she can't do anything.

"From now on, I will set aside two annas[3] every day. I need to buy an undershirt. Everything else is only after that," he said and went to the boat with the oar. He rowed hard to feel warm. The tremor left his lips and he hummed a tune as he relaxed.

He got to the jetty. Two or three people were waiting for the boat. "If you want to go across, get in," he said enthusiastically at the thought of getting two or three annas.

"We don't want to get into this small boat and drown in this cold water," one of the passengers said.

---

1   Mother.

2   Leaf of pandanus.

3   Sixteen annas made a rupee in the old currency.

"How can you drown? I will be rowing it. You get in." Kuttappan waited, looking at their faces anxiously. "Aren't you getting in?"

They didn't even show that they had heard him. They were looking at a big boat that was coming from the other side. He left them, murmuring, "This is not a good omen," and rowed to the other side. By that time boats with older boatmen started arriving at the jetty. Working till evening, he didn't make enough money for the evening meal. When all the people had gone, he bought some rice and went home. Tying up the boat by his house, he called out, "Amma, I am home."

"Did you get anything, son? I had put the water on the stove and was waiting, listening for your footsteps."

He washed the rice and put it in the pot on the stove.

"I think my mundu[4] is torn." He untied his mundu and looked at it in the light from the cooking fire. It was torn about a foot. Amma didn't say anything.

"Oh, oh! This is bad. I wanted to buy an undershirt, but I must first have a mundu.

This is sad."

"You will have mundu and undershirt, son. You bring me some thazha. Though I don't feel well, I will make a mat. You sell that and buy a mundu."

"Do I make my mother who can't even sit up weave a mat to buy a mundu? I don't want any mundu or undershirt."

"Don't talk like that. You are a boy. You will have everything."

"Yeah, I will have everything. I go around with this boat from morning till night and I can't make enough money for one meal. There are more boatmen than passengers. Then how can I make any money?"

"God will give you, son."

"Mundu and undershirt?"

"He will give you a mundu and He will give you an undershirt."

"OK. I will wait for that."

The next morning he went to the boat, again in the shivering cold. He noticed a package wrapped in paper, partially hidden from view. He opened it and called out, "Amma, what you said is true. God gave me a shirt and a pair of shorts."

Amma got up painfully, came to the door to see this miracle.

"See, Amma. They are of good quality. This shirt has no buttons. With the first half anna I make, I will buy some buttons."

"Oh, my son, I am getting scared seeing this."

---

4   A lower garment, consisting of a length of cloth.

"When you see me in these shorts and shirt, I look like a policeman, don't I? You don't have to be scared."

"They don't suit you, son. Take them off." Amma said.

"Who said they are not my size? They look as if they were made for me. Amma, touch the material. It is nice and smooth."

"Smooth, I believe. You don't have to wear such nice clothes. I don't even want you to touch them." Her voice was heavy with sorrow and irritation. "Where did you get them? Don't stand there wearing them. Someone may come and get you."

"You don't have to be scared of that. Even if God calls me, I won't leave you and go."

"Don't go. But tell me who gave you this."

"God gave me. They were on my boat. They were wrapped up in that paper. Why should we be scared?" The boy asked.

"God put them on the boat! It is not God. It is the devil. My son doesn't need them."

"Did you see the devil? Yesterday you said God would give me."

"I did not mean that God wiould give you like this. God is not going around distributing shirt and shorts in packets. You take them off, pack them up, and return them to where you found them."

"Why do we keep it in the boat? We will keep it in the house. Even if I find things somewhere, you won't let me keep them." His face became sad.

Amma said, "You may like these clothes, but I like you more than that. You have to look in the mirror to see your good looks. I don't have to. They don't look nice on you. Some passenger must have forgotten the package on the boat. He will come back to get it. That boat is your everything. That is your God. If anyone says that he lost something on your boat, it will be the end of your earning." Her voice was cracking.

Kuttappan stared at the floor. He packed the shirt and shorts in the paper and put the packet in the boat. Without saying a word he rowed the boat to the jetty. His eyes were on the packet. No one who got on the boat paid any attention to it.

In the evening when he got home he said, "I have had enough of these devil's clothes. I am going to throw them in the lake."

Amma didn't say anything. How can a boy who has nothing to wear carry around clothes with no owner?

He knew that Amma had decided. There will be no change in that decision. So he didn't bring up that topic again.

The next day one of Kuttappan's friends saw the package.

"Kuttappan, what is in the package? Did Amma send you lunch so that you won't waste money? This way you must have a lot of money saved up."

"Poda.[5] Don't make fun of me. Somebody forgot a shirt and a pair of shorts."

"You are kidding!"

"That is the truth."

"Then why aren't you taking the packet home?"

"Because it is not mine. The owner will come back for it.

"Does he know that he left it in this boat? You can use them. Wear them."

"If I go home wearing them, Amma will beat me with the broom."

"Then give it to me. I will give you four annas."

"I am not going to give it to anyone. If Amma finds out, she will kill me."

"How will Amma find out? Tell her that the owner came and took it back. You are stupid."

"Let me be stupid. If I tell her lies, who will tell her the truth?"

"Oh, an honest boy! From the time people like you started plying the boat, real boatmen can't find work. I believe we are going to get a bridge by next year."

"When they start building the bridge, I will start a beedi[6] shop," Kuttappan said. "There will be a lot of workers and good business."

"I will be your partner," the friend said. "Let me see what is in the packet. Give it to me."

"No."

"It doesn't have clothes. It must be green pepper or something. It has been two or three days since you found it. They must have dried up. We will open and see or throw it in the lake."

"Then you can take it, is that it? Very smart! Go mind your own business." Kuttappan rowed the boat to the other side.

For some time he rowed around with no customers. Then a man got in and saw the package and stared at it.

He asked, "What is in this package?"

"I have been carrying it around for two or three days to give to the one who can say what is in it."

"No one has said anything?"

"No one has said anything. When the owner comes, he will say."

---

5   Get out.

6   Cheap smoke made of fragments of tobacco wrapped in leaf.

"Did you open it to see?"

"Yes I did. If I find something on my boat, shouldn't I find out what it is?"

"What if the owner doesn't come? Does he know it is here?"

"If he doesn't come, it will stay on the boat. I am afraid that someone will take it from the boat at night. Amma won't let me keep it in the house. She says that the devil kept it there."

"The devil? Am I a devil? This is mine."

"Then you can take it. Just say what is in it."

"A shirt and a pair of shorts. I thought I had lost them and got another pair made for my son."

"You can take it."

"When you opened the package didn't you want them?" The passenger asked.

"Why do I need someone else's stuff?" After a while he added, "Amma will kill me. If I die Amma has no one else."

"Where is your house?"

"A little further, by the side of the lake. If you shout from here, we can hear at home."

"You don't have a father or an older brother?"

"I have only Amma and this boat. Achhan[7] used to transport people in it."

"Let us go to Karott. I am going there too."

Kuttappan continued, "Now there are a hundred boatmen at the jetty. How much can I make? In a short while this also will end. There is going to be a bridge here. Let the bridge come. Then I will start a shop–a beedi shop."

"If you want I can give you a job."

"I cannot come. If I leave, my mother won't have any help. I won't go."

When the boat reached in front of his house he said, "This is my house."

"Then let us get off here. I want to see your mother."

When the boat was tied, the passenger took the packet and got down.

"Here, take this. See how they fit you."

"I don't want to."

"You can have them. I am giving them to you."

"For bringing you this far? Don't tease me. Just give me two annas. That is enough."

---

7 Father.

"I am not teasing you. This is not the boat fare either. That is separate. This is a gift for your truthfulness."

Amma came out hearing the conversation. Kuttappan asked, "Amma, do you hear this? These are for me. If I wear the devil's clothes, will my friends make fun of me?"

Amma said, "Now it has become God's. Take it."

A Rented House
Sachidanandan

It is about a furlong from the front yard to the gate. The gate is built in the shape of a gopuram,[1] and its big wooden doors have started to show its age here and there. There is a narrow gravel road not far from the gate. It connects this place to cities far away. One can say that the house is by the road. That's all.

As soon as she got to the house, Vimala wanted to go sit in a corner where her husband wouldn't see her, and cry. But seeing all the rooms in this huge house was in itself an exciting activity, though there was something in the big doors fitted with brass ornamentation, the thick walls, and the high ceiling that repelled her. Other than the driver dusting off the dead car in the portico and the servant bringing in the luggage, there was no one in sight. The sun had already gone from the high roof of the house and tall greenery in the yard. Meanwhile her husband was talking about something while opening the doors, going in, and looking out of the window like a child playing.

"Look, from here you can see the sheep along the side of the hill moving like ants. Do you see them?" He couldn't help saying that when he looked out from the veranda. She wanted to ask him what was so great about ants crawling in a line. But by that time he came behind her, put his chin on her shoulder, and asked, "Are you angry at me?"

She laughed and shook her head.

"We won't have to stay here more than two months," he said. "If possible we will leave earlier."

"That is all right," she said. "It is not good to talk about leaving as soon as we get here. Always living in one place can become boring."

What she said was not sincere. From the tone of her voice, he must have understood that. She was not tired of city living. When one was tired of city living, that was like being tired of life itself. She was not familiar with any other life. When had she lived somewhere other than the city, except for a week or two on vacations? But he was ready to tell

---

1 Bell tower.

anyone and everyone that he was from a village. He was proud of that. He used to tease her, asking if she was aware that there was a world outside of Calcutta. But all that was before their marriage. Those days she just sat looking at him lovingly and didn't bother to think about city life or village life.

Even then, he didn't have the courage to tell her that he would like to stay in a village for some time to write his new novel. He had his best friend, the critic, sound it out. Vimala had only revulsion for this man with the narrow forehead and a French beard. But, when he mentioned the idea she agreed. Her husband jumped for joy at the unexpected consent.

Later she was thinking only of that while watching the movie at a theater. It was based on a novel written by him about village life. She asked him if he didn't write it while living in the city. She didn't understand whatever he said in response—the novel he wanted to write was not like the movie; if he lived in the city he couldn't focus on the writing and if she didn't want to go, he would go by himself. He also added that in her absence his imagination would not flourish as well. She felt that he cared more for the novel than he cared for her. When he talked about it, he would forget everything else. He believed that this novel he was going to write would be his best work.

When they were out of the theater, the critic was talking about the movie. According to him, the producers destroyed a great story. Vimala was glad that she didn't say she liked the movie very much. Then he asked, "So when are you starting on your trip? Take as much time as you need to write it to your satisfaction. Return only after that. Dostoevsky tried to save time and as a result, many of his classics don't have the sheen they could have had if he had taken the time to polish his writing.

"But," he said looking at her and smiling, "as your wife is going with you, the work won't finish quickly." She laughed at that joke so that her husband would not feel bad.

He said that his novel would be an epic about the thousands of villages in India—a quiet village, on the bank of a river, where the vegetation grew in abundance. It looked as if the river lifted a small wooded area from the mountains and set it on its bank. The life of the village people was inherently natural and beautiful. It is not that there was no wickedness, dishonesty, or immorality, but there was something in the village that brought them together like a family and connected them to one another. "Do you remember it took us almost a year to learn that Mr. Ghosh who lives next door to us is a doctor and that the woman who lives with him is not his wife but his sister?" he asked. "Even if they fight with one another occasionally, the villagers won't ignore one another." Some zamindar[2] had lived in this huge house a long time ago. Standing on the veranda today and looking around, no one would think that there were people living anywhere near, let alone get to know them or ignore them.

By the time they arranged the luggage brought in by the servant boy and had tea, they realized that daylight was almost gone. When the sunlight coming between the hills was also gone, it was as if a huge shadow had fallen before them. The valleys that seemed like lines stretched between hills extended to the narrow river beyond. The river that looked like a blue ribbon disappeared among the green trees. A canopy of darkness had quickly fallen over all these.

Vimala stood there gazing at that sight as if she saw something interesting in it. The hills and riverbed that were being attacked and subdued by darkness would be gradually redeemed by the morning light, she thought. As if from naught, the green trees and huts would slowly take shape. A traveler unfamiliar with the area coming here at night would not be able to say what things were concealed in the darkness. But she knew. At daybreak she could stand here and say like a magician, "Let some hills rise up here, let a river start flowing there." She couldn't wait for the morning.

Far away in the city, traffic must be flowing along the streets. On the walls of buildings, big pictures in neon lights must be going on and off. People in large numbers must be going in and out of restaurants and theaters. These thoughts seemed like a dream to her.

She pretended that she was unaware that he had come and was standing close by. But when the breeze blew the end of her sari on to his face, she laughed. Without trying to move the sari, he stood there with his hands on her shoulder. She didn't try to tuck away the hair that was playing on her forehead, either.

"Maaji,[3] I have prepared fish and vegetables for dinner. What else would you like?" Only when she heard the old woman's rough voice did she realize that she was leaning on his shoulder. He took his hands from around her waist. Showing more pleasure than she felt inside, she went down the stairs quickly.

The old woman advised her to be careful going down the stairs. She just laughed. The old woman was the caretaker of the building. She looked after the needs of those who came to stay there.

---

2 Landholder.

3 Madam.

Coming down the stairs one walked into a large hall with big mirrors and comfortable seats. Big lanterns that hung from the ceiling made clanking sounds. The skillfully carved, heavy wooden door led to the central courtyard, around which were servants' quarters and a kitchen towards the end. If one looked at the main building from the central courtyard, its walls seemed like huge fortifications. There were inner chambers and servants' quarters for women upstairs. The hall, veranda, and gardens were just for men.

When the lights were turned on, the room shone like a palace. The building had the quality of making those who lived in it seem insignificant. But the zamindar and his entourage who used to live there were not insignificant. Then there must have been scurrying and commotion. In the hall decorated with wall mirrors and lanterns they must have had dancing and singing late into the night. As they were being served liquor, there must have been the appreciative calls of "Wah! Wah!" The tabla[4] and bells must have gone crazy. To Vimala that noisy picture of this silent building seemed like magic.

When she sat down to a dinner of fish curry and rice, Vimala was hungry. In that large room, they were the only two at the big dining table. The old woman and the servant boy waiting on them stayed in a corner. The room was strangely quiet.

Through the window bars, two or three dry leaves from a banyan tree fell into the room. Blown around on the floor, they made a rough sound. Suddenly, fixing his eyes on her face and laughing lightly he said, "Taste better than the items at Park Street Restaurant, don't they?"

One did not go to a restaurant in the city because one was hungry. In the dim light, sitting at a well-set table, looking around was fun. Two or three people always accompanied them and they would discuss some book, drama, or movie. However long they might discuss Ingrid Bergman's love story, a new book of Sartre, or the youthfulness of Francoise Sagan, they would pick up the topic again at another time.

Getting up from the dining table, they washed their hands and went upstairs. He said, "That old woman ruled this house during the time of the zamindar."

She looked at him with astonishment. "I thought she was the servant here."

He told her the story he heard when he came to check out the house. The zamindar was a lonely man. Until this woman became a part of his life, his only companions were alcoholics and dancing girls. Once she

---

4   A set of two small drums used especially in India and played with the hands.

came into his life, he turned his back to that world, sent away most of the servants, and lived just with her. He didn't even want to see anyone but her.

"And today?"

"She didn't get anything from him. All his wealth, including this house, he had mortgaged for his relatives, friends, and the dancing girls. The zamindar did not marry her according to the law. She was the young wife of his driver. Some people say that he paid the driver to go away. Others say that he was killed and dumped deep in the river. Even after he became a pauper, she took care of the zamindar."

Vimala thought about the old woman and felt sorry for her. The lean body in the white sari must have been striking at one time. The face that was serious and sad today, must have smiled beautifully. That night Vimala forgot to think about the city or the restaurants and activities there.

Early in the morning, while he sat at the table set under a spreading mango tree and wrote deliberately, she stood nearby, leaning on a tree stump. At times his hand played with the cap of the pen, at other times it moved fast along the page. He looked into his notebook, turning its pages back and forth, looked around, sometimes over her head without seeing her. He was like that while he wrote; even if she went and stood by him, he might not see her.

Of his writings, the first story she read was a love story of a beautiful girl and an ugly man. She didn't read it, he read it to her. More than listening to the story, she paid attention to the way his lips moved while reading. Since their first meeting, her heart missed a beat whenever she saw him with the unruly hair that fell on his face, his chubby face and strong arms with prominent veins. His body was strong like that of a bodybuilder or a factory worker. When he talked his large mouth and thick lips moved fast. His eyes were always fixed on something; they never faltered.

The day he read his story to her, he held her hands together and asked her to marry him. That day she spent a great deal of time thinking about the beautiful girl the ugly man with the chubby face and unfaltering eyes left behind.

She played with one of the smooth stones she picked up from the many he had kept on the table to use as paperweights and looked around. The crooked, rusty iron works, the broken cement walls, and the over-grown weeds showed that long ago there was a garden that had deterio-rated slowly and died. The crater nearby could have been a pond. Dry grass three to four feet tall could be seen everywhere. On the walls there were long marks made by flowing dirty water. Many of the windowpanes were broken.

The sun rose in the sky and sunlight fell into the shadow of the trees, creating silver leaves. The sun was getting hot and the wind getting strong. The dust blown up by the wind settled on everything.

The sky was dark blue. The white clouds that passed by from time to time made the moving shadows seem like a flock of sheep. When he called her, she felt as if she had woken up from a nap. She was afraid that he would ask her if she was mad at him. While in town he repeatedly talked about wanting to go to the countryside. After coming here he started saying, "Don't worry, we will leave here soon." But he didn't consult her about anything. He stopped writing and was smoking a cigarette, leaning back in the chair. He was looking intently at her with mischievous eyes.

As she got up and went to him, he smiled and gave her the pages he had written. How did he know that she went closer to see what he wrote? She didn't remember having read any of his manuscripts before. Now she was curious to read what he had to say about villages.

"Listen, you can only say that it is well written. Never before was I able to write with such ease." She didn't like the way he joked. She felt that he never talked anything serious with her.

"I hope this will be completed soon. To write the next novel we will go to Kerala or Kashmir," she said. But why did she say that? Would she have been happy if he had decided on a program for Kerala or Kashmir? When he laughed out loud she felt annoyed.

There is a meeting of the Panchayath[5] in front of the Kali[6] temple in the village. There are the landowners, those who cultivate the land, and the poojari.[7] The topic is hot—a robbery in Mr. Chaudhary's house. He is missing 50 rupees that he had kept under his pillow. He is a rich landowner and is not upset about losing 50 rupees, but is angry that someone has played a joke on him. Everyone suspects the thief of the village, Charu. But he has been down with fever for the past four days and cannot even get up. Then how could he have taken the money from Chaudhary's house? Nobody has an answer to that question. Just then the village schoolteacher, Das Babu, walks in with another problem. It is not about thievery, but about caring. Charu is very ill. Even if he is a thief, the Panchayath has the responsibility to save his life. Charu needs 50 rupees

5   A village political unit.

6   Goddess Parvathi.

7   A priest, one who does pooja.

to buy medicines. Das Babu looks at Chaudhary. He and the members of the Panchayath are flabbergasted.

That was all he had written. She couldn't understand why the Panchayath was meeting over a matter like this. Didn't they have police in that area? Wasn't this something that should be investigated rather than resolved by arguments? She had so many questions. But she only read his books, never discussed them, and was reluctant to comment.

If a chubby, middle-aged woman hadn't walked in at that time, she would have stayed hesitant and he would have been quiet for a longer time. "This is our landlady," he introduced her.

The woman didn't look like the owner of such a big house and yard. She had on a dirty white sari that couldn't completely cover her large body, and her face was unattractive, lacking any emotion as she sat down on a chair. Vimala tried to smile, and the landlady smiled back with no emotion.

She said that she had bought the building only recently and that the owner sold it to raise capital for some factory he was going to set up in the city. She hadn't even seen the whole building. She wanted to demolish the building, but the cost would be prohibitive. So she decided it would be better to clean up the building and rent it for some time.

This huge building must be a burden on her and that must be why she was ready to demolish it or sell it. Vimala felt sad when she thought about the driver's wife. Even if she had to live like a servant, she would live there because the building was much more to her than the stone and wood used to build it. She lived in the house and was not capable of leaving it.

Two more people came in, two elders of the village who came to enquire after the well being of the new tenants. They said that the previous tenant was a rich businessman who came with his large family. They left after a week in three or four cars, just as they came. Before that, three hunters, including a white man who had come looking for uncommon birds reportedly found in that place, stayed there for almost a month. When they were leaving the oldest among them, a bearded man, complained that the guide had deceived them because they didn't find any birds there. Vimala realized that she and her husband came next as the third party to occupy the building.

When the visitors left, Vimala said, "It seems studying the people who come to stay here is a hobby for the local people."

"After we leave, they will talk about us to future tenants," he said laughing, "A crazy writer and his beautiful wife."

She felt uneasy thinking about the scene where the elders would talk to future tenants about the writer who came with his wife to write a novel.

He wrote from morning till night, sitting in different places. In the morning he wrote at the table in the shade of the trees, in the afternoon taking all the papers and going to the riverbank in a horse cart, and late into the night under the light of a lamp. He wrote page after page and made corrections and marks in the margins. The page number in the corner went higher and higher. The pages in the notebook were marked off in red. She brought him black coffee and cigarettes.

She read every page he wrote. On and off she would be deep in thought, looking at the valley meeting the riverbank. She would listen to the wordless music of the boatmen who moved the boats using long bamboo sticks. Her eagerness and apprehension increased as she progressed through the written pages, sitting at the door of this palatial building, while the whole world was asleep, and there was complete silence. How great it was to be writer! How lucky she was to be the wife of a writer! When going to sleep, she would ask him, like a little girl asking her grandmother, "What happens next?"

He would pull her close to him and say, "I don't know. They are all characters in the story, people on paper. Now I want my real heroine."

One evening he took time off from writing and took her out for a walk. The intensity of the sun was going down. They had to bend down to get through the cluster of bamboo trees by the side of the footpath. Each time they came out of such a cluster, he would burst out laughing like a child. He said that the life in the village was not as easy as life in the city. Then he had a long talk about developing villages, the troubles and tribulations of villagers, and the need to build roads and hospitals in villages. When walking close to him along the narrow path, she rubbed against his shoulders and took his hand and held it with love, while watching clouds gathering in a corner of the sky and the light fading slowly. At that moment she felt that in this wide world they had been linked together as an inseparable couple, and that together they could face all troubles and difficulties. She wanted to press her face on his chest and cry out that she was a lucky woman.

The villagers were returning to their huts driving their cattle. Those who were fishing in the pond had some more time to try their luck. Here and there smoke rose from huts and spread among the branches of trees. Villagers could live without clocks. Work as long as there was light or until they were tired, and sleep when it got dark or they were tired. They were beyond time and clocks.

Suddenly clouds filled the skies, and darkness filled the fields like a flood. The cattle bellowed loud. Children came out and shrieked, looking at the skies. Cold wind blew, whistling loudly.

"Today we are going to get wet," he said and walked fast, aiming toward a faraway hut.

But it didn't rain. The wind got stronger and blew away the clouds, clearing the sky before they could reach the hut. Warm light fell all over. The cattle stopped bellowing and the disappointed children became quiet. That day they got back without getting wet.

It rained the next evening. It poured as if water was coming from pipes fitted in the sky. The rain seemed like a curtain touching the sky and earth. The hills and trees beyond were indistinct. The air was filled with the smell of wet soil. The ground that had been giving rise to dust until a few moments ago now had streams of muddy, red water. Thunderbolts shook the whole world. She didn't try to wipe away the water droplets that came to rest on her face and hair. She wanted to go out and stand in the pouring rain. Later, when the rain stopped, she watched the skies and stars through the passing clouds.

After a long time she heard him and realized that he was not asleep. He was smoking a cigarette, leaning back on the chair with his feet on the table.

"Are you thinking up a poem?" he asked.

How does one think up a poem? She didn't know. She just laughed.

Leaning forward, he gathered the papers and gave them to her, saying, "Here, I have completed the last chapter. Don't you want to read it? I will copy it only after getting your comment."

On hearing "last chapter" she felt sad. She didn't think that the story would end. While reading, it didn't seem like a novel. But it was a novel that he was writing, and it had to end somewhere.

Surely somebody had died, she was afraid. All his stories were tragedies. But he always said, "No, nobody has died. Nothing has come to an end. These characters and this story will never die. They are eternal."

Trying to take her own time to read the story, she read each line deliberately. The teacher, Das Babu, who is a good man, has come out of jail. When he tried to stop the zamindar's henchmen from stealing a farmer's crop he was made the scapegoat. In his absence so many things had happened. The country gained independence, and the village zamindar has become a political leader. The farmer whom the teacher tried to help has come to some agreement with the zamindar. Money changed hands and the farmer left the village after testifying for the zamindar before the Panchayath Council. The smallpox that ravaged the village has taken the lives of Das Babu's wife and only son. As in jail, he is alone in the outside world too. He has nobody in this world.

One day one of Das Babu's former classmates meets him on the street.

He has become a rich businessman. "You should not return to the village that destroyed you. Whom do you have there?" he asks. He promises to find Das Babu a good job and a house in town. He thinks for a while and says, "My good friend, I might have lost my family and relatives, but that village is still there and a great deal remains to be done there. Life still has meaning in the village." Sitting in the night train, he looks at the city lights for the last time. When she read this, Vimala felt as if something was caught in her throat. The hero was returning to the village with pleasure. Then why was it that she wanted to cry reading it?

As she asked herself that question, he got up, came to her and, lifting her face, gave a long kiss on her lips and said, "The story has ended. What a beautiful night! Let us get to real life."

It was a cool moonlit night. While he led Vimala to the bedroom, with the story still on her mind, she couldn't laugh with him.

When she woke up at the crack of dawn, daylight had already seeped in because they had forgotten to close the drapes. Lifting her head from the pillow, she looked out. The small branches of the tall mango tree were slightly shivering. Cold wind was playing around in the room.

Because he had a sense of satisfaction from having completed an admirable feat, he was sleeping well. His chest was going up and down as he breathed in and out. Some of his very straight hair had fallen on his face. Slowly she lifted his hand that was resting on her and put it down before getting out of bed quietly and straightening her clothes. Without making any noise, she opened the door and went to the veranda.

When the curtain of darkness was lifted slowly, hills and huts came up. The ground, cool from the rain, seemed reluctant to wake up. As the daylight got brighter, stars disappeared one by one. The daybreak seemed like a great miracle to Vimala.

Only when she heard a light cough from the other end of the veranda did she realize that she was not alone there. The old woman came towards her, wiping her face with the end of her sari.

"Madam, you got up very early. Shall I bring you some tea?" she asked.

Vimala shook her head to say no. She didn't know what to say.

"Nice cool morning, isn't it?" the old woman asked.

"Yes" Vimala said. "The doors don't close tight in our bedroom. So the daylight gets in and I wake up."

"They were always like that. To this day no one could fix them. It is 25 years … yes, exactly 25 years! This is the month of Sravana."[8]

"Was it in the same room …" Vimala didn't complete her question.

8 A month on the Hindu calendar that falls in August or September.

"Yes. Huzur[9] was laid up for a long time. There was no one to take care of him and no money for treatment. But ..." The old woman tried to change the topic and asked, "Let that be. Do you like this place? People who come from the city are always in a hurry to leave this place."

Vimala didn't respond to that.

"I just want someone to stay here." The old woman was deep in thought, but continued: "I have no desire to have this big building closed up."

Vimala didn't have the heart to tell her that her husband had finished writing the novel and they were leaving. The old woman would have to close down the building. She kept on talking without realizing any of this.

She looked down to the valley where the daylight was spreading and said, "That tall building is an old Kali temple. Beyond that is a wooded area. Those houses you see on this side were all built recently. Long ago there were only trees in all that area. Then people used to ride horses to get to places. None of these pathways existed then."

The old woman stood there, her eyes fixed on something pleasant far away. The past was taking life before her. Immersed in that, she must have even forgotten Vimala's presence there.

Later when the old woman went to make tea, Vimala kept standing there. She could see a footpath that started far away, turning this way and that and stringing huts along the way. From a couple of huts smoke went up and disappeared. Far away, human forms were moving along the path. A man passed by the yard with a cow tied to a rope. Behind that a calf followed, running and jumping. On and off it bellowed loudly. Because it had no strength for long bellowing, it came in small fragments.

She didn't know when he came and stood behind her, but realized he was there upon hearing him yawn. Though sleep had not left his eyes, he tried to smile, standing there with his hands in the dressing gown pockets.

"Now we should think about going back. I will arrange everything today itself."

To the city ... in the city cars and buses must have started the daily run. People dressed well in clean clothes must be moving towards bus stops and train stations. In tall apartment buildings, movements of life must have started. In front of office buildings, Gurkhas[10] must be saluting men in suits getting out of cars. Vimala didn't like thinking about any of these. She stood there looking at the sunlight of the monsoon season falling on tall grass on either side of the footpath, sometimes bright and

---

9   Master.

10   People from the mountains of Nepal, famous as soldiers.

sometimes dim. When the wind blew, the grass moved in unison, like waves. Suddenly, she was sad for no explainable reason.

At noon when he was sitting under the tree and arranging his writing according to chapters, Vimala tried to tell the old woman about their decision to go back. For some reason Vimala's tone was apologetic when she told her that he had finished writing the novel and that they had to get back to the city to attend to some urgent business. But the old woman didn't show any sign of getting upset. She laughed and said, "Didn't I tell you that you people won't be able to live here long? But that is all right. Someone else will surely come."

Someone else will surely come!

Vimala couldn't laugh with the old woman. She remembered the advertisement that her husband had shown her: "Comfortable and convenient big house. Decorated in old-fashioned way! Enjoy a vacation in countryside at low rates." Who would be the next tenant, hunters or rich businessmen?

This was the turn of the writer. Do people here know that he came to study this village, its character, secrets, and diseases to write a book? Had they known that, wouldn't they have chased them out? She felt really bad.

When they got into the car after taking two days to get things ready, he said: "I wonder if there is any good movie in town. I had heard that a drama written by Samir Babu would open this month...we missed this year's Monsoon Dance at the club."

Vimala didn't say anything. Through the car window she was looking at the fields, woods, and waterways of the countryside. After a while she said, inadvertently, "It seems we came here just to write the novel."

"Certainly," he said right away. "Didn't I tell you we could go back once the writing was done?"

"Yes, you did. But I am wondering if it is possible for us to live in one place, just to live there. Live in one place because we want to live there."

"I don't understand." He was unsure of what she meant.

"I was thinking of that building," she said. "To its owner it is a property in which she invested thousands. She hasn't even seen all the rooms. But she can sell it or dismantle it. The old woman has no rights over it. But she wants to live there. She won't leave the place even if she has to live like a servant. What about us? We aren't its owners nor do we have any feelings for the place. For us it was just a rented house."

"But we can't live here. To buy that..." Suddenly he stopped. After thinking for some time he said, "What you said is true. We are not able to make something ours or love them as such. We keep everything at arm's length, even life itself … we like to live in rented houses … tell me, Vimala, did you like the countryside?"

She didn't say anything in response, just sat there with her head on his shoulder.

He pulled her closer to him and said, "I am sorry, very, very sorry. For us life is not a goal, just a means. We don't live. We trade with life, with this novel, this story, this love and all."

A kid jumped in front of the car and the driver hit the brake suddenly. With that the discussion was cut off in the middle. They didn't try to pick up on that topic again.

THE DAUGHTER OF MAN
Lalithambika Antharjanam

He had just come home, dead tired, from a long journey. It is three o'clock. At four there is a committee meeting and at five a public meeting. Between six-fifteen and seven there are some important visitors to meet and then a banquet. With the schedule so full, he didn't appreciate the number of people in the visiting room. He is a human being, not something made of stone or iron. How can he keep up with the schedule filled for every one of the sixty minutes in the hour? He is always on the run, sometimes as if he is in a competition. At times he regrets this life of marathon running.

When he went into the office and fell into the chair, he had an awful headache. Only then did he realize that he hadn't had a shower or a meal that day. He has not been able to keep his daily routines of late. Food, sleep, rest, and other such necessary activities were done whenever he could. He didn't have time even for the child he had awaited for many years. This is the life of a public official, of a political leader. He knew that to enjoy the comforts and status of a leader, one had to make personal sacrifices. Because of that, as he entered the visitors' room, he swallowed his anger and exchanged smiles and pleasantries as needed. But he screamed at the secretary who brought the visitors' cards.

"Go and tell those people who have nothing else to do, to come back tomorrow morning at eight. I don't feel well today, and I don't have the time to see anyone."

The secretary suppressed a smile and waited patiently, knowing that however angry he gets, he would have his meal only after meeting every visitor there. He might even go to the meeting without having his meal. Otherwise he couldn't have become who he is today.

The secretary was right. He met with everyone. When the last person left the office, the secretary went to him and said softly, "There is one more woman to see. She is sitting on the other side. She came from far away, a poor woman. She wanted to see you alone and that is why she was not called until now."

The leader was furious. He couldn't contain his anger and impatience and he hit the table with his fist. The inkbottle turned over and papers flew.

"If you want to see me dead, you can tell me that. Your woman and your recommendations! Ask her to come back tomorrow morning. It is already 4:30 now."

In a calm, tactful voice the secretary replied, "I think it will be a shame. She came early in the morning and waited so long. She hasn't had even a glass of water the whole day. The old woman walked a long distance to see you. She said she wanted only a few minutes of your time."

Silently, the politician waited. He glanced at the woman who moved the expensive curtain aside and followed the secretary into the office room. She looked strange, covered from head to foot in a shawl, with a dirty umbrella and long, swinging ears.

Like an eighteenth-century character she stood in the corner of that big room, embarrassed. Behind her, holding her knee was a six or seven-year-old boy.

The leader looked at her with wonder. He was thinking of something, as if trying to recall a friendly face from the darkness of the past...a reflection...a hesitation. Suddenly he got up. The woman was standing silently with her eyes to the floor. The politician controlled his agitation and said slowly, "Please sit down. Where are you coming from? What do you need? I don't have much time. Tell me quickly what you need."

When the visitor raised her head, the shawl fell off. She was shaking from fear and confusion. Her eyes reflecting dignity and nobility filled with tears. In a pleading tone she said, "I don't want to sit down, Govindankutty, and will leave right away. I just wanted to see you. You may not recognize me. You won't recognize me now. But...but..."

She was straining to get the words out. On her forehead was the traditional mark. Hands were calloused. Without thinking, the leader said, "Oh...my...Kunjathalamma!"

They stood looking at each other for a while. Her eyes caressed him with all the emotions of a mother seeing her long-lost son. There was no complaint in that look, no sense of being offended and no requests—just the sincere, humble look of love and confidence. She sighed deeply and the whole history of a life unfurled and fell to the floor.

In the presence of the unfortunate, poorly-dressed woman whom he had wanted to send away, he forgot all his programs for the evening. Now he felt a great sense of guilt and a heavy heart. It was like toppling the statue of a goddess mistaken for a stone. Stones do not feel happy or sad. They are to be broken. His success in breaking these stones raised him higher and higher. Why didn't he think of the helpless folks at the of the heap, struggling to stay alive? They had wounds that do not bleed and stomachs that do not beg for a grain of rice even if they suffer from hunger. She was one of the lambs sacrificed for the great yaga,[1] still showering him with the blessings of love.

He felt that he was getting smaller and smaller in front of this woman. Now he was not the politician speaking at the public meeting, not the expert attending committees. He was a little boy in a faraway village, playing sticks, collecting mangoes, and jumping over brooks. His father died early and the uncles left soon after. His mother tried hard to make both ends meet. Her goal was to educate him. She wanted him to get to a high position and do well in life. He went to school and covered the primary classes quickly. He remembered what this woman, Kunjathalamma of Manakkal,[2] told his mother: "Govindankutty is a smart boy, Lakshmi. He will go places."

Amma would say sadly, "How am I sending him to school? I don't even have enough to feed him. How can I get him books, pencils, notebooks and whatever else is needed?"

Kunjathalamma was quiet, thinking of something. "That is nothing, Lakshmi. We will find a way. Can this smart boy collect flowers for the daily pooja?[3] I will find the money."

Like a kind goddess she looked at him. He could remember that face only like that of a goddess. Is it because most of the times they saw each other in front of the temple? Or is it because she waited with rice balls like Annapoorna?[4] By the time he went through the bushes and climbed the trees to collect flowers for the pooja, he would be famished. Kunjathalamma's son, Unni, would be finished with breakfast. She would wait with these rice balls made by her fair hands, with yogurt and mango pickle. Kunjathalamma would put rice balls that tasted better than amruthu[5] into Govindankutty's hands, along with words that were even tastier. She would tell Amma, standing near by and crying, "Don't worry, Lakshmikutty, he will study well and become great. Then he will get tiles for your house."

He remembered with sorrow that when the house was tiled, his mother was not there to see it.

After his mother died, his only refuge was Kunjathalamma. She

---

1   Sacrifice done to propitiate gods.

2   House of a Kerala Brahmin.

3   Ceremonial worship.

4   The goddess who provides unlimited food.

5   Food of gods, ambrosia.

poured her affection over that boy. Often she gave him some change for his needs and set aside the special rice cake made for Durga pooja. Giving that to him she would say, "Don't show it to Unni. I kept this for you. That haughty boy has a bottomless stomach."

Govindankutty continued to reflect on this long-ago time. Did she consider these acts as charity work? As far as Kunjathalamma was concerned, these were a necessary part of her life. She did not find anything unusual about it. She was living just to give. It was not just her thinking, but her neighbors, Mathai, Muhamad, and Chathanpulayan, thought so too. She was born to give. If she didn't give, who will give? In that village this became the norm. Everyday, after dark, one can hear the call from the Mana: "Anyone who has had no dinner?"

People considered that house as the common granary and dining hall, and eating there as their right. And so Govindankutty did not consider it necessary to say even a word to Kunjathalamma when he left after completing high school. By that time he had grown big, read many books, and heard many speeches. He had learned about communal conflict and that love, obligation, and gratitude were meaningless. Fulfilling Kunjath-alamma's predictions, the smart young man's star was rising through speakers' platforms and elected positions. But he had no time to think of his old village. Years passed, and events turned things upside down.

Recently, as he was being driven to a reception, he saw that the place where the sprawling Manakkal house stood was vacant, full of weeds and thorny bushes. The temple pond was half filled, and the gatehouse tilted and crumbling.

"This family perished by giving," one of his companions said. "They didn't realize that times had changed. Whoever went there was fed well. When the rent and taxes couldn't be collected, they sold the properties to buy food. When there was no more property to sell, they sold parts of the house and continued their charity work. At the death of the eldest Namputhiri, they sold the house to feed the largest group of people ever. Unni is down with arthritis. A younger brother who finished high school was tired of looking for a job and joined some political party."

He also learned that Kunjathalamma had moved to a small house far away with the sick son and his children. She was able to do that only through the kindness of one of her former tenants.

As a leader he used to raise the slogan "Down with big land holdings!" Now he understood that big land ownership was shattered without any-one's help.

He had thought of visiting her to find out how she was doing. Kunjathalamma fasted often: on all sacred days and Mondays—about twenty days a month. Those days she cooked and fed many people. Her face, taut from fasting so often, had the smile of satisfaction. She used to sing:

"When people are hungry
Cook and feed them gladly!"

One day a poor woman said, "Kunjathalamma, I have a question. We starve because we don't have anything to eat. Why are you not eating?"

Kunjathalamma thought for a while and replied, "It is to know the pain of being hungry and not having food to eat. Poverty is a terrible thing. Just think of hungry children crying and the parents having nothing to give. Oh Bhagavan![6] Don't let that happen to anyone!"

She prayed to some God in her mind and paid abeyance. Seeing that, everyone around would do the same. It is this Kunjathalamma, who fed the poor and fasted for many reasons, that is now ...

The leader felt dizzy.

Outside, the car that was to take him to the meeting was honking. Impatient secretaries were trying to see what was going on. The mother and son who were embracing each other with their eyes, without saying a word, but understanding a great deal, woke up to their surroundings.

Amma said, "Govindankutty, you should excuse me for coming and troubling you. Before dying, Lakshmi said that I was the only help for her son. I was happy to hear that. I was happy you made the best of it."

She stopped and said hesitantly, "Unni was bedridden eight years ago. The house is all destroyed. The younger boy finished high school and has been searching for a job ever since. I heard that the upper caste is not supposed to get any help for education or jobs any more. So he has gone to work for some political party. There is a girl of marriageable age at home. People have been telling me that you can make things happen."

With a long sigh, she pushed her grandson forward and said slowly, very slowly, "If nothing else, get him admitted to a school. At least he will get lunch at school. Oh, God, protect us."

The leader was stunned. Kunjathalamma, who provided food to so many poor people, had to beg for her grandson's lunch? Is this the reward for giving? The palace of nobility has been ruined!

His tears came down freely. He knelt before her, touched her feet and said, "Amma, forgive me, forgive me! Govindankutty is a vicious man. He is a sinner. He is an ungrateful man! Yet, you don't curse him.

---

6   God.

We destroyed your home. We were the reason for your not getting rent. In our fight for the poor, we forgot the hands that fed them. Even now you do not curse us. Instead you are showering blessings on us. They are more powerful than your curse.

"I don't know if I can help your son. Even the lunch program is not under my control. But I have one request, please be a mother to the motherless Govindankutty. Pass on this love, affection and sincerity to the next generation. Only your heart is still filled with these."

He turned to the secretary and said, "Tell the driver to take Amma home. Then call the people involved with the meeting and tell them that due to some unforeseen circumstances, I am unable to attend the meeting. There are some more important matters that I must finally deal with. I am the son of the Daughter of Man."

WOODEN DOLLS
Karoor

The census enumerator stood in the yard and read the name and address to himself—312 Aasaariparampil—and called out: "Anybody home?"

From a room divided by a palm-leaf screen, a woman came out.

"Is your name 'Ummini'?" the enumerator asked, looking at the list in his hand.

The young woman's naturally big eyes got even bigger. She was afraid that it was a summons or police matter.

"I am taking the census. How many people live here?"

"Now only I am here. Amma[1] just left to cut thazha.[2] My brother went for his construction work."

"Whose name is Ummini?"

"That is my Amma's name."

"OK. Is Ummini male or female?"

She laughed. It was a sarcastic laugh, but a beautiful one.

"Amma and I are females. My brother is a male."

"How about your father?"

"He died."

"So Ummini is a widow."

"Now she is."

Then she said, "When you are doing census work, maybe you are not allowed to use an umbrella. But if you do this work in the scorching sun, there will be fewer people to count. Why don't you sit on that bench?"

He moved to the veranda, besmeared with cow dung, and sat on the bench.

He got all the necessary information about Ummini and recorded them.

"And your name?"

"My name is Nalini." She acted a bit shy while giving that response.

"Age?"

---

1 Mother.

2 Leaf of pandanus plant, dried and used for making mats.

"What do you think?"

"I don't think anything."

She smiled.

"Twenty-three."

"Are you married?"

"Yes."

"You have a husband?"

She hesitated.

"He is not here now. Have you been to the Thirteenth-mile area?"

"Someone else has that area. So you have a husband, don't you?

"You can write that I have or I don't have," she said in a careless fashion.

"Those two responses don't mean the same thing."

"Then you can write that I have a husband, but write it very lightly."

"The marriage must have been recently arranged. Then it should be recorded not as 'married', but as 'unmarried.'"

"We got married all right."

She scratched the back of her head, making her dry, dirty hair fall down as a backdrop for her beautiful face.

"Your husband?"

"I have a husband, but not really."

"He has divorced you. Then you are 'husbandless.'"

"That word sounds like one you can use. Say it one more time. This is a complicated case. He did not divorce me. If he had, why would he send a messenger every week?"

"Then you must have divorced him."

"I didn't ask for this marriage to begin with nor did I ask for a divorce later. You can write whatever you want. You know everything."

"I don't know anything about your husband. I will record whatever you tell me. You have a husband."

"That sounds better."

"This is not a book to write things as sounding good or bad. I have to write down facts."

"What I said is true," she said as she tied her hair into a bun. He watched her do that.

"Have you given birth to any children?"

"I have given birth to no boy or girl."

"Have you terminated any?"

"Within six months of my getting married they started termination. I didn't spend one day there without it."

"Termination every day?"

"That's why I came away."

"What are you saying? Termination means abortion. Have you aborted a pregnancy?"

"What shameless things you talk about. It is good my brother is not here."

That didn't sit well with the enumerator. "If he were here what would have happened? This is government business. You can have your brother or even your uncle, I will ask all the questions to be asked. You have to give me true responses. If not, it is a crime. Whatever you tell me will be kept confidential."

"If you feel very hot you can fan yourself with this," she said as she put a fan made from paala[3] on the bench. "I only meant that I will feel shy to say all these things if he were here."

"So, what do you say?"

"No."

"Meaning you won't respond?"

"No, no. Didn't you ask me about abortion? That. I haven't had one."

"I see that your in-laws wanted the marriage terminated. What is your monthly income?"

"My brother gets a daily wage of three rupees."

"Not your brother's income. What is your income?"

"I don't go out to work."

"So you don't have an income. You are a dependent."

"Me, a dependent? Who told you this? It must be Katha at the boat jetty. I have a few things to say about her also."

He was amused by her response and smiled.

"Who is Katha and what did she say? You didn't hear what I said. If a person has no income, he or she has to live on another person's income. You have no income. You have expenses for food, clothes, etc. You are dependent on the person who provides these things. You depend on your mother or brother for your livelihood. True?"

"These questions sound like the ones asked in the court."

"Have you been asked questions in the court?"

"That malicious man did that also."

"Your husband, right?"

"Some husband! Just write down that I have no husband. I will give you something for that."

"Let that be. You don't have an income, right?

"I have an income. I don't depend on anyone. I have an income of at least 15 rupees a month."

---

3 Spathe of the areca palm that attaches the leaf to the tree.

"OK. What do you do?"

"This government business is getting too personal. I do not do just one thing, but many things."

"Go ahead and describe them all. I have plenty of room here to write all that."

"I prepare the meals in this house. I am the one who besmeared the floor."

"You did it well. The floor shines like a mirror."

"Once my Panikkan,[4] no he is not anyone to me, told me that my cheeks shine like the mirror. So the floor must look like my cheeks." She laughed at her own joke.

He also laughed.

A girl from next door came and stood there staring at the enumerator.

"She is only ten years old. Look at the way she looks at you. In two years she won't leave anyone who comes this way."

The girl was angry. "Just because I looked at him, did you lose anything? Hey, I am leaving." So saying she went back the way she came, muttering something.

Nalini said, "She is just upset. If anyone comes to the house, I don't know how she knows, but she is here in no time."

The enumerator was feeling uncomfortable to stay there long.

"Then? You didn't say what you do"

"Didn't I say? Whatever there is to do in a house, I do all that."

"I want to know about work that gives you an income."

"If I don't have work that gives me an income, will you give me something?"

"If you ask that way," he was reluctant to complete the sentence.

"If I ask, you may give, right?"

He looked around.

She said, "When someone comes to the house, one should show some courtesy."

He said suddenly, "Did I say anything discourteous?"

"No, you didn't. I am the one who was discourteous. I think you like to chew betel leaves." Saying that she went into the house and he could hear her getting some things.

After a little while, she brought betel leaves and other things for a chew. He was getting it ready, while she went into the house and came

---

4 One who works on articles of gold, iron, or wood.

back with three wooden dolls. Then she said, "This is what I do. I can make one of these in a day."

He took the dolls and examined them. They were images of women, about nine inches tall, beautifully painted to a shiny finish. They had pretty, chubby limbs, raised breasts, strong abdomens, narrow waists, and plenty of hair, with an attractive smile—delightful statuettes that attracted his complete attention. Then he looked at her.

"All four are the same. Amazing!"

"What is amazing is seeing three and counting four," she said. He didn't respond to that.

"Do you make these in a mold?"

"Casting from molds is not our tradition. We are carpenters."

"You must have milled these dolls. They look like Lakshmi the Goddess who came out of Paalaazhi[5] when it was churned."

"I was not part of Paalaazhi churning. So I have not seen Lakshmi. I was just showing you my work. Why did you count these as four?"

"These lifeless three and the live one who made them make it four. What is amazing is how similar they are."

"Does that mean the living one looks like the lifeless ones? There is nothing amazing about it. That is my fate."

Her eyes flashed. She went to the room again and came back with flushed face and another doll in her hand. She put it near him. He took it and examined it carefully.

"Is this Krishna who killed Kamsa[6] or someone in Krishna's get up? If this were bigger, we could have put in the vegetable field instead of a scarecrow, so that no one would cast eyes on the produce. If it were smaller—"

She interrupted him. "This is how it turned out by the time I made about 50. At first, people bought them for three or four annas[7] each. Slowly, the face changed, but everything else was like Krishna's. The face became like that of another Krishna, my husband. Thinking of him made me angry, and when the doll was finished it looked like him. All my anger reflected on the doll's face. Slowly, people didn't want to buy the doll. So I stopped making them and decided not to make a man's figure.

"Then I made Sri Parvathi's[8] statues. Meaning, I made a woman's figure and called it Sri Parvathi. I have not seen Parvathi either, and that's the

---

5   The mythical ocean of milk.

6   Lord Krishna's uncle, who was killed by Krishna as predicted.

7   Sixteen annas made a rupee in the old currency.

8   Consort of Siva.

best I could do. I have heard about Parvathi's meditation and penance, and how she danced with Shiva. I have seen some of these in the cinema also. I understand that Parvathi and Parameswaran[9] have had disagreements. Sometimes, I sit before the mirror and imitate Parvathi's different facial expressions and make the dolls. I pretend to be Parvathi while making the dolls. In the end, Parvathi looks like ..."

Before she could finish the sentence he said, "You and Parvathi are equals."

"How can I be equal to Parvathi? The dolls look like me. I am beginning to feel embarrassed selling these dolls that look like me. If I make dolls in my likeness and sell, who will ..."

He added quickly, "Lots of people will buy them."

"I have seen that. Even those who buy make fun of me, saying that I am selling these dolls in my likeness to attract men. I mentioned Katha a while ago. She said that to my face. I used some choice, abusive words in response. Then I wondered how I would abuse people who say such nasty things behind my back. If someone else had made money like this I might have said the same thing."

"That may be true. But your ability to recreate your image so accurately is amazing."

"You flatter me. If you make one, using it as a sample, you can easily make as many as you want. You should make the first one looking in the mirror. It is no big deal."

"That is not true. Not many people can make an image of self as you do."

"Most of my neighbors used to agree with whatever I said, though I was scared of them."

"You are not scared of me, are you?"

"Now I am not scared of anyone. I don't even think that there are people other than me."

"Most artistic people are like that."

She went into the room. Before she returned he completed that statement in a soft voice: "And that is called arrogance."

She put four more dolls before him. They were in her likeness, but showing emotions: compassion, amazement, ferocity, and romance at their height.

"If I say these are first rate, will you make fun of me, saying that I am inclined to flatter?"

"I can refrain from saying that. Why do you say that they are first

---

9 Another name for Siva.

rate? I don't sell these any more. I do these so that I don't sleep during the day. Some day, these will become popular.

When they get to people who don't know me, no one will say that this is publicity for a woman looking for men. I am sure of that."

"You have a talent and you use it well. It is a shame that you have no way of making a living out of it. Why are you afraid of scandal? Let people say what they want. Any blind man will give a rupee for a doll. You can meet your needs without anyone's help. I am going to write: profession—wood carving."

He wrote that and more. He asked about her brother and wrote down everything. Meanwhile, she took all the dolls in, except one. That she held in her hand.

He chewed another betel leaf. "Did you say you don't sell any of these dolls?"

"I don't eat them or burn them. So what else do I do with them?"

"Do you have many more?"

"Is it one of the census questions?"

"I will see you. Your husband may get ang ..."

She interrupted him. "I told you about that already. To a stranger how can I say anything more? He is an animal. He drinks and becomes like a mad dog. He will fight with everyone he comes across on the way and get beaten up. Until he sobers up, that means till morning, he is in the police station. One night, the head constable sent a policeman, saying that I should go and bail him out. I said he could come out in the morning. The policeman said that knowing that the carpenter was not home someone might come and attack me. If that happened, he didn't want me to go to the police to complain. I told him that if anyone came in, I would use the broad chisel I keep under my pillow. The policeman left.

After a couple of hours, my man came in, unsteady on his feet. I didn't ask him anything or say anything. In the morning I told him, "I am going to my mother's house."

"Why?" he wanted to know.

"If I stay here, I might use the broad chisel to kill someone. That is why I am leaving," I said.

"I am not going to take it lying down," was his response. Saying that I was not willing to live with an animal, I left. I went to the road, got on the bus, and came here. There are many more stories that I don't want to talk about."

When she stopped talking, he got up to leave.

She said, "You can have this, if you want," and gave him a doll.

He accepted it with pleasure. But when he saw that it was the angry doll, his face changed. Still, he thanked her and put a piece of paper on the bench and said, "Look at this."

She did. He had sketched her! She looked at it carefully.

"You drew this while we were talking? Amazing! Please give me that doll." She went inside, brought back a slightly bigger statuette of Parvathi, in a difficult, penitential pose, and presented it to him. He accepted it with great pleasure and gratitude.

"OK. Thanks for coming." She stepped down to the courtyard. He started for the next house. In his heart a veena[10] was being strummed!

---

10 A stringed musical instrument used in India.

THE DAWN OF ENLIGHTENMENT
M. P. Sahib

Two more years must go by.

"Please read that again," she said moving a bit closer on the doorstep
where she sat.

"We are taking a ship to Korea next month and will come back only
after two years. I will get home leave soon after we return..."

The mailman read that part again. Handing the letter to her he said,
"Keep this carefully, he has given an address."

"Next time you come, please bring a stamped envelope," she
requested.

This was the first letter Ameena got after Asanar left home. He wrote
many things that made her feel embarrassed when the mailman read the
letter to her. But she listened to every word he read and felt as if her husband was talking to her in person. She looked at his photograph on the
wall, at the familiar uniform and smile, remembering the way he talks.
The mailman would read some and then cast a side-glance at her. Quickly
she would look away. She still feels bashful thinking about it.

She held the photograph in her hand. What stature! The way he
stands with the gun resting on his shoulder is something to look at! He is
smart! He travels by plane and ship. When he looks down from the plane
he can see the mosque in Mecca. Two more years... With a deep sigh she
put the picture back on the wall.

Asanar left two months after he and Ameena got married. It was not a
marriage approved by the family. When they met under the mango tree
among the rocky hills, they stared at each other, forgetting everything.
The goat had gone down the hill pulling the rope that was in her hand.
When the cigarette he was smoking, held between his fingers, burned
him, he threw it down. She ran away laughing. She went up the hill and
looked back to see him standing there with another cigarette he had lit.
After grazing around, the goat came back. Asanar tied it to a tree stump
and gave it a couple of berries he had collected. Ameena could feel the

taste of the fruits in her mouth and, without realizing it, she stroked her chest.

When it became necessary for them to get married, the family members closed their eyes, but wondered where she would live. He couldn't take her with him. So he bought a piece of land and built a hut for her. How could she live there alone? She was brave about it. There were houses close by and if the relatives were not willing to help, there was an old woman who could be called to give her company for the night.

The mailman comes to her small village only once a week. On Friday afternoon the bicycle bell can be heard on the road continuously. Then the children playing under the trees gather around him. Their leader might try ringing the bell without the mailman's permission, and the children would scatter away. He delivers one or two letters after calling out the addressee's name. But that is not the end of his responsibilities. It is his responsibility to read the letter and explain it. Usually the letter will be from the tax collector. The responsibility of responding to the letter also falls on the mailman. He fulfills all these responsibilities with pleasure. So the villagers give him the best reception possible. There are about 60 houses scattered around, but few people in the village are literate. The children have just begun to go to a primary school two miles away.

On Fridays when the prayers are over and the people disperse, Ameena will come out of the house and stand outside looking at the road. Here comes the bicycle! Her face brightens when she sees that helpful man who is the go-between for her heart's secrets.

The young man in uniform, just like her husband, came fast to her house. She went in and put a grass mat on the floor, took a scarf and covered her head, and stood behind the door.

"Very hot." Taking the bag from his shoulder and putting it down, he said, "Please give me some water."

Ameena went to the kitchen and brought some water in a jug, put it on the floor, and pushed it towards him. Then she sat by the steps all ears for what he was going to read. After quenching his thirst, the mailman opened her letter and started reading:

"Ameena, the love of my life, do you know how my heart aches? Last night I had a dream. You and I ..." As he continued to read, she felt embarrassed, yet thrilled. Enticing memories were tickling her mind. She was full of pleasant memories! Sitting there with her head down, she listened carefully to every word being read. On and off she would direct a bashful look towards him. What would he think of her? Why was he looking at her in between? He had a long mark of chandan[1] on his forehead. She didn't like his looks in the least but had to put up with it.

She gave him a piece of paper to write the response. She talked long, giving a lengthy list of news items. Like a newspaper reporter, he stored everything into memory and wrote down only a few notes. She had many more things to say, her hopes and dreams were coming to her mind. But how could she say all that to him? But there was one thing she had to say. The child in her womb was blowing a trumpet. Even that she couldn't say openly. In the end she had an idea. After writing everything, he read the letter to her. She reminded him that he had forgotten to write about the cow giving birth.

"That's it?" He was pressed for time.

"When you come, bring a small pair of knickers..." She didn't complete the sentence.

However much she tried to hide it, now he knew her secret. With a wicked smile, he looked at her. She pulled her head in like a tortoise.

"Oh, I almost forgot. I have to give you money." He pulled out a money order form.

"How much?"

"Thirty. Sign this." He tried to give her the form.

"I don't know how. You can sign it." Showing her helplessness, she gave him that responsibility also.

He laughed. He made her understand the need for the recipient to sign the form. But she didn't know how to write her name.

"Then show me your hand." He took out a tin box from the bag.

Ameena was shaking all over. She has seen the old wife of Meeranadima taking money. A kafir[2] touching her! She couldn't even think about it. As a child, when the vaccinator asked her to show her hand, she ran away. Bapa and Umma tried their best, but she was not going to let him touch her "even if I am to die of smallpox." She could say that then. What could she do now? He might leave without giving the money.

"Are you going to show me your hand or not?" It was an order.

Before she could think about it, her hand stretched out without her knowing it. She sat there with her face turned and eyes closed. It was getting hot. She was perspiring all over. He dipped her thumb in the ink. Iblis[3] has got hold of her!

---

1 Sandalwood paste.

2 Infidel, one who is not a Muslim.

3 The Islamic name for the devil, the representative of the powers of evil.

"Rabb,[4] forgive me," she prayed. Iblis was pulling her to the fire of hell. She tried to pull her hand. Very carefully, he was pressing her thumb. He pushed her black bracelets up her arm. She felt something going to her head, and a sweet sensation went through her heart. Her whole body was aroused. Another wave of emotion swept over her, and then she began to feel cold and numb. After counting the money and giving it to her, he stepped down.

"Don't forget to mail the letter," she called after him.

"I won't." She watched him until he disappeared.

Quickly she took some water and sprinkled it on her hand saying "Kalima."[5] Like a culprit she prayed again: "Forgive me, God."

She counted the new bills backwards and forwards. Her husband was smiling at her from the wall. She went and stood by the picture. "Aren't you ashamed to write such things? Some people!" She covered the picture with both her hands.

Every Friday she would get a letter from Asanar. Now the mailman was coming twice a week. She would sit with her head down until he finished reading the letter. Like a student who has learned things by heart, he would sometimes look at her while reciting from the letter. When there was a money order he would take almost ten minutes to get her thumb imprint. If there were 30 rupees, he would press the thumb almost 30 times. Biting her lower lip, she would sit there with her eyes closed.

Ameena often says with a deep sigh, "Too bad I don't know how to put my signature or write a letter."

The cashew tree spread out like a canopy produced fruits three times. The cow gave birth to another calf. Ameena got a baby that was ready to play with the calf. Contrary to expectations, her baby was a girl. The day it was born, Ameena told the tiny baby who was crying while she was being bathed, "Don't cry my precious. I will send you to school." That was a promise.

When Asanar came on leave, Ameena said, "We must send our Farida to school."

"Why are you so particular about it?" Asanar was surprised.

"So that she can read Bapa's[6] letters."

Asanar was dumbfounded.

---

4   God.

5   The Islamic oath: Allah is the only God and Mohammad is His messenger.

6   Father.

As her husband was preparing to return to duty at the conclusion of his leave, Ameena went close to him and said softly, "If you want to tell me anything, say it now. Don't write such things in the letter, dearest."

What she got back in response was a look full of love.

When Farida was five years old, she joined the school. Every morning Ameena would bathe her, dress her up, and send her off. She would sigh looking at Fareeda with her head covered, laughing and walking to school with the other children. Ameena's heart would break seeing those tiny feet getting tired. But she had a goal. My child must study. She should not be handicapped like her mother.

The number and size of the books increased each year. Farida was in the fifth grade. In the evening she went to the Madrasa[7] to learn the prayers. That little beauty is growing up!

What a pleasure it is to listen to her read. Farida would open her book, point out each picture, and explain things to her Umma.[8]

Farida was reading a piece of paper used for wrapping the red pepper: "American ship capsized along the coast of Japan."

Ameena heard that faintly as she was preparing rice. She said, "Read that, again, child," and came to the doorway. Farida managed to read that again.

"Warship capsized." A lightning bolt went through Ameena's head.

She raised both her hands and prayed, "God almighty, please don't let anything bad happen to Farida's Bapa."

"Umma, it is not our ship, it belongs to America." She made Umma understand.

Ameena picked up her daughter and kissed her. Two teardrops fell on Farida's forehead, but she could not have understood their meaning.

The dawn of enlightenment was coming into that little hut. But it was against the law. Usually Muslim girls are not sent to school. Their education is complete when they learn to recite all thirty sections of the Quran. It is required that they complete it. Arabic was used for court hearings and questioning by "Malaks."[9]

Ameena had completed her prayer recital. She correctly recited

---

7   Traditional Islamic school.

8   Mother.

9   Angels.

whatever the priest had taught her. She would recite "badarulmunir"[10] in a singsong fashion. But she didn't know how to hold a pencil.

"Girls will become bad if they learn kafir's language," next-door neighbor Aisha warned Ameena.

"That is true," she agreed. "But to live in this world, you need to learn that too. No one knows what I had to put up with. My daughter shouldn't have that problem."

Her experience had taught her.

"What did you have to put up with?" Aisha asked, wrinkling her forehead.

"Nothing." Ameena refused to clarify that. After being silent for a short while, she said, "Kafir shouldn't touch her." She sounded determined.

---

10 A love poem.

THE LULLABY OF DREAMS
Martin Eresseril

The creeper with the blue flowers had grown well over the gate. The flowers seemed to be trying to keep the bright deep colors of the sky.

She sat on the stone seat in the veranda to escape the boredom of waiting. When the sparrow flew away disappointed that there was no honey in the flowers, she got up and tried to walk on the footprints her young friend had made the day before. Hearing the bicycle bell on the street, she looked out. Was it him?

On days like today, she would think of talking to him about it when he comes: "You should not be late like this. You don't know how monotonous this waiting is."

But she has never said that. She has not been able to say it was closer to the truth. Suppose he asks, "Why do you wait?" What could she say?

From among the din and clamor on the street, she picked up the sound of her husband's scooter horn. The scooter got to the gate by the time she walked to the gate and opened it. She wondered how she could come up with the smile of a girl waiting with a plate full of flowers, ready to receive him returning home.

Her husband asked, "Are you tired of waiting?"

"No."

She could smile and say that because she was not waiting for him. She knew that however late, he would come home. Then why should she wait?

"I ran into Poulochan. You remember our friend who gave us a camera as a wedding gift, don't you?"

She didn't say that she remembered him or she didn't. She just gave one of her winsome smiles.

He went to the sitting room, sat on the sofa, and started untying his shoe lace, talking about Poulochan. She sat across from him, trying to remember what she had been thinking. What was I thinking of? Oh, yes. Monotonous—mono-tone. She dislikes even saying the word.

He said, "While I take a shower, you get ready. There is a good movie at Shanti."

She gave him a bath towel and took his shoes and put them in the proper place. She was thinking how she might miss seeing her friend if she went to the movie. He didn't come yesterday, either. So he will come today, most probably. If she says she has a headache, she wouldn't have to go to the movie. She lay on the sofa, turning the pages of *Femina.*

Where would he be now? He doesn't stay home when he gets back from college. He must be roaming around the city on his bike. She tried to imagine him smoking cigarettes and joking with his friends at the crossroad. The Women's College was near his house. When she thought about that, she felt uneasy. Then she scolded herself. Why was she feeling jealous?

When her husband came back after taking a shower, she was still lying on the sofa.

"Aren't you ready, yet? Don't you want to go to the movie?"

She said that she didn't feel very energetic and had a headache.

He joked, "You are a doctor. How can you get sick?"

She tried to smile. She had to try to smile. Three years ago, such a small joke was enough to make her laugh out loud. One Sunday evening while they took a walk, he said something and they were on the street laughing when the young man went by on a bike. At that time they were tenants in his house. That night when he got back home, he teased them in front of everyone, "All newlyweds have their honeymoon in Ooty or Kashmir or their bedroom. These two have it on the street. I saw them today, at the crossroad—"

The unfinished sentence implied that they were doing something more than just laughing.

When everyone laughed at this, she became angry and pale. But her husband came to her rescue: "Don't pay any attention to him. You know he has a loose tongue."

It had taken a few days to get over the anger she felt towards him. Today, if only she could get angry at him! She can't. How did this change take place? Even not seeing her baby did not make her feel so uneasy.

She got up in a hurry hearing the gate open. Did he come?

Her husband looked through the window and said, "Your colleagues, Kamala and Ramani."

Oh, she forgot. As she was leaving the hospital they had said that they would come to pick her up to go to the beach.

She changed and went out with them. Walking along the road, she said as if she remembered something, "I forgot to lock the cabinet. The money from this month's salary is all there."

Her husband said, "You go ahead. I will take care of it and catch up with you."

She ignored his offer and went back. She wanted to leave a message with Lakshmi, the servant girl, for her friend—they had gone to the beach and he should join them there. That could not be done if her husband went back.

As she turned around after leaving the message with the servant girl she wondered why she was making up things. Prior to this, she had left a similar message with Lakshmi in front of her husband. She did that even last month. But now...

While on the beach watching the sunset she thought of herself as a burning sphere, and the young man as the deep, calm, endless sea. She would be satisfied if she could dip into a corner of that sea.

She wanted to sink into the depth of the sea and be a burning sphere there. Then the sea will embrace her.

(Who said that love doubles the strength one has?)

Ramani asked, "What happened to you? You don't seem to be as lively as you were when you left the hospital."

Kamala said, "Why are you so quiet? Did you two have a fight?"

"No," her husband said, "she said she had a headache. That must be why."

"Why are you so uneasy?"

"Nothing."

"Not true. Your face says otherwise." She wanted to say that she was uneasy because the young man had not come and he didn't come yesterday either. Do you know who he is to me? He is the sun and I am the earth. Haven't you seen the earth becoming dark when the sun sets? Night is when nothing shines. But she didn't say any of that. She shouldn't. When she realized all the things she was thinking about, she smiled. A while ago she thought she was the burning sun. Now he is the sun.

"Why are you smiling?"

"Oh, nothing."

"Why are you smiling for nothing? Remember I joined medical college after getting a master's degree in psychology."

"Didn't you say that I was uneasy? Isn't that a joke? I smiled thinking of that."

Returning home, she asked if he had come. The negative answer made her sad. Who is she to him? No one. That is why he is not coming. She remembered the day one of his college mates named Cecily was going to Trivandrum to participate in some camp. He was anxious to get to the bus stop to see her off. Seeing him hurrying, she got angry and asked, "If you don't get there, she won't leave? Are you in love with her?"

He laughed. It was a loud laugh made up of numerous small tunes as in a symphony. Then he said, "This is why I say that you have no common sense. Look, Chechi,[1] she is going to represent our organization. Isn't it my responsibility as secretary of the organization to see her off?"

Is that the only reason why he went? Why is he not as anxious to see me? When there are girls of his age to have fun with, why would he want to spend time with me, an older woman who is a wife and a mother?

The young man had said that he had no big sisters and would like to consider me as his Chechi. He is cheating me by saying so. Nonetheless, I will be happy even being his Chechi, but why is he not coming to visit me?

Her husband changed the clothes he went out in, and came to the room in a lungi.[2] He asked, "What are you thinking about standing here? Aren't you going to change? What has happened to you?"

She smiled so that he may not read her mind and said, "Oh, I forgot."

Walking to the dressing room she thought, He will surely come. Could he be sick? No. If he were, he would have sent his servant with a note saying: Chechi, I am sick. Come quickly and give me some medicine.

She thought she could ask her husband if he had seen him, but not now. If she were to ask now, he may sense that she was uneasy because he hadn't come. She decided to ask him while having dinner. The next day was her birthday. She purposely did not tell him, to give him a surprise. Now it seems he may not even come the next day.

While having dinner, she pretended as if she just thought about it and said that it had been a couple of days since the young man had come.

Her husband replied, "He is very busy. I saw him on my way home from the office. You know that they have an arts club. They have scheduled an evening of music. He gave me all the details. He is running around for that."

She got very angry at no one in particular. Who am I to him? No one. To him the arts club and girls going to camp are important. Not me. Am I that old? While getting ready to go to the beach I looked in the mirror. I am not old. There are no lines on my face.

When he comes praising the girls who sing for the arts club I will say, I don't want to hear this. Can you stop this boring topic and leave?

1   Elder sister.

2   A lower garment, consisting of a length of checkered cloth.

And if he leaves? Let him go. He can go to his favorite girl.

She realized that her husband was watching her. He asked, "Why are you moving your lips and talking to yourself?"

She took a few seconds to respond.

"I...I...When you said an evening of music, I was trying to sing a song."

He laughed and said, "It is good that you didn't sing it aloud." He continued, "In Shakespearean dramas there are people who speak out what they are thinking—soliloquy. You have no idea about literature."

She laughed just to please him. She loved him more at that moment. She wanted to love him more at that time just to feel angrier at her friend. She said, "When you come to the bedroom, I will pay you back for saying what you just did."

"We will see. You know that I always win."

They laughed together sharing the pleasure in doing so. She thought of her friend even at that moment. "I am going to take revenge on you tonight. You won't know how I am going to do that. That is the secret of our bedroom."

The next day when they sat down for lunch her husband said, "Because our baby Sajimol is not here, I will sing 'Happy birthday' to you."

She laughed. When she remembered that a two-year-old couldn't sing, she laughed all the more. As they were having lunch, she said that it would have been nice if her friend could have joined them.

He said, "On my way home, I stopped at his house. He is not there. He had to go somewhere and left early morning, saying that he would be back late."

Pretending to use the authority of a big sister she asked, "Why is he running around for the club and association instead of studying?"

"He is a grown up boy. We don't have to remind him."

When her husband left for the office after lunch, she went to the bedroom to take a nap. She had to get to the hospital only by four p.m. That means she had two more hours. She had no idea how far her thoughts would go if she didn't take a nap. Her friend had spoiled the excitement of her birthday.

She woke up with a start when something fell softly on her chest. When she put her hand on the chest she got a bunch of flowers–Arali[3]

---

3   Nerium.

flowers. She looked up and saw him standing at the door laughing. And she thought he wouldn't come!

She pressed the flowers to her chest. He said, "It is time to get up, madam. How can you be sleeping at this time?"

She got up and arranged her sari. As she was tying her long hair into a bun, he said, "Many happy returns, Chechi."

She stood there tying her hair as if she didn't hear what he said. He continued, "I didn't have to wish you. Don't you see the flowers? They know how to speak. Do you understand the language of flowers?"

She controlled the smile that came to her face. Arali flowers are for lovers and not for birthdays. She wanted to laugh thinking about that. But keeping a serious face, she passed him and went to the sitting room. She sat on the sofa, looking out of the window. He went and sat across from her and snapped his fingers in front of her face to get her attention.

She said, "I am not talking to you. I am angry at you. Where were you yesterday? Where were you the day before?"

He laughed as if to say "oh that's all" and replied, "I had some things to attend to, Chechi. However, this morning I had to go 60 miles for something urgent, but hurried back. Do you know for what?"

"For what?"

"To wish you a happy birthday."

Within seconds, her anger subsided and she even forgot being angry at him for going to see off Cecily. She asked, "How did you find out today is my birthday?"

"I remember the 11th. Do you remember going to the circus last year?"

She was delighted with him. He remembered her birthday! If she were nobody to him, why would he remember that? Even her husband remembered it only when she mentioned it two days ago.

She said, "I thought you wouldn't come. Because of that I had no interest in celebrating my birthday."

She saw that his face brightened up. When he sat there and stared at her, she felt like a dewdrop melting in the sun. It reminded her of her child's cries of hunger as she tried to breastfeed. Without drawing his attention, she put her hand under the sari and touched her breast.

As they sat there lost for words, she wished to tear down the fine curtain that separated them—

"I..." She was lost for words.

"Yes, Chechi?"

Suddenly she remembered that if she didn't control herself...

"Oh, nothing."

She tried to change the subject. "Have you had lunch?"

"No. On your birthday, why would I have lunch somewhere else?"

"Then wash your hands and come. It is past three. Even though I thought you wouldn't come, I have kept lunch for you."

While he was having lunch, she asked, "How do you like the curries? I made that fish curry."

"I knew that as soon as I tasted it—no salt, not enough chili or tamarind."

She was provoked. "You don't have to eat it."

"I didn't get what I like most."

She got up, went to the cabinet, and brought out a bottle with the picture of a Kathakali[4] character on the label. His face brightened.

"Tender mango pickle! Chechi you are great!"

"I wanted it to be a surprise. I bought it just for you."

He poured it into his plate and said, "I will finish this. Aren't you having lunch?"

"I finished lunch."

"That won't do. There is no fun in eating by myself."

She took part of the rice he had set aside and sat down. He served all the curries to her. She had an appetite like never before and ate with gusto.

He asked her, "How old are you now?"

When she gave the date of birth, he calculated and said, "There is a difference of four years and four months between us—to be exact, 1,568 days."

"Do I look old?"

"To me you are like nature: perpetual beauty."

She was reluctant to believe it and asked, wondering, "You mean it?"

His eyes widened. He just looked at her, but did not respond.

After lunch when they were in the sitting room, he asked, "Isn't it time for you to go to the hospital?"

"I must go. I have half an hour more. If not, I can take the day off for you."

"For me?"

"Yes. Don't you believe it?"

He sat there staring at her. She was intoxicated by happiness. How do you say that in English? Ecstasy? Yes, ecstasy.

---

4 Kerala classical dance.

"What are you thinking about?"

"Thinking about ecstasy."

"Why now?"

"Have you ever felt ecstatic?"

"No. When do you feel ecstatic?"

"Have you ever loved anyone?"

"Do you experience that only if you are in love? Then I am unlucky. Chechi, I have never experienced that."

She knew that his voice was cracking. She remembered what he had said about feeling like a stranger in his own home. He felt sad about not having found an honest friend, ever. He had a philosophy about people who create small islands of selfishness to survive in the swift current of life.

"You are not being honest. Don't you feel ecstatic now? I do."

He sat there not believing what he heard, looking at her face, her eyes, and her quivering lips.

She was losing herself. She realized that the house and the sofas they were sitting on were disappearing. All that was left before her, like a speck of energy, was him.

She asked, "Don't you understand? I love you. You are Paramatma[5] and I am Jeevatma.[6] Aren't you the one who taught me about Hindu philosophy?"

In the ensuing silence after she stopped, she saw him melting, and she continued,

"Don't you understand? I said I love you. I tried very hard not to say this. But I couldn't. Do you understand? I can't help ..."

She stopped, panting, "I am totally helpless."

He got up and walked around in the room. He realized his blood was flowing faster in his veins and he was breathing faster.

"Can't you say something?"

"What do I say? What did you say? Was it about ecstasy? Yes, I experience it, now, at this moment. Do you understand?"

"Yes. Only when you love, can you understand each other."

He said, "I can't believe this. I am talking about this experience. None of the people I loved, loved me back the way I wanted them to."

He came back and sat on the sofa. Looking into her eyes with intense feelings, he asked, "Whom do you love most?"

"You."

---

5   The Supreme Being.

6   The individual soul.

"More than your husband?"

"You."

"More than your baby, Sajimol?"

"You."

"More than your mother?"

"You."

He got out of the room and started walking around in the veranda. He was adding more footprints to the ones she had been following the previous night.

"Why did you go out?"

"It is too hot in the room."

"I can turn on the fan."

"No, thank you."

She got up and went to the door and stood there looking at him. He was walking around, deep in thought.

"What are you thinking of?"

"Of the excitement of Bruce after he won the war."

"Are you feeling happy?"

"No, I feel sad, very sad."

"Why?"

"This love is not free. I am sad about that."

She didn't respond. If he were in love with an unmarried girl, he could have proudly walked around the college campus. She realized that now he had lost that freedom.

Words took a break. On the veranda, more footprints made their mark for her to follow when he was not there.

Finally he said, "The earth is mother and lover to the farmer. I am a farmer and you the earth. Let me go. If I stay here, snakes will entwine my feet."

When he went down the steps, words from her mouth came in the form of a question, "When will you come again?"

"Tomorrow."

He left. She watched him until he and his black bike disappeared.

When her husband came in the evening, he said, "Get ready. We will go to a movie."

"No, we will go to the beach, again."

"We went yesterday."

"I want to see the sunset."

They went to the beach. Sitting in the dry, white sand, away from where the waves break, she watched the sunset. As the blazing sun was sinking into the sea, she thought, "I am the sun and he the sea. It is not enough that I sink into a corner of that sea. I want to be the sun that is submerging into the whole sea."

At night, as they were getting ready for bed, her husband said, "Victory is always mine. Today, being your birthday, I will give you that honor."

She said, "No, I want to sleep."

When he embraced her, she gave in without the usual protest. She embraced her husband, trying to imagine that she was in her friend's arms. Without realizing that he was sleepless and crying into the pillow, she slept in the languor of dreams.

ROSEMARY

K. L. Mohana Varma

Rosemary had no desire to go for viewing Thampuran's[1] body.

But Sonny insisted, "Aren't we neighbors? If nothing else, he is not like the others who have come to this mountainous area. True, we have had our differences of opinion. We have had our quarrels and disagreements. But that is something else. It is common among people of culture and class. Emperors and kings fight battles among themselves and kill one another. Does that mean they are angry at one another? No."

"None of that bothers me. No argument," Rosemary said.

"Then get ready," Sonny said.

It was half an hour since she was asked to get ready.

Rosemary pressed the green plastic bindi[2] on her forehead and looked at herself in the mirror.

Ready.

"But, why am I not feeling even a little bit sad?" she wondered.

The fog over the hills she'd seen earlier had changed into fluffy clouds here and there. Before long it would all change into tiny droplets of water. What will happen to the whiteness of the fog?

"If I had asked Thampuran, he would have had an answer. But if I ask Sonnychayan,[3] he would say I am nuts," Rosemary thought.

"Rosemary, I think even after all this time, you have not got used to the blustery weather here," Sonny said some months ago.

I could not get used to the mountain, the woods, or the dreadful silence of the night, until last year when I met Thampuran.

Rosemary smiled.

Sonny was ready and waiting in the jeep. Hearing the door opening, he looked up from the newspaper.

"See, there is a report and a picture in the obituary. The reporters

---

1   A male member of the royal family.

2   The small dot worn on the forehead by women in India.

3   "Achayan" is added to the name to show respect for the husband.

must have prepared it when he became serious. The cremation is at 11:30," he remarked.

As Rosemary was getting her slippers, Sonny said, "Gee, you should have selected another color. I am not saying you should wear a black sari, but one with a black border or design or something appropriate for the occasion."

"Oh, this is OK. If I go back to change now, you will be late."

"People will notice us, that's why I said it."

Rosemary got into the jeep and sat down.

"This is OK," she said.

Sonny folded the paper, put it on the back seat and started the jeep. From the back of the jeep a little bird was startled by the noise, flapped its wings, and flew away.

Rosemary said, "It is the little bird I was looking for all over the place last night. It hit on our fan and fell down. Didn't I tell you? Poor thing! It was not yet ready to fly. I picked it up and put it on the sofa. By the time I turned around it was gone. For some time I could hear a faint cry."

The driver was waiting at the gate.

"Sankaran, you get in the back. Did you order a wreath?"

Sankaran closed the gate and jumped into the back.

"Yes, I ordered one. But today they have too many orders. Kumaran doesn't know where he can get flowers for so many wreaths. Also, the market is closed today."

"Why?"

"In Thampuran's honor. All political parties are together on this clos-ing. The schools are also closed. We will know about the wreath only when we get to the shop."

"Thampuran doesn't need any wreath," Rosemary thought, but kept the thought to herself.

One day Thampuran had said, "Rosemary, I always mess up long names. My daughter-in-law is from Maharashtra. Her name is Arundhathy. I always messed it up and finally started calling her Aru. Like that if I can call you just Rose, it would be easier."

Thampuran always spoke in a melodious, singsong fashion. One had to listen carefully to understand. If you go to the southern side of the hills and listen to the brook, after a while you can hear the brook and its singsong flow. Thampuran's way of speaking haltingly was just like that.

"Rosemary, you know that these plants and flowers have life. We studied that in our botany class." Rosemary nodded.

"But the plants and flowers that grow freely in these mountainous areas have not just the ordinary life but also a culture and energy of their own. Because of that they can communicate, in a kind of telepathic language. Many times I have felt that the plants express their culture and history through the flowers."

Then Rosemary did not understand any of it.

"You must talk to plants. The flowers must realize that we can understand them. Stop along the turn near the Kattimala hill, Rose, no, Rosemary, stop and listen. From where you can reach them on the side of the hill, the whole area is full of hibiscus. I should say 'was' because half of it is cleared. Between January and February suddenly that area becomes red. All the plants flower at the same time. If you go there at that time and listen, you won't believe the tumult. Have you attended Trichur Pooram?[4] You have heard of the commotion there, the noise from the crowd, the merchants calling out their wares, children's laughter, the sound from the microphone, and the bands with their drums and wind instruments that beat all these. The tumult of the flowers is similar."

Rosemary smiled.

"The flowers speak in many ways, not like us by sound alone."

At the age of 40, Rosemary was back in school. During the last five years there was not one day she didn't regret coming to this mountainous area to live. She hated the mountain and the wooded acres with her whole heart. Every day she thought that she could have settled in Bangalore had she insisted just a little. She could have convinced Regi. If Regi had agreed, Sonnychayan would have too. She thought it would be a month, six months, or a maximum of two years. Sonny was reluctant to leave what his father worked so hard to make with some stranger. "Until we find someone who will give a good price, we will stay there," he said. The price was going up almost by the day. Before meeting Thampuran she never thought she would make friends with nature here.

To take in every word that Thampuran was saying, Rosemary intently watched the movements of his lips.

Thampuran took a sip from his crystal glass, a small sip.

She had never seen anyone take an alcoholic drink like that.

If it were Sonnychayan, he would have had his fourth drink by this time and then would have wanted to make love.

She asked, "Then?"

---

4   A festival in Trichur famous for its fireworks, bands, colorful umbrellas, and decorated elephants.

"Then there is the fragrance. The same flowers send out a different aroma into the breeze at different times," Thampuran said.

Rosemary still did not understand.

At first she didn't understand anything.

The tarred road had huge potholes. One had to be very careful while driving. Here and there concrete slabs were laid to direct water flow, but they had shifted and were now sitting very precariously.

A bus was going very slowly in front, without giving way to the jeep. Sonny sounded the horn frequently. But the bus driver went very slowly over the potholes. The road was not wide enough and the footpath was at least six inches below.

"Sankaran," Sonny asked his driver, "who is the driver on that bus? Is he deaf? If we go at this pace, it will be ten o'clock by the time we get there."

"The bus is going to stop," Sankaran said.

The bus pulled over at a bus stop, giving as much of the road as possible to the jeep. Three or four people were running to catch the bus. Sonny edged the jeep in front of the bus and turned around to look at the driver.

The driver laughed.

"Good morning, you must be going to Thampuran's house," he said.

It was Mathaichan, an ex-serviceman. When Thampuran started the bus service, he was the first driver. When that route was sold to someone else, he was retained. Everyone in this place knew Mathaichan.

Sonny also laughed and said, "Yes."

"I am also coming. Right after this trip I will get there. There was no one else. That is why I had to do this trip. Otherwise..."

Sonny increased the speed of the jeep and pulled away.

The mountaintops had changed color. The fog had melted, giving way to the green color of the leaves. The river that one could see on and off flowing along the valley received direct sunlight and shined like molten silver.

Rosemary was happy. She thought, "Today, nature will wear all its ornaments to say farewell to Thampuran. What month is this? January, after the fifteenth... there is still time for the hibiscus bushes to flower, or would the plants start the commotion and give a tumultuous send-off to Thampuran?"

"What are you thinking of?" Sonny asked.

"Oh, nothing," she said.

A car sounded the horn behind. Sankaran turned around.

"Everyone is going to Thampuran's," he said.

"At least some of the ministers will come. He was an active member of the Communist Party," Sonny said. Sankaran kept quiet.

Sonny continued, "Long ago, he was involved in a notorious murder case. Do you remember? He was in hiding for a long time."

But recently he was not involved in any "ism."

"I am scared of blood. I can beat up someone and am not reluctant to use force to defeat the enemy. But blood..." Thampuran had said.

That day Rosemary had asked a question for the first time. "Why is that? Isn't blood part of causing pain to someone?"

Thampuran said, "Maybe. It is something I cannot figure out. I cannot watch even a small living thing covered in blood struggling for life. That must be why I cannot eat non-vegetarian food."

"Did you do that even when you were in hiding?" Rosemary asked.

"Yes," Thampuran replied. "My mother taught me to practice 'Vratham.'[5] It is not difficult for me to live for two or three days just on water. That practice helped me a great deal while I was in hiding."

The market was closed. Kumaran had closed his shop, but waited outside with the wreaths. He said, "It is good that you came early, Sankaran. I couldn't get enough flowers. This is all I could do. I don't know if you like it."

"This is fine." Sankaran took the wreath and put it inside the jeep.

He was saying, "The hibiscus plants near Kattimala are all in bloom. They came out early this year. But hibiscus flowers are not good for a wreath."

Sonny started the jeep and remarked, "He was a great man." He then laughed.

"I appreciated him most for the way he handled alcoholic drinks. We, I include myself, have no limit to the amount we drink. It is as if we are anxious to get whatever is available inside. But he was not like that. Rosemary, do you remember him coming to our house the day the workers had the fight? It took me two, two and a half hours to go to the police station and see the lawyer to take care of everything. During that time all he had was a peg-and-a-half of scotch."

It had been a boundary dispute. It ended in the workers beating and stabbing one another. There were mistakes on both sides. Thampuran came to where the fight took place. Sonny and Rosemary were also there. As part of settling the case out of court, Sonny invited Thampuran to

---

5   Fasting.

come home. He agreed to Sonny taking care of everything at the police station and with the lawyer.

That day Thampuran said, "God must have chosen this fight as a means for me to get to know you better. It is good it happened."

While having lunch, Thampuran said, "The area where they fought is the most fertile area in Kerala. There are many types of vegetation growing there. Some are not even named yet. I have an idea in mind, to set up a nature treatment center there. You can even call it a monastery. With all the necessary medicinal herbs, plants, and trees around, with sunny days, breeze, rain, and mist this place will be ideal. Don't know if the idea will work."

Sonny was in a good mood after four drinks. He said loudly, "It will all work out, Thampuran. You shouldn't worry. We will start such a center. This Sonny will see that it happens."

Rosemary looked at Thampuran. There was no impatience or scorn in his eyes.

All of a sudden Rosemary felt that she was falling in love with Thampuran. She wanted very much to embrace him and kiss him. Years of emptiness inside her disappeared suddenly.

Rosemary looked at Thampuran and suppressed a smile.

She realized what she had been waiting for. She didn't have to go searching for it anymore.

After lunch when Thampuran washed his hands and turned around Rosemary handed him a towel. Unexpectedly, her fingers touched his and suddenly she felt like a 16-year-old over her whole body. She blushed.

The next day Rosemary asked Sonny, "Are you serious about the Nature Cure Center that Thampuran was talking about?"

"What?" Sonny asked.

"What did you say yesterday?

"Am I supposed to remember whatever I say when I am drunk? You are something else," Sonny said.

Rosemary thought about Thampuran.

The spacious huge front yard of Thampuran's house was full of cars, jeeps, and people. Sonny walked in front and Sankaran followed him with the wreath.

Rosemary hesitated for a moment. But then she left her slippers in the jeep and followed them. As she was walking, she could hear thousands of harmoniously blended sounds coming from somewhere. She covered her head with the end of her sari.

Amidst the light from the nilavilak[6] a ray of sunshine came through. Thampuran's face! Under the closed eyes, his nostrils were stuffed with cotton. Those lips!

Rosemary stood at his feet.

She didn't know how long she stood there.

Suddenly there was a slight movement.

Rosemary felt that his lips moved.

From behind, Sonny touched her on the shoulder.

Rosemary turned around.

"Come, let us go," he said.

She went around Thampuran's body from the right, once, and went out. Her chest felt heavy. Something was missing. Everything was done right, but something was lacking.

She didn't turn around to look at the body again.

She felt like crying.

She was not sad because he died, but because she didn't do for him something she was supposed to do.

Sonny said, "Come on. You are very emotional."

Some acquaintances smiled at them.

Rosemary's eyes filled with tears. The heaviness in her chest increased. She thought she couldn't hold on. They got into the jeep.

Suddenly without a warning raindrops fell on the windshield and on her body. It started to rain. "To give a good send-off to Thampuran the only thing missing was the rain," Rosemary realized. She was happy. Nature cooperated fully in this send-off.

Rosemary felt like a lover who had realized her love.

The jeep went slowly through the crowd.

The rain continued.

---

6   The traditional prayer lamp.

Sandalwood for the Funeral Pyre
Madhavikutty

The one who arranged for sandalwood for the funeral pyre was the dead woman's rich first-born son. Her youngest son came with his wife and young daughter and walked through the gate watching the pyre burn like thousands of red flowers blossoming in the southern yard.

Neighbors and relatives who were starting to disperse stayed back a while longer, seeing the young man, his beautiful wife, and the child she was carrying.

The youngest son looked again towards the burning pyre with dry eyes and asked his older brothers, "Couldn't you have waited till I got here?"

"Amma[1] died yesterday. How long could we keep the body? We expected you to come before noon," the oldest brother said. He had not shaved his face for two or three days, and the lower part of his face looked dark. He had on a mundu[2] and a mesh t-shirt.

His ten-year-old daughter looked at her little cousin and smiled. "Anjali, look at me and give me a smile," she said to the little girl. The little one was not pleased with the request and turned her face away.

"I won't be able to see Amma's face again. We went to the airport early in the morning. Someone telephoned that there was a bomb on the plane. The authorities got everything out of the plane and all of us off the plane. They checked us all, again. The plane took off three and a half hours late," the youngest son said.

"It is good that you didn't see her face. It was not the beautiful face that we remember. She looked as if she was frightened by something she saw. The face had gone darker and her eyes seemed to bulge out. You are lucky you didn't have to see how she looked. I can never forget that look," the second son said.

"What Appu said is true. I wish I didn't have to see the look on

---

1   Mother.

2   A lower garment, consisting of a length of cloth.

her face. Even at this age, Amma was a beautiful woman. But she had changed to a different person before death," the eldest son's wife said.

"Did Amma ask for me?" the youngest son asked.

"How could she? She was unconscious for two days. Just before she died, she opened her eyes and looked around as if looking for someone. She must have been looking for you," the oldest brother said.

"I am an unlucky person," the youngest son murmured.

"When Amma started to struggle for breath, I called Thankayya in Mysore and asked him to send sandalwood for the cremation. He sent it the same night by truck. It reached here this morning by 10:15. We started the funeral service soon after that," the eldest son said.

"We were afraid that the truck would get caught in rain. The wood won't burn if it gets wet. Even covering it with tarpaulin is of no use. Luckily, it didn't rain," the second son said.

"Where is Achhan[3]?" The youngest son asked.

"I saw him ready to go in for a shower. He has a slight cold and fever. I asked him not to take a shower. But he doesn't listen to anyone. Amma was the only one who could control him," the eldest son's wife said.

"How will Achhan live in this big house without Amma?" the youngest son's wife asked.

"He has to, nothing else can be done. It will not be right to make him travel in his old age," the eldest son said.

The second son said, "You should not misunderstand what I say. I think it would be better if you took him to Bombay."

"Achhan cannot live without help. His hands tremble much more than last year. While having his meals, he drops food on his shirt," the eldest son said.

"There must be very good neurosurgeons in Bombay. They can treat him and get him back to normal," the second son said.

"What nonsense are you saying, Appu? Vimala and I go to the factory early in the morning. Our daughter goes to school. Very often we go out to dinner parties. By the time we get back it is past midnight. If we leave Achhan with the servants what will others say?" the eldest son asked, his voice rising.

"It is true. Achhan will hate Bombay," his wife added.

"Have you all forgotten that Achhan lived in Bombay for forty years?" the second son asked.

"Today's Bombay is not the Bombay that Achhan knows. There is no

---

3 Father.

place to stand. The streets are full of people. Sometimes my legs shake with fear while crossing the road," the eldest son's wife said.

"My hands become cold like ice when I cross the streets," the ten-year-old daughter said.

"Is Amma's cabinet locked?" the youngest son asked his sister-in-law, who nodded in reply.

"Amma had said that her diamond earrings will go to my daughter because we gave her Amma's name," the youngest son said.

The eldest son's wife looked at her husband.

"Didn't you name your daughter Anju?" the eldest brother asked.

"We call her Anju, but her real name is Amma's name, Soudamini." the youngest son said.

"Amma never told us that her earrings will go to Anju. If she wanted to do that she would have told us," the oldest brother said.

"I am not going to argue about it. She said she would give the earrings to my daughter. I just remembered what Amma had said to me." the youngest son said. They were sitting at the dining table. Flies were flying around the half-empty coffee cups. The youngest son's wife took out a feeding bottle from her bag and started to feed the child.

"You give her only milk, even now? Isn't she over one year?" the second brother's wife asked.

"Sometimes we give her Farex in addition to milk. Milk is convenient while traveling," the child's mother said.

"The diamonds in Amma's earrings are blue jaegers. Such high quality stones are rare now-a-days. You could see all the colors of the rainbow in them." the eldest son's wife said.

"They suited her face well. The way they glitter at night is a sight to see," the second son's wife said.

"I am willing to pay for those earrings. I would like to see my daughter wear them. She is Amma's oldest granddaughter," the oldest son said.

"Amma wanted my daughter to have them," the youngest son said.

"Go and see what Achhan is doing. It is three hours since he went to take a shower," the oldest son said.

"Tomorrow I plan to go to Nagarkoil to get the grocery needed for the sanjayanam[4]—split peas, sugar, oil, etc. If you like you can come with me," the second brother said to the youngest.

"Then I will pay for the taxi," the youngest brother said.

"I slept on Amma's bed for eight years. So I asked Thankayya to send

---

4 Ceremony to gather the bones of a cremated person as part of the funeral rites.

good sandalwood, however much it might cost. He sent it by truck covered with a tarpaulin. I was determined to do something for Amma," the oldest son said. His wife came back.

"Amma's diamond earrings are not in her jewelry box. I looked everywhere in her cabinet. There are four bangles, her wedding ring, and the thali[5] chain in the jewelry box. What happened to the rest of her jewelry?" She asked everyone in the room.

"Amma has not given us anything since we came three years ago," the second son said.

"I came here on the 90th day after Anju was born. Amma did not give us any jewelry. She said that the earrings were for Anju. She might have said that when she learned that we had named the child after her," the youngest son said, looking towards the still-burning pyre.

"Amma might have sold her jewelry. Achhan's treatment was very expensive. In addition, she had to hire a taxi to take him to the hospital and back every time. She needed money," the youngest son said.

"Amma could have written to me. Not once did she ask me," the oldest son said.

"Amma was a proud person. Her self-respect did not allow her to ask anyone for money. She never asked me," the second son said.

"Had she asked me, I would have sent her two or three thousand rupees every month," the oldest brother said.

The child laughed as if she had heard a joke.

"She has some features of Amma," the second son said, looking at the child.

"Amma loved little children. I could have come home more often," the youngest son said.

"You couldn't take leave from work," the second son said.

"I always wished to do something for Amma. That is why I telephoned Thankayya for the sandalwood," the oldest son said.

"I have heard Amma tell the neighbors with great pride that her oldest son is a millionaire," the second son's wife said. Whenever she thought about Amma her face lit up with a smile.

"I have told my friends that my husband's mother is an extraordinary woman," the youngest son's wife said.

The oldest son's eyes brimmed with tears. He got up and stood near the window.

"When Amma was alive I did not do anything significant for her. But

---

5   Wedding string or chain tied around an Indian bride's neck by the bridegroom.

now I realized one wish. I was able to afford sandalwood for her funeral pyre. I am a lucky person. There is no doubt about it," he said.

No one spoke for a long while. But the faint cracking sound from the pyre could be heard in the room.

FRACTION
Gracy

She felt as if something was expanding in her head like a balloon, and realized that she was on the verge of an explosion. Thinking that a warm shower would give her some relief, she shuffled into the bathroom.

Her fever started three days ago. When she finally left the office, she had a throbbing head, burning eyes, and sore body. All she wanted to do was to curl up somewhere.

As soon as her husband walked in she said, "I can't even raise my head. Please make the tea."

He walked into the kitchen muttering something. After a long time, he brought her tea, but it tasted like some medicinal decoction. As soon as she swallowed a mouthful, she vomited that and more. Her husband stared at her with obvious irritation.

He picked up the newspaper that he had only glanced at in the morning and lay down on the easy chair. Realizing that he was not showing any signs of getting up, she dragged herself from the bed into the kitchen. She made a few items for dinner and put them on the table, murmuring, "Even when lying dead, one won't find peace in this house. These days are there men who won't do a few things in the kitchen when necessary?" Her husband showed no sign of having heard it.

Though she got three days off from work at the office, there was no relief from her work in the kitchen.

As she got out of the bathroom, her daughter came to her with homework problems. "Mommy, please tell me how to do addition of fractions."

Suppressing the anger rising inside her, she said, "Ask Daddy."

"Daddy will just stare at it. He won't explain anything."

She scanned the text, scribbled something on a piece of paper, and tried to explain as much as she could.

The girl became upset. "I didn't understand a thing."

Her head started throbbing. Holding her head in both hands, she turned to her husband, "Would you explain this to her?"

With his feet on the coffee table and a vacant look he mumbled, "I have forgotten all that."

Her face hardened. She cried out angrily, "Yes, you have forgotten a lot." But she remembered ...

The intensity of their love during the first days of marriage, the arguments they had for no reason at all that grew like bubbles until they burst, driving them to irresistible laughter ... the excitement and pleasure of sucking for breast milk, with the relish of a child finding a lost peacock feather. There were many memories like that, but they all changed. She watched these stars turning into lumps of coal, and her laughter became tears. He said she was crazy, and just yawned.

Now she has become really crazy. She sat down cross-legged and said, "OK. Then I will teach you first."

Though she repeated her explanation two or three times, he couldn't remember any of the old math lessons. She felt that he was not paying attention to what she was saying. Her anger burnt up whatever was left of her dreams.

Hitting her head repeatedly, she cried, "My fate!" She has had it!

He just continued to sit there with a vacant look, paying no attention to her.

She had a wild look in her eyes as she got up and rushed to the bedroom. After closing the door and locking it, she selected an old sari. She stood on a stool and tied one end of it to a ring in the ceiling that was meant for a light fixture. After making a knot at the other end and putting it over her head, she cried out,

"Come here. I will teach you."

She laughed at the faces that appeared at the open window. They were unnerved by the rage leaping from that laughter.

She touched her head and said, "This is numerator."

Then she touched her chest, "This is denominator!"

She continued, panting: "When you add two fractions together, see, like this ..." Suddenly she kicked the stool with her foot.

ARYA REBORN
Chandramathy

The wind said to me, "It has started. A sharp metal arrow is on its way to destroy your glass tower." On the wings of the wind, sound bites scattered saying, "Watch out! Battle plans are being drawn up on the south side." A bird talked about the weapon factory expanding on the northern side. I also learned about people on the east and west getting war masks ready.

I am Arya, woman of Aryavartham.[1] Will I be able to fight off the people in war masks?

See, this is my ancestral home. This is where I grew up. Hanging from this decaying A-frame for the roof was a kuvalakkudukka[2] that had the ashes for ceremonial uses. Muthassi[3] fell down and died right here in the yard when Muthassan[4] kicked her from behind as she was getting ashes from the kudukka. That day I was imitating the steps for sword-fight, using a broomstick as my sword, dressed in a towel. Muthassi left us that very night the drumstick tree opened its flowers with a cruel red color. Muthassan followed the funeral procession with tearful eyes and burst out crying at the cremation. Everyone was pushing to reach him and console him. How sad! They felt that instead of helping him through his old age, she had left so soon! Why did God create the human heart so tender? But inside the house there was hushed discussion of what really happened.

When the 16th-day ceremony for the dead was over, the cook who used to sleep at the foot of the stairs went upstairs and moved into Muthassan's bedroom. Amma,[5] with her tear-stained face full of anger and shame, just stood there watching it. After that she and my uncles held long discussions in the yard and by the bathing pond on how to

---

1   India, the land between the Himalayan and Vindhyan mountains.

2   A globular pot with a small mouth made from the hard outer shell of a gourd-like fruit, used for keeping sacred ash.

3   Grandmother.

4   Grandfather.

5   Mother.

handle the situation. When the light was out in Muthassan's room they continued the discussion in the front yard, sitting in comfortable chairs. They took out their anger on my broomstick cars by throwing them away and on me by boxing my ears for no reason.

Kavu the cook became Kavamma. She went with Muthassan to the temple in the next town dressed in a sari with gold border and big earrings. She ruled the house, supervising the servants and jingling the bunch of house keys along with her gold jewelry. Saris in her chest that smelled of paraffin balls overflowed.

Achhan,[6] who came for weekends with the welcome smell of cigarettes, was like a short dream. He joined my uncles under the jambu[7] tree in the front yard for the discussion while keeping me in his lap and stroking my hair. He said, "The law cannot do anything. All loopholes are cleverly blocked."

That Sunday, when getting ready to leave, Achhan asked Amma to go with him. "For what are you staying here? Bring Arya and we will go to my small house."

When Amma refused, Achhan smiled as if he had expected it. I was the one who was fuming with anger.

I always liked my father. He was just the opposite of my mother, who would scream about the smallest thing and hurt and curse me. I have never seen him without a smile on his face. Every weekend I waited for his special smell with all my senses open.

He had talked to me about the school in town with high walls around it, its shorthaired students, and nuns who spoke in English. Many a time I asked him to take me with him so that I could study in that school, become fashionable with a short haircut and speak English. If he took me, I could stay with him in the house with the guava trees and the jasmine and nerium flowers and sleep hugging him.

He always laughed and said, "Your mother should hear this."

I have a blurred memory of staying in that small house just once. Is that the only time Amma went with him to share the bliss of married life? What I remember most is Amma driving away the school children who were throwing stones at the guava tree. She used to cry to be taken back to her house.

After Muthassi died, Achhan raised his voice at Muthassan with the blessing of my uncles. That week Kavamma's loafer brother, Anirudhan,

---

6   Father.

7   A tall tree (Eugenia jambolana), common in Kerala, that bears a dark crimson fruit.

moved into the house. He took the room with the ovara[8] that Achhan used when he came home. Achhan threw out Anirudhan's red-checkered shirt. When I ran to Achhan and Muthassan, their eyes were red, and they were still at each other.

When he left with his suitcase, just as he had come, Achhan put his hand on my head for half a minute.

The next weekend Achhan didn't come home. He never came again. One night my uncle, whom Amma called Kochappu, came from town and told Amma, "Sankaran Nair[9] won't come. He is stubborn. He wants you to go there, if you like."

"I won't go," Amma cried. "I am also stubborn."

Every weekend I waited for him under the shade of the jambu tree. I was sure he would come with the cigarette-smelling kiss.

Sometime later, we heard that Achhan was living in a small house with a beauty who could play the veena[10] and always wore flowers in her hair.

"Devil!" Amma cursed. "Blood-sucking race! She will suck every drop of his blood and leave. Then only I will be here."

Much later when I was in college in the nearby town, I saw them in a fabric shop. She was buying material for a safari suit for a boy who looked like Achhan. She was a beautiful woman, a bit heavy, fair complexioned, dressed in a silk sari with flowers in her long hair. Achhan was wearing glasses. The few hairs he had on his bald head had gone gray. His characteristic smile was gone. He was sitting there looking sad with a crinkled forehead, but surrounding him like a halo was the cigarette smell that I loved. That was the only thing that had not changed. That smell woke up memories deep in my heart. Hiding among my friends, I stared at him for a long time.

My friend Gita saw Achhan's picture when it accidentally fell out of my diary and said, "He is my neighbor. Drinks a lot and beats up aunty. Vijayalakshmi Aunty is a nice woman. She makes such tasty sweets. Doesn't complain, always wipes her tears before coming out."   .

I did not tell Gita about Amma, who did not care to wipe her tears. One by one, my uncles built small houses and moved out and Amma was left there to be the servant. She had to cook and serve Kavamma and Anirudhan's children and take care of Kavamma when she gave birth to her baby. All this took a heavy toll on Amma's health. With eyes deep

---

8   Urinal for night use.

9   My Achhan.

10   A stringed musical instrument used in India.

inside dark circles and a skeleton that could barely support her body, she cooked, swabbed the floor, and washed countless articles of clothing. She cursed everyone in a voice that had become hoarse. When Muthassan died Amma didn't cry. When she became tired of being neglected in each of her brothers' houses, she came back to the ancestral home. In the end, one evening she vomited blood, fell into it, and died.

I was in the middle of my college studies at the time. My youngest uncle brought me the news of my mother's death to my hostel veranda. Looking at me, not shedding one tear, he pressed my hand and said, "Chinnu's[11] hopes were all in you. She saw the end of her misery in your bright future."

I didn't say anything.

Amma's body was laid out in the foyer of the ancestral home, covered with a new shawl, showing only her face decorated with chandan[12] and ashes. Although she was the same age, Kavamma, looking much younger, walked around jingling the keys to everything in the house.

I sat at the head of the body feeling no emotion. Nobody had tears for her. Amma's face seemed unfamiliar to me. I never liked this woman, I thought, looking at her face. How did I get into the womb of this woman who had only curses on her lips and anger in her heart?

She used to scream at me through her clenched teeth, "Go, you go with your father and be damned!" and then cry before the prayer lamp, "Oh, God! I don't even have you." On those occasions, more than sympathy I felt disgusted with her. Without realizing it, I wished for Vijayalakshmi's womb. When the smell of cigarette mingled with the smell of liquor, I longed to wipe the tears from her cheeks. Why didn't God put me in your womb? Why didn't you bring me up as my father's daughter? Though I was sitting before my mother's dead body, I was sorry about losing out on the smell of the flowers and the veena music.

I am carrying the name of my great-grandmother who was a woman of class. As a result of the lucky horoscope of Arya Devi (my great-grandmother), the family found wealth and prosperity and its gold collection increased. My mother used to keep her hand on her head and ask, "Why did this unlucky one get that name?" She used to curse me.

My Muthassi always objected to her doing it. "Don't," she used to say, "She will make the name Arya meaningful; she will redeem us who had no backbone to stand up to ill-treatment."

The resourceful Arya Muthassi who could do anything she wanted,

---

11 My mother.

12 Sandalwood paste.

even make the sun rise at midnight, was a great myth to me. With her long, thick hair, eyes made attractive with black liner, and bare, round breasts, she was supposed to have commanded two husbands, one on either side. Leaving that commanding power that could make everyone obey her at the cremation ground, the other women went into corners of the inside rooms. Every night women's cries from Muthssan's bedroom could be heard. To block out the sound, Muthassi recited her prayer louder and louder. With a heart that clung to something, Amma cursed herself and wandered around inside and out like a dead person. She didn't love anyone. When her body was taken out, I felt the freedom of the last link being broken.

Now the only burden was the name I inherited, a name that attracted attention wherever I went.

"Arya Devi is an old-fashioned name," I said to one of my uncles. "I would like to put a notice in the gazette and change that name."

"Don't do that. Old names are coming back."

My uncles gave their children new names. No one had to bear the weight of a name like Arya Devi. I did not dare to protest because my future was hanging on their kindness.

Vipin said that he liked the name Arya Devi. I didn't have any desire to have a love relationship with him. Neither of us could believe that our relationship would go beyond a sincere friendship. Sitting on the sandy beach, I talked to him eloquently. From the myth of Arya Muthassi through the prayer recitation of Muthassi and Amma who could only curse, the vocal talent stopped with me.

Even that friendship couldn't save me. In a phone call that came for me from my oldest uncle to the hostel, his anger flared. "You dirty girl, if you spoil the name of the family, we will kill you. How did you, bearing the name of Arya Muthassi, have the courage to take drugs and roam around the beach? If we hear anything more, your studies will end that day."

I heard the pitiful cries of women rising out of Arya Muthassi's house. Tiny skulls were turning under the foundation of that splendid house. Muthassi's cremation fire, Kavamma's naked chest, Amma whose face did not let go of the anger inside even after death—what possibly could I add to destroy the name of this family?

I had never seen ganja.[13] When I heard that Vipin had connection to drug sellers, I had not taken it seriously. He was just a good friend. But that day I said, "I want to know what ganja is. Please help me."

---

13 Marijuana.

He was taken aback.

"Arya...I...once in a while try it just for fun. I am not an addict."

Later he gave me a white tablet, instead, and said, "For the time being this is enough. You should melt it under the tongue. This is the key to a wonderful world. There will be many kinds of wonderful creatures and experiences. You shouldn't get frightened or cry out loud. If you won't misunderstand I would like to say that it is better to come to my lodge. You can experiment there. Nobody will know."

"I don't want to do that," I told him firmly.

That night I was sitting on the terrace of the hostel, trying to decide if I should take the drug or not. What came clear in my mind was Vijayalakshmi who did not have me in her womb. Looking very kind she said, "No, Arya. Don't."

"What right do you have to say that?" I was angry. "My Achhan is caught among the petals of your lotus flower. Your future is safe with your son who is a medical student in the neighboring state, gaining admission by paying a huge donation. What does Arya have? What has she achieved? Your wish to punish yourself makes you worship my Achhan. Do you know the little girl who used to play sword fight with a broomstick is dead? I always detested my Amma who could only curse. But her shame of having to wait for kindness in someone else's house... you are partly responsible for all these problems. You bitch!"

Impatient, I put that tablet under my tongue.

Slowly I danced around and started to rise. Like a mother singing a lullaby, someone was caressing me, making my whole body move slowly. With the ease of a butterfly rising between the wings, I floated among the clouds, rising above the hostel building. Arya Muthassi in army uniform, eating some pudding that looked delicious, was ordering her husbands: "Number one, cut off the head of little Arya's uncle and bring it here. There shall be no internal dissension here. Number two, widen the boundaries of the southern province." The husbands saluted her and left. The pudding was dripping from the corner of Arya Muthassi's mouth. Tap-tap-tap-tap. Who is there? Grate the red chandan, and fill the kuvalakudukka with ashes. Muthassi was praying with the thulasi[14] rosary. Arya, when you grow up you should buy me a rosary with a thousand and one beads for me to recite the Vishnusahasranamam and Lalithasahasranamam[15] without mistake. Even after all this prayer, the gods haven't even turned towards us. Muthassan was calling Chinnu,

---

14   Sweet basil.

15   Repeating invocations to Vishnu or Lalitha (Durga) a thousand times.

"Come Chinnu, today I want you." Glass bangles broke in Muthassan's bedroom. Jani came out tying her loose hair. "Why are you hiding here, Arya? Can't you go out and play?"

Kavamma was screaming, "Girl, if you come here again, I will break your legs. Let me see who will come to question me on that." Muthssan was roaring, "Arya, get out you idiot." Amma was waiting with a cane. "What did you want to see there? Will you go to that door again, ever again?" Muthassi was praying to the gods, tears streaming down her cheeks, and calling on the gods, "Sinduraruna Vigraha ... Thrinayanam ... it is because you don't pray." Amma got so angry. "Anything can happen inside that room, and you just want to recite your stupid prayer."

"What do you want me to do Chinnu? You should have advised me on this."

"If you are a woman you have to be clever too."

"Yes, yes. You were too clever, that's why Sankaran Nair is living with another woman."

Amma raised the broom. "Shut up, woman." Muthassi was crying. Bhum! With one kick Muthassi was in peace. The sword fight turns into a cry for help, into Arya! The smell of cigarette melts into the sound of veena. "Arya, who is the bitch, you or I?" Achhan was a baby with bald head and glasses, sitting in Vijayalakshmi's lap.

"Arya, look. Do you know me?"

They told me that my crying was ugly. The lights in the hall that were turned off were turned back on and people were terrified. At the end of the search, they found me lying on the terrace, kicking my hands and legs and frothing from the mouth.

I met Menon at the sanitarium where my uncles took me, with anger inside and on their faces. The welcome smell of cigarette was around him. He was free of the sound of veena. His wife, with red lipstick and a hand-bag on her shoulder, sat near my bed and talked to me in good convent English. I shouldn't worry, she said, the women's organization in the city would be with me.

Chempakam, the women's organization, would resettle anyone, Menon said: prostitutes, recovered addicts, the mentally unstable, anyone like that. Arya realized that it was her family that needed resettlement.

Menon came to see me again without his wife's company. He talked to me about his children living well abroad, his vacation home on the hillside, and his loneliness. "One day I will take you to my house," he said. "I will show you the beauty of the old and new, when old architecture combines with the new. But you may see loneliness in the unusually large rooms."

I used to ask Menon to light a cigarette whenever he came to my room.

"Doctors have asked me not to smoke. But that is OK," he would say and light a cigarette. The security of my childhood came rushing to me.

One day, as we sat talking, I took his hand in a sudden urge and said, "I am not a drug addict. I have taken it only once. That was to defy my uncles. Please believe me."

I couldn't control my crying. Even to this day I don't know why I behaved that way. Menon told me later that it was a moment of discovery for him. When I cried with my face in his lap, his heart filled with kindness. His short fingers ran around in my hair. I remembered the touch of my father who put his hand on my head for a second or two as he was leaving the house.

The door of a small, tiled house where Menon's mother lived on the edge of the city opened for me.

Now I have someone to wait for everyday, with flowers in my hair. A consoling touch was transferred to my shoulders while imprinting the stamp of love on my lips.

I must learn to play the veena and become successful. I must provide comfort to him when he comes seeking the cooling sound of brooks to escape the intolerable lipstick and shoulder bag. I should give birth to children who look like him.

Arya found peace on his hairy chest with the gold chain.

But...

The wind said to me, "An arrow is on its way, a swift arrow to shatter your glass tower."

Tell me, when not one, but a thousand shouting fighters are coming near, how can Arya find peace?

WHEN A STAR IS FALLING
Gracy

His life starts ticking when the world is at rest in darkness. He has magic at his fingertips. At the touch of his magic hands, bars on windows gave way and safes and cabinets opened up.

That night, as he was standing quietly in the yard of a house he had selected earlier, he was stunned by the sight of the housewife standing outside. He doubted she was waiting for her lover. Though rarely, he has seen her before. She did not have the beauty to attract a man. She was dark and skinny with big eyes full of sadness. He wondered why a woman who has a house that looks like a palace, a husband holding a high position, cars, and other luxuries would look so sad.

Soon he understood that she was not waiting for a man. Raising her face to the sky, she was observing something. Out of curiosity he moved closer to her and turned his face to the sky. He could not find anything special.

Suddenly she realized his presence. Though excited, she asked in a subdued voice, "See, see, do you see that falling star?"

Moving to make him stand close to her, she pointed her finger to the sky. He was seeing a falling star for the first time. He disliked starry skies. Light was always his enemy.

She started walking close beside him. Her eyes were still in the world of stars. Going beyond the limit of the big yard, they stepped on to a footpath. But the bars on the gate stopped them. She thought of the stars, now out of sight, and sighed.

"That star must have reached someone else's life, do you think?"

He just stood there, silent. In the faint light he saw tear drops shining in her eyelids. She put her head on his chest and closed her eyes.

"It is supposed to be bad luck to see falling stars. But I consider it a great wonder when I see it. Whenever I look at the sky, at least one star is falling. It has been like that from the time I can remember. My beautiful younger sister used to tease me, saying that the stars got scared seeing me and were running away."

A wave of affection went through his body. He still didn't have anything to say, and he just patted her on the back. She continued in an emotional tone, "This sky dotted with stars scattered all over reminds me how insignificant I am, and I begin to forget all my problems and pain. Around midnight, when the owl sitting on a far-away tree cries out without getting a response from its mate, comfort flows into me."

Her words fell into silence. He was beginning to wonder if she was falling asleep. Then, as if waking up from some dream, she asked, "Who are you?"

He could not have said anything but the truth. It was the first time in his life that a woman found refuge on his chest.

"I am a thief."

She did not startle or cry out as he had expected.

Instead, in an emotionless tone, she said, "My husband is also a thief. What he steals is women's chastity. What about you?"

His heart flickered like a flame in the wind. With a scattering sigh, his rough face pressed the top of her head.

Then, slowly moving away from her, he melted into the darkness and disappeared.

WHEN BIG TREES FALL
N. S. Madhavan

"When big trees fall the earth trembles." –Rajiv Gandhi, speaking after the
assassination of his mother, Indira Gandhi, and its aftermath

Whenever I go through the records of the convent, one thing surprises me:
most of the deaths occur during the months of November and December.
It may be that the hearts of the old residents of this convent get tired and
stop as they struggle to provide their old bodies more warmth during
these cold months.

Sister Philomena was the only person who died in October 1984.
When she didn't show up for breakfast I asked, "What happened to Sister
Philomena?"

Sister Katherine rolled her wheelchair away from the dining table
and sat under the Gothic window. The rosary in Sister Margarita's hands
moved faster. Sister Martha bowed her head and drank her milk carefully,
sip by sip. There was no need for me to go to the hall where the sisters
slept in two rows of beds. I called the bishop's house and asked Thomachan to come immediately.

I clearly remember October 31, 1984. That morning I had gone to the railway station in Meerut, near Delhi, to meet another nun coming to live
in the convent. By the time I reached the station, the train had already
arrived. A young nun and an old one with many wrinkles on her face
came forward when they saw me.

"Are you a Malayalee[1], Sister?" the old nun asked me.

"Yes," I said.

"Where are you from?"

"Varapoly, near Ernakulam. And you, Sister?" I asked.

"I am from the north. Thiruvampadi. My father settled down there."

The young nun was from Orissa. She was to go back the next day.
She said that Sister Angelica, the old nun, was diabetic and should not be

---

1   One who speaks Malayalam, a person from Kerala.

given anything with sugar. Sister Angelica said, "I was always in Orissa—Cuttack, Rourkela, Kalahandi, and Bhuvaneswar—teaching math and science." Looking at the many crosses in the cemetery on the way to the convent, she added, "Everyone ends up in Meerut."

The bishop of Meerut, who died the previous year, established this convent for the old nuns in the order. Before that, the nuns spent their retirement days in convents where they lived. The bishop had received many complaints about the nuns not getting the care they needed.

When I returned from Germany after higher studies, the bishop sent for me. "You are a child of the church," he said. He was from Kerala and knew that I had grown up in an orphanage and had joined the convent when I was still very young. The nuns had sent me to Germany for higher studies.

"I had you in mind when I thought about this convent—a last resort for the nuns who are too old to work for God."

That night I couldn't sleep. From my childhood whenever I had problems, I prayed to Archangel Gabriel for solutions. That day I prayed for a long time. Finally I felt I heard the flapping of wings behind me. "Jesus built the church on Peter, the rock. Will this convent last if it is built on me, a mere pebble?"

"Sister Agatha," my own mind spoke to me in the voice of Archangel Gabriel, "This is the opportunity that God is giving you to be the salt of the earth." Salt, salt, salt without savor, I cried bitterly, beating my head on the bed.

From the first group of nuns who came to live here, only Sister Karuna is alive. She is a Spanish nun who ran a center for training poor girls in Bihar. When she came here she brought a large piano.

By the time I got the beds ready for the nuns who came from Orissa, it was past 11 p.m. A phone call came from Thomachan at the bishop's house. "Did you know that Indira Gandhi has been shot?"

"Oh, my God!" I was stunned.

"People say she's dead. But the radio news is only that she was wounded."

"Oh, Jesus!" Sister Angelica said when she heard about it. "The day we were leaving Orissa, she had come there," she added.

While spoon-feeding Sister Davies some light green soup, I told her that Indira Gandhi had been shot. Her mind had left her a couple of years ago. She just opened her mouth for more soup, without saying anything.

As soon as she heard the news, Sister Karuna went and sat in front of the piano. Its open lid gave her an abode, like a tree. She was turning the pages of the music books without playing anything. At two o'clock, Thomachan called again from the bishop's house. "Radio Australia said that Indira Gandhi is dead. Some Delhi newspapers have come out with special issues about it."

"What does All India Radio say?" I asked.

"Only that she was wounded, still."

"And the TV?"

"Same news."

When I came out of the phone room, the first person I saw was Sister Katherine, sitting in her wheelchair on the veranda, reading from her prayer book. I spoke to her in Malayalam about Thomachan's phone call regarding Indira Gandhi.

After Sister Philomena died, Sister Katherine had almost stopped talking. They had come here together from Delhi. As if to ask something, she raised her face, but didn't say anything. It seemed it was too much of an effort to form the needed words. Rolling her wheelchair she went into the convent. I made a mental note that the wheels needed some oil.

When I went into the office I saw Sister Margaret standing in front of an open cupboard with an awkward look.

"Sister," I called to her in an admonishing tone, "what are you doing?"

"Oh, nothing."

"Not true. You are looking for your tablets to throw them away."

It was the gardener who found out that she was throwing away the high blood pressure pills she was supposed to take. He was surprised to see blue pills among the petals of the chrysanthemums and dahlias. He picked them up and brought them to me. As soon as I saw them I knew what they were. From that day on Sr. Margaret had to take the medicine in front of me.

Sister Martha came into the office room. Whenever I see the energetic way she walks, I wonder if she came to this convent a few years too soon.

"Is it true?" she asked.

"Yes."

"How sad! She once came to the playground of the school in Indore where I used to teach. She threw back all the garlands and bouquets she received to the children. I believe that is her custom. The poor Aadivaasi[2] children ran around barefoot and caught them like little monkeys. That

---

2   Tribal.

sight seemed to excite Mrs. Gandhi. She broke the flowers from the bouquets and threw them also. The children caught every one of them without letting any touch the ground."

The evening news on TV, for the first time, said that Indira Gandhi had been assassinated.

That night very few came to the dining room for dinner. Sister Karuna played the piano for a long time. Sister Mary, who usually had her dinner in bed, walked to the dining table with the help of her cane. "I want to sit with everyone. It has been too long," she said smiling.

The senile Sister Davies stared into the TV without muttering as she usually did. Sister Katherine rolled her wheelchair away from the TV.

Sister Martha was crying. "I cannot forget that volleyball game with the flowers," she said.

The nuns went to bed warmed by the red glow of the room heaters. I went upstairs, said my prayers, and turned off the light. I shivered under the woolen blanket, not because of the cold November weather, but due to the fever that gripped the whole country.

After a while, someone knocked on the door. When I opened the door, I saw Sister Cecilia, who had brought Sister Angelica.

"Sister Agatha, I am scared," she said.

I looked into the darkness behind her. It seemed like the ocean created at the beginning of the universe. God only had to give it sound.

"You can sleep in this room, Sister," I said.

The next morning Thomachan called from the bishop's house and said, "The trouble has started. The Sikhs are being killed in large numbers. Close all the doors and lock them. The sister who came from Orissa should not leave today."

The Gothic doors and windows with their conical tops were all closed and locked. Sister Cecilia, Sister Angelica, and Sister Katherine sat around a room heater warming their hands. The 96-year-old Sister Mary lay on the bed hugging a hot water bottle. Ever so often they would all look toward the infirmary. We could hear Sister Wilfred struggling to breathe. When that sound became unbearable, I went in and gave her oxygen.

Then the shooting started. We could hear the sound. When I looked out of my upstairs window, I could see many smoke trees shivering in the cold. By evening the single smoke trees had become a huge forest.

The Gurkha[3] gatekeeper locked the iron front gate, chained it, and waited inside. He gave us news continuously:

"The shops near the clock tower that belonged to the Sikhs are all destroyed. All their taxis on the main road were burned. You can see dead bodies of Sikhs along the way to Sadar Bazaar."

All through the night we could hear gunshots. We could see the redness of the fires reflected in the horizon.

By November 2nd, the sound of gunshots had only increased. All of us spent the day together in the long hall. We could see fear written even on the face of Sister Davies.

On the third, we saw Indira Gandhi's funeral procession on TV. Sister Cecilia was describing whatever she saw on TV to the 96-year-old Sister Mary, who could not see well.

"The crowd is small," Sister Angelica said. "People are scared to come out because of all the troubles. You should have seen Nehru's funeral procession. I was in Delhi at that time."

Sister Cecilia's recounting of what was on TV continued. In addition to Sister Mary, Sister Martha and Sister Margaret sat nearby.

Now the funeral procession moved through Vijai Chauk in Delhi. These pictures on TV were translated into Sister Cecilia's words. I couldn't bear for too long this unfortunate event being played simultaneously on three different stages. My stomach churned and I felt nauseated.

I went into the bathroom and threw up. For the first time in my life, history had a physical impact on me.

The next day, November 4th, curfew was declared. Everyone stayed in bed. Sister Cecilia and I gave them dinner in their beds.

At night Sister Katherine rolled her wheelchair and came to me.

"I want to go out," she said.

"No, you shall not."

"All the lights are off. I have to go out. I am feeling suffocated," she said.

"OK. Then I will come with you."

No one raised her head when the hinges squeaked upon opening the door.

The sudden burst of cold air that came through chilled the slight warmth in the room.

---

3   A person from the mountains of Nepal.

"I am just going out." Sister Katherine rolled her wheelchair and moved to the far end of the veranda and then went back and forth.

Suddenly, I heard her cry out for help. "Killers! Help!" The wheelchair came fast as a train.

She was panting, "In the darkness... killers..."

I ran to the kitchen. Sister Karuna came out quickly and wheeled Sister Katherine in and closed the door. I took out the sharpest knife and hid it in my clothes.

The nuns were quiet. In the infirmary, Sister Wilfred was trying hard to pull her muscles in to reduce the sound of her breathing. Then someone banged on the door. I took the knife out. Sister Karuna and Sister Martha stood close by me. The banging grew louder.

"Open the door! Please open the door!" a woman was crying out in Hindi. Suddenly, we heard a boy cry.

We heard motorbikes roaring into the yard and stopping. Their headlights played on the wall of the convent like searchlights.

"Please open up! They have come to get me," the woman screamed.

When I opened the door there was a woman in salwar-kameez[4], her head covered with a shawl. Beside her was a young boy with his hair tied on his head in a white scarf.

"They killed my husband and this boy's older brother, Babu. They said they would kill me and him too." She spoke as if she was going crazy.

When those who came on motorbikes started to knock on the gate, Sister Karuna took the woman and boy inside and closed the door. Until they left, after speaking with the Gurkha for some time, no one said a word.

Sister Martha broke the silence: "Who are you?" She asked in Hindi.

"My name is Amarjit. They killed many who lived in our colony where the Sikhs did not celebrate Diwali[5] this year as a protest against the army attack on Harmandir Sahib.[6] For that reason people were very angry at us."

"Didn't the police come to help?"

"The police station is right in front of our colony. People went to see the one in charge. But he said he couldn't do anything because he didn't have enough policemen there. He hates us."

"And then?" Sister Martha asked again.

---

4   Long, loose pants and top.

5   Festival of lights.

6   The Golden Temple at Amritsar.

"We left our homes and went to the Gurudwara.[7] Nihang[8] Sikhs wearing blue turbans with insignias made of steel stood guard all around.

"Some played the harmoniums hanging from their necks and all joined in singing Gurusthuthi[9]. Everyone had kripan[10] hanging from his waist. Some even had guns.

"The Adigrandha Sahib[11] was on a seat covered with red silk. Grandhis[12] fanned with venchamaram.[13] Devotees threw coins in front of it. Donations of wheat flour for the community kitchen were being gathered in a corner.

"Only one Akali[14] member spoke. 'Khalsapandh[15] asks for blood today, blood of the Guru's own Sikhs. You are wearing the armor of Amruth[16] so that you are not dead even when you die. Guru wants surrender, sacrifice.' Genes that carry the memory of their race showed their strength in the blood of the listeners. Everyone chanted 'Sat Sri Akal!'

"When the police started circling the Gurudwara, some of us returned home. The rest stayed in camps at the Gurudwara."

The attack came at night. They hunted Amarjit's husband down and killed him, and then the elder son. Someone caught hold of Amarjit's hand. But she bit deeply into his forearm and he had to let go.

"I ran dragging my son," Amarjit continued. "As I was running, I remembered the face of the man I bit and suddenly realized who he was: Ramji, who has a shop next door to our shop that sold metal parts for buildings. Ramji had been trying for a long time to get our shop. If the two of us also die, then he can just take over."

The people stayed at the Gurudwara one whole day. But Ramji and company were freely going around it in jeeps and motorbikes. They had bought off the police. When night fell, Amarjit and the boy ran away from the Gurudwara. In the darkness of the night, they climbed through the cracks in the wall and came to the convent.

---

7   Sikh temple.

8   Fundamentalist.

9   Hymns praising the Guru.

10   Ceremonial curved knife.

11   The Sikh's holy book.

12   Priests.

13   Fans made of the tail-hair of white deer.

14   Sikh.

15   "Our faith."

16   Ambrosia.

Sister Cecilia brought a cup of milk from the kitchen and gave to the boy. He gulped it down.

"What is his name?" Sister Angelica asked.

"Joginder Singh. We call him Juggy at home."

"Do you want some more milk?" Sister Katherine asked him.

Without any hesitation, Juggy nodded yes. Sister Martha brought more milk, some bread, and a couple of boiled eggs.

"We are not safe here. We have to leave this place and go to Delhi," Amarjit said. "There at the camps in Fateh Nagar Gurudwara we have relatives. May we stay here until we go to Delhi?"

Remembering that Jesus gives us opportunities to be kind to others, I took her by the hand and led her to the bed vacated by Sr. Philomena. "You can sleep here," I said. On the floor we spread a quilt for Juggy. After eating the long loaf of bread all by himself, Juggy came to bed and instantly fell into a deep sleep without dreams. After prayers, the nuns also went to bed.

The next day, November 5th, the nuns woke up earlier than usual. It seemed that they were waiting for Juggy to get up.

Juggy's attention was drawn first to Sister Karuna, who looked different from the others. Her light blue eyes were a wonder to him. She took him by the hand to the piano. He stared at the black and white keys for a long time. Sister Karuna touched a key and sang, "Do."

Reluctantly at first, Juggy also touched the key and sang, "Do." For the first time we heard his voice.

"Re, mi, fa," Sister Karuna touched the keys and sang the tune.

Laughing, Sister Angelica went to Juggy and lightly pressed his hair bundled up in the white kerchief. She turned to me and said, "Looks like a spider's egg pouch."

Juggy's face turned red; he pushed away Sister's hand and then pushed her away. From that moment, Juggy's hair was forbidden territory for us. We realized that the sense of history of a race was entwined in that hair.

That day Sister Margarita asked for her medicine and took it. Sister Katherine was in the wheelchair hovering around Amarjit and Juggy. Sister Karuna was busy making a cake for the boy. I contacted the bishop's house for permission to keep Amarjit and her son in the convent. Thomachan said that he would discuss it with the bishop and call back. I was wondering what the bishop would decide when the phone rang.

"The bishop's order is for you to follow the way the Lord has shown you," Thomachan said.

As the curfew was in force, we opened the doors and windows without fear. After many years, the 96-year-old Sister Mary came out to the front yard. Juggy was holding on to her walking stick. Sister Mary's blind eye seemed to have caught a ray of the healing sunshine.

"What is the name of this flower?" Juggy asked.

"How does it look?"

"Like the moon, round."

"The color?"

"Yellow."

"Does it have many petals?"

"Of course. More than the lotus. Small, narrow petals."

"Then the flower is a dahlia"

Juggy and Sister moved to the next flower. The nuns looked at them with delight. When they got back into the convent, Sister Mary said, in spite of her wheezing, "Juggy became Adam and named all things today."

The next day the curfew was lifted. The trains started running. We sent Amarjit and Juggy with the nun who had to go back to Orissa, along with the Gurkha as their escort to the station. As they were stepping down from the veranda, Sister Wilfred came out from the infirmary. "Juggy, Juggy," she called. She put a medal of Mary into his hand. He took that, looked at everyone, waved, and ran back to his mother.

Hours later, as life in the convent was getting back to normal, an army truck came into the convent. The Gurkha, Amarjit, Juggy, and Sister Cecilia got out of the truck. The Sister took Juggy's hand and walked into the convent, and he disappeared somewhere.

"What happened?" I asked. The Gurkha told me the story:

"We had gone only a short distance when a jeep came and stopped us. A man jumped out and tried to drag Madam out. Then Juggy Sahib cried out loudly, 'Mommy, Mommy.' The mother and son started running."

"They had been there waiting for us for hours," Amarjit said crying.

"The jeep took after them to run them down." The Gurkha was shaking with fear, but his Mongolian face, with its small eyes, thick eyebrows, and sharp jawbones, was limited in its ability to express emotions. "Luckily, at that time an army truck came by and saved these people."

"It's all right," Sister Karuna said. Sister Martha found Juggy hiding quietly in the darkness behind the foot of the stairs.

"You can stay here as long as you want," I said. "Nothing will happen to you here."

I immediately regretted what I said without God's approval. Later that day I got an anonymous phone call: "You agents of the CIA, if you don't let the Sikh woman and her son out, we will bomb your convent and destroy it." My throat was dry and by the time I tried to say "Hello, hello," the caller had put the phone down.

Although police protection was arranged, that night stones were thrown from behind the convent. The window with the picture of Christ the Shepherd holding the lamb was broken at the Shepherd's heart.

Early next morning Thomachan called from the bishop's house. "They broke the statue of Our Lady of Lourdes in front of St Mary's school. They telephone here repeatedly asking that the Sikh woman and her son be handed over," he said.

"Will they cause trouble, turning the situation against us?" I asked. Thomachan did not answer that.

"What should I do?"

"The bishop said that the Lord will continue to show you the way."

I hurried to the prayer room and knelt down. "Archangel Gabriel, give me a message. Don't you have a message for me from the Lord?" Shadows moved through my mind like refugees. I didn't feel anything.

My mind was blank. I started crying. After a while I calmed down completely. By that time the other nuns and Amarjit came into the prayer room.

I asked George, the ambulance driver, to get a casket.

"Here is the way the Lord showed this sinner," I told the members of the convent. "Amarjit will dress like a nun. Juggy will lie in the casket in the ambulance. Some of us will sit around it and pray. The ambulance will enter the cemetery from the east. When no one is paying attention any more, we will drive through the western gate and go out to the church near the railway station. It won't be difficult to go to the railway station from there."

Sister Cecilia brought Juggy. Sister Angelica held his hands tightly. Sister Martha sat on the floor and held both his legs. Sister Mary held him at the knees with the curved end of her walking stick. Sister Margaret covered his face. When he started crying loudly, Sister Karuna covered his mouth.

Amarjit untied the knot in the white kerchief on his head and opened the hair. It was shoulder length. I sprinkled some water to wet the hair. Then with a pair of scissors I started cutting his hair. As the hair fell to the floor, strand by strand, Juggy was becoming more and more naked.

"Vah Guru Vah," Amarjit recited sobbing.

Juggy became even more helpless, but he stopped crying. Sister Karuna removed her hand from his mouth.

"Jo bole so nihal[17]," Amarjit recited for him.

"Sat Sri Akal, " Juggy responded mechanically. By the time I finished, he had very short hair.

When the haircut was done, I noticed that his skin under the turban, never having seen sunlight, was almost white in the outline of the head-gear. That would be a sure giveaway. I mixed some soot in mustard oil, rubbed it on his forehead and ears, and made them the same shade as his face.

By then the ambulance had arrived. Juggy got into the casket in the ambulance. We closed it, making sure he could get air. Amarjit dressed like a nun, Sister Cecilia, who was returning to Orissa, Sister Angelica, Sister Karuna, Sister Martha, and I sat around the casket and started praying. The trip was peaceful at first. But when we had gone some distance, motorbikes came speeding towards us. They drove alongside the ambulance and told the driver to stop. George started to speed up instead. The sound of the motorbikes changing gear was deafening. Sister Karuna touched George on the shoulder with her long hand and asked him to stop.

She opened the back door of the ambulance and stood on the step. Her headdress, caught in the cool breeze, flew like long, open hair. Her blue eyes, which did not go with the looks of Meerut, surprised the cyclists. Raising the incense burner in her hand she asked in Hindi, "You devils, don't you leave alone even the dead?"

Sister Angelica and I sang a Malayalam hymn even louder. After hesitating for a while, the cyclists drove away. The rest of the trip to the cemetery and out to the church was uneventful. When the ambulance stopped, Amarjit and I opened the casket.

"Get up, Juggy," Amarjit said. He got up like a butterfly coming out of the pupa. He felt his head, sorry for having broken the tradition of his religion. The realization that the hair I cut off was what he got in his mother's womb was disturbing.

Amarjit, Sister Cecilia, and Juggy got into the women's compartment of the train. Juggy stood at the window pressing his face against the window bars. Unconsciously, his hand touched his head again.

The next day was calm. There was no curfew during the day. Sister Mary didn't get up from bed. Sister Katherine rolled her wheelchair away from everyone. Sister Margaret refused to take the medicine. Sister Angelica tried to tell old stories. Sister Davies lay in bed muttering

---

17 The one who speaks is blessed.

something. Sister Karuna sat before the piano without ever touching the keys. Sister Martha prayed the whole day. Sister Wilfred went back to the infirmary.

I could feel the deaths that were to take place in November in the air. I went into the prayer room and closed the door.

BABY DOLL
Gracy

On her way out Nalini reminded her daughter again, "Whoever might come and ring the bell, don't open the door. Even if it is someone you know, open the window and talk to them. Your Achan[1] and I will be back soon."

The girl nodded in agreement. Before going down the steps Nalini waited to hear the sound of the door being closed and locked.

When her father and mother had passed the gate and were out of sight, the girl said to Baby Doll, "Did you hear that, my beauty? Whoever may come, don't open the door!"

Baby Doll closed one eye and smiled. The girl kissed its silky hair, starry eyes, and shiny cheeks and remembered with a smile how angry Amma[2] had been when Achan presented her with this beautiful doll on her twelfth birthday. That night they had an argument.

Amma cried, "Whatever I say, you don't understand. Look! Our daughter has the looks of a 17-year-old, but she behaves like a seven or eight-year-old. If you don't let her grow up what can I do? How would you know the anxiety of a mother?"

Amma had started the argument thinking the girl was asleep. But she was awake, wondering what would happen if she laughed out loud. Then she decided not to. "Let us listen to what Achan has to say." But his voice was full of sadness.

"This time too she made me promise, Nalini." After being silent for a moment, Achan slowly opened the tiny door to his secrets. "I don't know why. When I see baby dolls I can't help buying them, Nalini. Chubby baby dolls take me away somewhere. My childhood was bereft of toys."

Hiding his face in his hands, Achan sat there, hunched up.

In a sad tone Amma murmured softly, "But times are bad, Ravi."

Then she sighed, combing Achan's hair with her fingers.

---

1   Father.

2   Mother.

While wondering why Amma got so anxious about every little thing, sleep came creeping through her eyelashes like dew.

The next day, the girl repeated that question to the dolls lined up in the almirah[3] in the bedroom. She had acquired all those dolls by being stubborn about them with Achan. And she shared her happiness and sadness with them.

Yet all of them just stood there in silence, smiling, turning away from her question, staring towards some other world. Suddenly her big eyes brimmed with tears.

One day, when she was ten years old, she got scared seeing blood spreading on the floor in the bathroom and cried out. Her anxious mother came running, but stood there shaking. Then she held the girl close and consoled her.

"Never mind! This happens to all girls. It means you have become a big girl."

But her daughter didn't like it one bit. She always liked to press her face to her mother's stomach and to sit in her father's lap and dish out all the tidbits about what had happened in class.

After the incident her mother scolded the girl often. "That's enough. You are not a little girl any more."

Achan always protested mildly. "Nalini, why the unnecessary objections?"

Amma stared at Achan. "Unnecessary?" By then Amma's eyes began to fill up and her voice became hoarse. Oh, God! How will this girl face the world!

With a faint smile, Achan patted Amma on the shoulder and said, "Don't worry. Everything will be fine."

When the doorbell sounded its birdcall, the girl moved the curtain aside and peeped out. It was her neighbor, the cricket player. Though a college student, he smiled at her whenever he saw her. He would make some small talk and come close.

Pressing her face against the window, she asked, "What is it?"

He asked in a low tone, "Where did your Achan and Amma go?"

"Didn't you know that the uncle and aunt next door were in an accident? They went to the hospital."

"Why didn't you go?"

---

3 Cabinet.

"I am scared."

Looking at the doll in her hand, he asked, "You like baby dolls, don't you?"

She gave a shy smile, and said, "Yes."

Looking around quickly he said, "I will give you a live doll."

Her face brightened like a flower in full bloom. "Really?"

His voice cracked, "Yes."

"Where is it?"

The curiosity in her tender voice fell on him like a heavy weight. Still, he mumbled, "It is in my room. If you come, I will give it to you."

Slowly putting the baby doll down, she pulled open the door with great delight.

Amma

(Mother)

Johnny Plathottam

"Regarding your mother, everything was quite normal...like an engine that was tired of running, a quiet cardiac arrest, but..." The professor did not continue. That day Appachan[1] and I ignored that "but." Later on that word started to haunt me.

Amma's[2] death did not bother me much, as it was not untimely.

After getting a document registered, I was returning to the office along with my lawyer when I heard about Amma's death. I found the news difficult to believe. That morning, as usual, I had left home after a sumptuous breakfast that she had made. The servant girl found her lying on the floor. There was no one else in the house. One of the neighbors telephoned the office and showroom without success. Finally, someone took the car and went around looking for me.

Amma called me down that morning, as usual, after getting the breakfast ready. I came to the dining room from the second-floor bedroom, ready to go to the office, loaded with the necessary papers and files. While having breakfast, I looked through the morning paper. That day I called out a question to Amma. It was not about the breakfast. There were always more items than necessary on the breakfast table. Like a big factory, one could hear the loud noises of the blender and the milk churner. Amma could not have heard my question. I was a bit upset about not getting a response and looked up. I remember that my question was about the time Appachan was expected back. Recognizing that Amma would not know the answer, I did not repeat the question, but returned to the newspaper and my breakfast. I realized that my perception of having talked to her was not correct; it was a one-sided talk. I was disappointed.

Feeling guilty, I recalled something else. It had been years since I had gone into the kitchen, which was Amma's world. It was the world of my

---

1   Father.

2   Mother.

tender childhood memories, and that of my siblings. It was the beginning of my life's journey. Following her to the grinding stone, from there to the stove, to where she drained the rice, to the corner where the salt was kept .... My senses still remember the mouth-watering smells of the kitchen, its sounds and sights as if yesterday. However, one day during my boyhood, I left the kitchen. Maybe because I could go there anytime I wanted, I never went back. Chechi[3] and my younger brother did the same thing, one by one.

When we started going to school, Appachan allotted us rooms upstairs. All we had to do was to study. When it was time for meals, Amma would call us in her affectionate tone. Life had many new activities–learning to ride a bike and play tennis, etc. Yet, whenever we sat down for meals, I would mentally take a tour of the kitchen. Like the other rooms in the house, the kitchen was spacious. Huge cabinets of six feet or higher stood like storied buildings. There were cupboards made of black wood with glass and wire screen doors. Shelves full of crockery stood high. The cooking vessels of steel and aluminum were stacked up like pillars. Between all these there was a narrow path, wide enough for one person to walk. When I was a child, I used to run along this path and play hide and seek, feeling like the little people of Gulliver's world. Appachan had brought back many additions to the kitchen from abroad, things that were rare in most houses in those days—a refrigerator, an oven, etc. When I grew up and went to the city for the first time, it reminded me of our kitchen. Amma was in the kitchen like a small being in a world of concrete.

There would always be more than one person to help Amma, milking the cows, grinding the spices, and cleaning up. But they never got into the kitchen or dining room. Only Amma was allowed in there, one of Appachan's aristocratic stipulations. It was Janu the servant girl who found Amma dead. So I asked: "Why did you go into the kitchen? Was it because you did not see Amma come out?"

She started saying, "I saw Kochamma[4] even this morning," but stopped and corrected herself, "If not this morning, yesterday I saw her a hundred times."

"When you saw her yesterday, did she look sick?"

"I did not see her yesterday either...Kochamma was busy inside... the day before yesterday also she was busy..." I did not ask her any more questions. Was it just her imagination that she had seen her?

---

3   Elder sister.

4   A term of respect for the mistress of the house when used by household help.

When did I see her alive last? My memory was going back, further and further. After many years, last September Appachan had said, "The day after tomorrow is your Amma's birthday. I won't be here. But you should celebrate it."

"How old is Amma now?" I asked.

There was no response to that.

I bought the cake and other things the previous day. But I could not get home that night or the next night. It was not that I did not want to. To deal with the problems with one of our tenants in town, I had to use some force and go to Trivandrum to meet with a Minister.

The next morning I felt bad when I saw cake crumbs on the dining table. The soot-covered light bulbs in the kitchen made things even more unclear. But I knew that Amma was in that abode of shadows. The washing machine and the blender were humming. I believed that I could distinguish Amma's footsteps and her sighs amidst all that noise. From the dining table I called out to Amma: "Sorry I could not get home last night, Amma." As if in response, the hum of the machines got louder. Of late, Amma had not been talking much, and I did not expect a response.

One day some years ago, Appachan and Amma started to sleep in separate rooms. Even then, Amma never complained. Before that, my sister, her only daughter, got married and went to the States. Two years later my brother got a job there and followed my sister. The last six or seven years he wrote to Amma regularly. The last letter said: "Next year around this time we will definitely come for a visit." I knew that for a few days Amma would make items that her younger son liked and set them on the dining table.

I discontinued studies to join Appachan's business and took on some responsibilities there. I spent very little time at home. But I saw Amma through the food that appeared on the table regularly and heard her when she called me down for meals. Of late, she sounded feeble, as if her voice, though loud enough, was a weak echo of the old sound.

When Janu saw her, she had fallen in one of the narrow paths amidst the abundance of the kitchen. Amma could not get to where she was going or reach what she wanted to get. There was a cooking spoon in her right hand that was stretched forward. Her head was slightly turned as if looking at something. The lifeless eyes were open and the leg in front buckled under.

Even though her dead body was now cold, had Appachan been home or come soon after the event, many things could have been avoided. For the post-mortem Appachan's friend, a forensic professor, joined the surgeon on duty.

The next day, after the funeral and related activities, the professor came home late in the night. He said that Amma's death was like the engine that stopped working because it was tired of running. Then he got up and started walking back and forth and continued, "There was one thing unnatural. We were not able to figure out the time of her death. I want to tell you this only because of my integrity to my profession. Her dead body was very old ... as if the death took place months or even years ago. Yet, it was more unbelievable that the dead body had not deteriorated or was not attacked by ants or anything else ...

As soon as the doctor left, I asked Appachan, "Is your friend an alcoholic?"

But today, I have less faith in my senses. I am not certain of anything. These days I even fear that if Janu had not found Amma's body, she would have kept on getting food to the table and calling me down for meals.

NERCHAKKOTTAN
(SACRIFICIAL ANIMAL)
Moidu Vanimel

Sulaiyakutty remembered the small island that disappeared under water at high tide. She quickly forgot all the things that she was reluctant to remember. What was left were just a few memories that had no roots or stem, just like an orphaned grass patch floating on water. She searched every room in the house for her Bapa,[1] but he was dead. The only thing she remembered was Bapa going to the market. Then she asked for the lamb that was killed and divided among family members as blessed meat for baliperunnal.[2] She had fed the kid and cared for it from the day it was born. It was white as milk with black dots, and eyes that looked as if made up with mascara.

✻ ✻ ✻

When Sulaiyakutty was eight or nine years old, she came running from the grazing sheep nearby. As she was out of breath and couldn't talk, she tried to tell her older brother something by using signs. Sulaiyakutty was shaking as if she was scared by something she had seen. She was sure that Umma[3] would tie a blessed black thread to keep the jinni[4] away from her.

Her eyes were large, reflecting her fear, and she cried out haltingly, "Ikkaka,[5] brother and sister ..."

She stopped for breath. Her words sounded much like the last cry of a lamb being slaughtered. Tears started flowing, and she felt a huge lump in her throat.

---

1 Father.
2 Bakrid or id-ul-adha; festival marking the end of the 30-day fast.
3 Mother.
4 Invisible spirits.
5 Elder brother.

Ikkaka looked out of the window and saw two kids mating. The mother was eating leaves without paying any attention.

He realized the gravity of the sin committed by the brother and sister. But he didn't know if he should laugh or teach her. How could he explain to his younger sister the realities of animal life and sin?

Sulaiyakutty stood on the veranda with staring eyes and shaking body. Then full of anger she got down to the yard, cut a stick, and severely beat the brother and sister. They cried not knowing the reason for the beating. When she cooled down a bit, she threw down the stick and ran to the kitchen where she emitted a long, heart-broken cry.

For a long time she didn't even look at the kids that had committed the sinful act. Then she regained their friendship by stroking the marks her beatings had made on them and by feeding leaves from the jackfruit tree. But she didn't forget to tie the he-goat tight on the stake. Breaking the rope of precautions, the brother and sister mated again, and gradually these sinful acts stopped bothering her.

❋ ❋ ❋

Sulaiyakutty was put to bed with the last sleeping pill. That whole day she was agitated, asking for Bapa and the he-goat. Ikkaka entreated the almighty not to wake her up. If she awakened during the night, she would cause hell to break out. In a mental hospital, one patient's middle of the night cries and screams wake the others up, making the night become day.

❋ ❋ ❋

Sulaiyakutty's growing up was sudden. When she returned from the summer vacation in the yatheemkhana,[6] Ikkaka saw a younger sister whose body had blossomed like a flower. He saw her combing her hair for hours in front of the full-length mirror and smiling at the reflection of her body. With her bright colored clothes and made-up face she was like a peacock with its tail fanned out. It seemed that she was celebrating the beauty of her body.

Her dressing up and attractive looks made Umma uneasy and she scolded Sulaiyakutty for putting burning coal into Umma's heart. But she passed on her anxiety to her son.

---

6 Orphanage.

* * *

One day Umma tied a red pouch to the neck of the he-goat and sent it to the market. It was reluctant to leave the yard and cried pitifully for Sulaiyakutty.

Sulaiyakutty's he-goat became nerchakkottan, a sacrificial animal. It would roam around with the offering pouch around its neck until the festival. Coins would be put into the pouch and the goat would be fed as offering, and no one would harm the goat or kill it before the appointed time. People would fatten it up by feeding and taking care of it until the festival.

Through the small window, she saw her he-goat crossing the henna fence on his way to the market, crying all the way. A sigh that came from deep inside shook her all over.

* * *

"Relatives and religious leaders will have to answer in the next world for every drop of tear shed by a girl whose father is dead," Umma reminded Ikkakka on and off. In the end, the elders in the village took a collection and raised enough money for the orphaned girl's dowry and offering.

When they tied the gold pendant from the boy's house around her neck, Sulaiyakutty said, as a joke, "Now I can also be sent out like nerchakkottan!"

On the day of her wedding, Sulaiyakutty passed the henna fence with her friends, singing the traditional oppana.[7] As Ikkaka watched his younger sister, he recalled another sacrificial giving away. She was a grown-up housekeeper who had to manage someone else's kitchen.

* * *

Umma and other relatives were more proud than happy that the fatherless girl got a man working in the Gulf.

She remained like a beautiful flower, but became imprisoned in a smoke-filled kitchen. She had to hide her body inside the purdah[8] and scarf. Her husband would come only after two or three years to enjoy his married life. Thirty-five months of separation and one month of married life! How many months of married life would she have in all her life? His

---

7 Wedding song.

8 Long, loose garment used as a cover-up by Muslim women.

younger sister's future was always on Ikkaka's mind. He felt responsible for each drop of this fatherless girl's tears.

She accommodated herself quietly inside the high walls and shed tears looking at the sky, waiting for her husband's arrival. She was full of dreams. During the days and nights of separation and waiting, without her knowledge, a peacock woke up inside her and spread its tail. She was shocked by that alarming realization. Then with ruthless pleasure she would step on it and stamp on it and then press her face to the pillow. Every time she killed it, the peacock would come back stronger. She hid this scary vision in the deepest part of her mind.

❋ ❋ ❋

With the help of sleeping pills, Sulaiyakutty slept well, snoring. On and off she would groan and moan. Through the small window Ikkaka could see her pained expression. It seemed like the sorrow of a mother with her son's dead body in her lap.

It was past midnight. Ikkaka, who was staying as guard for Sulaiyakutty, was sitting on the wet veranda of the mental hospital, deep in thought.

One day when there was no one else at home, while breast feeding her child, Sulaiyakutty felt a kind of fluttering in her heart like never before. That day, for the first time, she undressed in the shower room and looked at her body in the mirror, bewildered. Then she got dressed in her wedding sari, put mascara in her eyes, and went to the shade of a tree in the front yard and loosened her hair. When her husband opened the gate, she was standing there in a rage and combing her hair, oblivious to what she was doing. He saw two eyes licking her up through the small window of the two-storied building across the street, though she was unaware of it. What followed was a scream that sounded like a thunderbolt.

That night, when she was fast asleep, her husband came with a scissors and cut her hair into a thousand pieces. The wind blew the hair into her mouth and nose and she could not breathe. Sulaiyakutty beat her head and cried aloud. Her cries came like the screams and incoherent mutterings of the insane.

❋ ❋ ❋

A week later, her husband brought Sulaiyakutty to her mother's house.

He got angry at the mother for inquiring about the baby. He screamed, "Your daughter will kill that child. She is insane, crazy!"

Lightning flashed in Umma's eyes. She cried embracing her daughter tight. Ikkakka stood there helplessly watching the two. Suddenly, Sulaiyakutty pulled off her head cover and threw it at her brother. Instead of beautiful long hair, she had the hair of a child in a nursery school.

On the third day, a letter from her husband came in the mail, giving the news of their divorce. That day the island of her memory went completely underwater.

✳ ✳ ✳

On the eve of the Baliperunnal, Sulaiyakutty was fast asleep under the effect of the sleeping pills.

Perhaps she heard the cries of the sacrificial lambs in her dreams or imagined someone giving her loving kisses. Whatever the reason, that night Sulaiyakutty disappeared from the closed ward of the mental hospital. Where could they look for her in the twilight?

Ikkakka was burning with anxiety. He searched every nook and corner of the hospital. Some people made their own torch with palm leaves and searched everywhere.

Ikkakka sat down exhausted, like one paralyzed, when some people returned. He got up and followed them.

On a dark veranda along the street, Sulaiyakutty lay unconscious with her sari torn and drops of blood everywhere. Her face had the tortured look of a nerchakkottan whose meat had been divided up.

THE LIES MY MOTHER TOLD ME
Ashita

The person who has told me the most lies is my mother. This knowledge is smoldering in my chest like a fire that refuses to be put out.

Amma[1] is in the pooja[2] room sitting in front of the oil lamp and reading the *Ramayana.* Sitting in the patio, I can see her face clearly: the bhasmam[3] mark on her forehead, the glasses sliding down to the tip of the nose, the wrinkles on her cheeks, and the barely-moving lips. In her old age she looks like a big wrinkle in my memory. Her index finger with the broken nail is moving along the line as she reads.

When school got out and I was walking home, Ahmed Ikka[4] gave me a few pieces of candy. Amma took them from me and threw them out angrily. "What do you mean by calling him Ikka? Who is he to you? Taking and eating what someone hands out! Wait till Achhan[5] gets home."

Ants carried away the candy that fell on the ground. It is only later that I learned the hard way that it is the sweets that strangers give you that are the sweetest. But that day it seemed unfair.

Ahmed Ikka is not anyone to me and my Achhan, who is, does not say even a kind word or give an affectionate look, but comes home and makes the whole house tremble with fear.

When I get home after school I can see his rough hand going over his bald head, everyone can hear his loud belching after meals, the shouting at the workers and then the counting of the beating for whatever wrongs we did. This was Achhan.

Achhan was pleasant only to Amma's close relative, Chellammakka. If Amma was a bhasmam mark and its mild fragrance, Chellammakka was the alluring scent of jasmine flowers and the magic of beautiful smiles. Even before she started laughing, her chest would shake, the dimples in

---

1   Mother.

2   Ceremonial worship.

3   Ash from burnt camphor.

4   Elder brother, used only to show respect.

5   Father.

her cheeks would become clearer, and her diamond nose ring would scatter light like her laughter. I don't remember her coming home ever. However, she was always there in Amma's curses, Achhan's unusual silence, and the jasmine buds I once saw in Achhan's pocket. I like Chellammakka, but when the fights between Achhan and Amma became louder, I would hide under the table or bed and pray, reluctantly, for her to die.

One day Chellammakka committed suicide. I was relieved that Amma wouldn't have to cry again. I put on my best clothes to go to her house. But Amma gave me a faded, ordinary blouse and said, "We are going to visit a house where someone died. What will people think if you are all dressed up?" Not knowing how to compromise two conflicting feelings, I looked at Amma's face. But it revealed nothing, like the mark on her forehead.

It was the fall. As I walked beside Amma kicking dry leaves, she said quietly, "When you get there you are not to talk or laugh. Remember it is a house where someone died. Sit somewhere quietly."

Then I asked, "Are you happy she died?"

I thought she was taken aback. Achhan, who was ahead, turned around impatiently, with a sad face. Amma blew her nose and pretended to be wiping her eyes with the end of her sari. I thought it was an astonishing sight.

When Amma was pretending to be wiping her tears, it seemed someone was mocking her by laughing, with the dimples getting bigger. When we were returning from Chellammakka's house, I ran and walked fast to keep up with Amma. Then I asked her the question that was beginning to baffle me: "Amma, can I also lie as I like when I grow up?"

Amma's face and the sinduram[6] on her forehead wrinkled at the same time, as if breathing in the mild fragrance of jasmine flowers. She was furious. "Awful child! Only shocking questions come out of your mouth. Only bad children have bad thoughts. God will question each and every thought you have. Don't you see..."

That afternoon the sun shone like left-over laughter.

I bent my head from a sense of wrongdoing. Now I feel Amma was trying to escape by making me feel guilty. There was a reason for this sense of guilt. It was a time when I was acquiring some secret know-how and learning about a secret world without Amma's knowledge.

Close to Amma's uncompromising world of don'ts, orders, and total obedience, I had found another world–from the homes of my friends, in Chellammakka's laughter, and from the people who worked in our house

---

6 Vermilion-colored powder applied on the forehead by women in India.

and fields. It was a poor, uncultured, unreal world, but definitely more free and happy. I was confused not knowing what was the truth and what was a lie. But I leaned towards the colorful lies rather than to the gray truth. Like water searching for its own level, whenever I could I searched for that world. When I had a ball of rice from the bowl of a worker, when I hung on to Chellammakka's hand in her fields during the harvest and learned bad words the workers were saying to one another, I tasted the pleasure of breaking Amma's don'ts. The more I tasted it, the more daring and stronger I became. I can remember saying "bitch" ten times at a stretch, after reciting the prayers before the lit oil lamp, without worrying about God's punishment.

Then I lay awake at night fearing God's punishment for a bad girl who had bad thoughts, biting my nails. When I slept I had awful dreams of swishing canes. The god who was ready to punish me had Achhan's face.

Then Achhan was carried home from the field one day, one side paralyzed and one side of the face gone crooked.

That was the day God died within me, a helpless God with a crooked face. Achhan died many days later like a nobody, a worthless truth, before my marriage.

For my marriage, my mother presented me with a stone-studded lie. On the day of my marriage, Amma came into my room—an unusual act. Like any bride, I was also shining with a bright inner glow. She looked at me from head to foot. It was sad enough to surprise me. She put her hand on my shoulder and said, "From this day onwards, you cannot live in a dream world. You must remember you are going to another house. It is not child's play to manage a house, cooking and feeding on time." She stopped and held me close and continued, "Don't forget that it is the only way to a man's heart." I didn't forget.

My husband was educated and cultured. He was a poet, and a politician in free times. So while he was reading the newspaper four or five times to evaluate a piece of literature, or in despair of democracy, I ground masala[7] and washed dishes and clothes. I left my dream world. In time the route of my movements was from the kitchen to the children's room and to the bedroom. I was searching for the way into my husband's heart. But at the end of the day, when I got into the bedroom after being in the smoke and soot of the kitchen the whole day, he was dissatisfied

---

7 Spices for seasoning food.

and wanted bigger breasts and thighs. I realized that, just like preparing food, I had to prepare for love also. I felt harshly betrayed by Amma.

Without my knowing it, my love disappeared somewhere, and I felt as if someone spat hard on my truth. I learned that there is only one way to a man's heart. The truth that Amma didn't tell me was like a lie to me.

That is how I acquired the language of Amma, her mother and all women before them, the language of silence. We learned the art of talking contradiction and denial when we had to talk, and practiced self-denial.

People in the neighborhood and family members started saying that I was looking more and more like a copy of my mother. Once in a while, without thinking, as I pass a mirror I happen to look and realize the shocking truth of what they say. It was like small lies joining together and I was becoming a big lie.

Sifted lines from the *Ramayana* reached my ears. Something serious was melted into Amma's voice—or was it my imagination? I saw Amma taking off her glasses and closing the book. The door of the bedroom opened suddenly. The light was on. Standing in that light was my eight-year-old daughter, dressed clumsily in one of my silk saris and holding a doll on her hip.

"Look Amma, don't I look like you?" It was as if someone just emptied a gun into my chest. Amma came laughing in agreement and sat opposite to me. Cleverly she asked me the question that had been bothering her for some time now, in a tone meant for ordinary talk: "Why didn't Balu come with you? He hasn't written either. Is there anything between ..."

A moment of silence!

Then I responded, with great ease, "Nothing Amma. These are not olden days. Girls are living well these days, very well."

The person I have lied to most is Amma.

ONE STILL PICTURE CANNOT CAPTURE A LIFE'S STORY

Gita Hiranyan

Sometimes when she lathered a sponge Azhakamma felt she was holding a wet kitten in her hand. It was just a fistful, but as soon as it was put in the bucket, it stretched out and slowly grew into a cat.

Light yellow in color.

And so, her classmate came to mind. She studied up to the eighth grade with that Padhani[1] girl, golden-colored skin, curly, copper-colored hair, and gray cat's eyes—Sherafuniza Begum.

Begum was also called Cat. That name was not given by her parents, but was the gift of the clever boys who were infatuated by her beauty and perturbed by her disregard for them. German Cat.

Where is that beauty? How is she? Who knows?

Azhakamma cannot waste time thinking about the German Cat. She has to go to four houses to do the daily chores. To add to her distractions, there is the local TV's white van in the front yard of the first house, and a few men scattered around with electrical connections, lighting equipment, and other instruments—white, black, and colored items.

She wants to watch them too. Watch the cameras. Watch the shooting.

So she told her friend, "Cat, I have to stop my reminiscence of our trip to Vivekodaya School in long, blue skirts with plaited hair coming down on both sides, and carefree attitudes. Let the memories of that trip end half-way." Still, those memories brought her pleasure.

But when Azhakamma tried to wipe her hands on either side of the checkered mundu[2] to dry them, her school English came back: "Ouch!" Actually, it was the universal language of pain. All palms that have lost the blistered skin on them will understand it. Only stay-home mothers who pamper themselves with hand cream would not understand it.

---

1 Of Afghan origin.

2 A lower garment, consisting of a length of cloth.

But the kitchen worker Parutty Chechi is not like them. For her to turn her face on seeing those hands...

Though the sponge in Azhakamma's hands carries many pleasant memories, playing with the sponge cat makes them look awful.

When they touched salt or pepper she felt as if she were carrying burning coal in her hands.

Azhakamma lost her self-respect when Parutty Chechi turned her face in disgust. Though she works in four houses, she was burnt by that.

"Are my hands so filthy?" she thought.

Parutty Chechi said, "You should try for some work in the government. You say you finished middle school, eighth grade. In olden days that was good enough for a Thahasildar.[3] You must be able to get in at least as a peon."

Parutty didn't say that out of sympathy. She meant something else. She doesn't believe that the girl did indeed finish the eighth grade. These days the world is full of double talk. But that doesn't bother Azhakamma. No one needs to believe that she went to school.

But Ramyakutty, the girl of the house, believed that she went to school. That's why she asked the cleaning girl for the spelling of a word: whether it is "bougainvilla" or "bougenvilla." Ramya was arguing with the gardener who was mixing some slightly poisonous substance in water to sprinkle on the rose bushes to kill the little creatures on them.

Azhakamma carried the washed plates and cups into the house when she stopped and asked the gardener as if just remembering something:

"Sashi, why don't you stand in front of the house, taking cuttings from plants or something? That way, they may include you in the movie and you will come on TV."

He just laughed.

Parutty, who was crushing onion and green pepper on the grinding stone, said, "From this morning this girl is all excited and can think only of TV. I have had enough of it."

So what, what did Azhakamma care! She was very excited. She had seen film shooting only once before.

It was ten or fifteen years ago, when she worked in a house on Marrar Road.

As she was going home at noon, seven or eight bicycles came down the narrow road like birds flying in formation. They were all pre-degree

---

3   Revenue officer.

students. One of them slowed down and barely touched the ground with one foot and asked, "Chechi, you want to go where they are shooting the film?"

What a question! Still she asked, "Where?"

The boy was back on the bike. "In front of Vadakku Nathhan Temple," he said.

When she got there the crowd was big, mostly college students waiting eagerly to see Mohan Lal, or to see Parvathy.[4] Even after waiting for a long time they didn't come. But she saw reflectors. She saw cameras. She was flabbergasted! Even the cameras had class! There was one on top of a ladder, almost as high as the banyan tree.

One of the girls waiting there asked the boy standing next to her, "Bejoy, why is this camera up there, so high?"

Bejoy, a fair young man wearing sunglasses, took his glasses off, wiped them and his eyes with a handkerchief he took out of his pocket, and put the glasses back on. He looked at the camera once again and said, like a learned man, "It is to get long shots. Suppose Mohan Lal and Parvathy are coming from that side, they can be photographed even at that distance."

Azhakamma was impressed. Though he is young, he knows all this. Silently, she congratulated him.

Long ago, Begum went to Jana Studio to get her picture taken. The photographer moved the camera set on a tripod back and forth several times. She stood away from the view of the camera, looking at the black, pleated camera. But because she didn't have 300 rupees to shell out for the picture, the camera did not blink its eyes at her that day.

Somehow that original camera changed and developed into the one that was in front of Vadakku Nathhan Temple. One camera was fixed on the tall tripod, another one running along a track, and a third one-eye on a platform hung from a tree. A bearded man in a loose blue shirt with circles of sweat marks under his arms went and looked into the cameras on and off. Whenever the children saw him they shouted, "Padmarajetta!" Either because he hadn't had enough sleep or because he was dreaming, his eyes were puffed up, but at times the blue-shirted man smiled at the children and waved his hat. But at other times, he just didn't bother. That was the only picture shooting she had witnessed.

Life's difficulties had pushed that memory down to the depth of forgetful-

---

4   Mohan Lal and Parvathy are movie stars.

ness. But it surfaced to the top when Ramyakutty told her about another group coming to shoot a movie.

Today, luckily, she was able to see film shooting–the wonders a camera could do–with no problems from college students.

How could she not be excited? Parutty Chechi could not understand that. But how could she get the front door opened? Even when it opened, it was not easy for her to get inside. Both she and Ramyakutty were equally crazy about cinema. Because Ramyakutty was the girl of the house, those who were getting the set ready excused her and let her in, but when Azhakamma tried to follow, they closed the door on her face.

She had come to tell the cook, who was watching the grinder going round and round, about the wonders beyond the closed door. But she needed patience to even talk about wonders to these dirty faces that showed no interest in anything.

Someone was thirsty on the patio. Ramyakutty came with a message: "Do we have any jeera[5] water? It is for them."

The cook got mad, "Where is your Amma?" she asked angrily.

The mother of the house was nowhere to be seen.

Ramyakutty responded, "Amma is upstairs. Some discussions are going on there."

"Discussions! Why are they drinking so much water? I have only two hands. There is a limit to the number of times I can get them water."

Ramyakutty, who was playing hopscotch on the black and white tiles of the kitchen floor, paid no attention to the complaints. She had heard many such complaints.

It must be because she knew that people would be coming for shooting that Ramyakutty was well dressed. She had a bindi[6] to match her pleated skirt. Azhakamma called her close and, while adjusting the bindi, she asked, "Are you going to act?"

Still jumping on one foot, she said, "Not me."

"Then who?"

Looking back to see if she missed a square, Ramyakutty said, "Amma."

Parutty Chechi looked at her and winked knowingly.

It is true that children study the grownups well. Not able to hold back her eagerness to find out about the woman who was upstairs, Azhakamma asked, "Who is the other woman?"

---

5   Cumin seed (water boiled with cumin seed is a common drink).

6   A small dot worn on the forehead by Indian women.

"Oh, that is Sunanda Nair." That eight year old wondered at the ignorance of the kitchen help.

"That silver saucer's name is Sunanda?"

That well-dressed woman had on silver ear ornaments the size of saucers, and the name Parutty Chechi gave was suitable. With that, Ramyakutty got a tune to jump to.

"Vellikkinnam thulli thulli."[7]

"Shhh!" Parutty put her finger on her lips. "They will hear you."

Still, Ramyakutty didn't stop humming the tune as she took a jug of jeera water back.

The gardener came to the kitchen at that time and said something to Parutty Chechi. They both went to the back veranda. He sat on the floor and said, "Good for the old people."

Thinking it was about her, Parutty was about to say something when he continued, "Because of independence celebrations."

She was not into politics; what did he have on his mind?

The politics enthusiast said, "Otherwise, would the TV crew come here?"

Azhakamma was flabbergasted.

"Did you think they are shooting a movie?" he asked.

She didn't respond.

"Do you know what they are going to do? First, introduction of the topic—our Chechi will do that—the history of Indian independence."

"How do you know?"

"I heard them talk. Then they will interview Kochutyamma."

"Chechi will also do that?"

"Yes. They have to go somewhere else too. There is an independence fighter there who is old, can't see or hear well."

"Still, they want her to act on TV."

They all laughed.

Ramyakutty heard the laughter and wanted to know the reason. But without waiting for an answer, she said, "They are looking for you, Sashi. They want two green plants."

"There are two in the sitting room."

"They are not bushy enough."

When the gardener got up and left Azhakamma said, "I have to go to all these houses. I was thinking of waiting till they start. But they are taking their own time. I am leaving, Parutty Chechi."

---

7   The jumping of a metallic lid on a boiling pot (used only for the rhyme).

"Wait a minute, you were supposed to clean the toilet."

She pretended not to hear that. After a while she said, "I am not going to clean the toilet with all those camera men there."

They saw the veettamma[8] in the dining room. She had changed her clothes. She had on a shiny sea-blue sari with wide, vaadaamalli[9] purple border. Her diamond earrings, shiny hair, and eyelashes were sparkling, and her body was of a golden color.

How beautiful she looked, even in her middle age! She smiled at Azhakamma. The one with the silver earrings looked at her, but did not smile.

"You can go upstairs and clean now, nobody is there." Nobody means no master or guests.

Azhakamma liked the upstairs–to be exact, the staircase. There were long fluorescent lights there that were on even during the day.

A huge mirror covered the middle wall, and she stood in front of it. Azhakamma was her own beautician. When no one was looking, she would sneak upstairs to stand in front of the mirror and consult the beautician.

"You are working too hard," she scolded herself. "Look at you! The body is all black and blue. Getting old, the hair on the side is getting gray," she said pulling out a gray hair. "Why don't you wear a bindi? It doesn't take long." She touched her forehead. Still she liked the Azhakamma in the mirror.

Today she came upstairs with a broom and a blue plastic dustpan. She looked at herself in the mirror and smiled. From the dressing table she wiped the powder that had fallen on one side and powdered her face.

"Why don't you do your hair? What if someone comes in suddenly?" She continued talking to herself, "I know there are ways to make one look fair and the hair look black. But they are only for those who have money and time for such things."

The Azhakamma in the mirror didn't say anything. She left her in the mirror and started to sweep the floor.

In a little while she heard the woman with the silver earrings on the stairs. She must have been speaking English. The veettamma said in the same language, "I have selected some patriotic poems. We will quote some of them at the beginning. Do you want to see? Come."

She heard their footsteps. They were coming to the wall mirror. She couldn't bear to see the queen in a blue sari with purple border in the

---

8   Mistress of the house.

9   Amaranth.

mirror. When she looked up the queen was straightening the gold border on the sleeve of her silk blouse.

As soon as the queen saw Azhakamma, she turned and said, "Before you go, you have to clean the toilet. Don't forget."

Did her royal highness come up here to say this?

Azhakamma hated cleaning the toilet. The veettamma accused her of waiting till it became slippery for someone to fall and break a leg. Once before, when they were arguing about it, the veettamma had said, "What is there to be ashamed of? Even Kasthurba Gandhi cleaned her bathroom."

She remembered that. "But today this patriot is not going to teach me history," she thought and didn't respond at all. Silence is not always the sign of agreement. In time she would know.

When she finished her chores and came down the steps, the veet-tamma and her friend were turning pages in a book, standing near the window. Downstairs the parlor was open. The cane chairs were set in the right places. Electric lights were shining in every corner of the room.

A young man who was setting up the room came and asked, "Is there a painting we can use?" The question was not addressed to Azhakamma, for she was not of the house. Still, she pointed to a picture on the wall, above the dining table.

Actually, Azhakamma did not consider it a beautiful picture. It was the picture of a poor old man staring at a money purse, with rays of greed coming from the pupils of his eyes.

But before he could take it, Ramyakutty, who was watching all this, said "Let me ask Amma," and ran upstairs.

Hearing her say "That is ok, he can use that," the young man pulled up a stool and got on it to get the picture.

Something that she didn't want to hear followed. "Ramye,[10] ask her to clean the toilet before she goes." Her! She has no name. She got angry, ready to explode.

As a precursor came her mumblings like the rumblings of the sky about to burst.

Ramyakutty heard that first, as she came down the stairs.

"What are you mumbling?" she asked.

In her anger Azhakamma forgot her surroundings. "I have told you a thousand times that I don't want to clean the toilet."

---

10   When you address someone in Malayalam, you add an "a" or "e" sound to the person's name.

The young man was getting down from the stool holding the picture. He was stunned and looked at her.

"They pay me, that's true," she complained, forgetting that she didn't know him.

"Workers are also people," she continued. "Do you think it is fair to make them do what they don't want to do?"

Ramyakutty was embarrassed. The eight-year-old child-veettamma was familiar with the servants' outbursts of anger. But she also knew that it should not be done in front of guests.

Quickly, Ramyakutty sought the help of the cook. "Parutty Valyamme,[11] she is saying some nonsense there. Call her here."

When Parutty came in to see what was going on, there was no audience. Still Azhakamma spoke with gestures as if there was a big crowd listening to her.

"I have your tea ready, come," Parutty said.

"I don't want your tea."

"Come, it will go cold."

"When have you given me hot tea? You can say that to trick little children."

"What do you know about tricking little children?" Parutty mumbled, but Azhakamma heard that. It was true that she had no husband or children, and all that was needed to break her heart was such a sharp insult. That would break her spirit as well.

She was angry and did not accept the breakfast. The cook put a couple of pieces of fried fish from the previous day into a plastic bag as Azhakamma changed her checkered mundu[12] for a sari. She threw the fish into the rubbish pile. The cook had to pilfer things to give the workers who come in. That was how she showed her regard for them.

"That is stolen fish. If I eat that, the fish bones will get stuck in my throat," Azhakamma said to put the kitchen help in her place. She was full of anger when she went down the steps carrying a broken vanity bag in her hand, to get to the next house.

She didn't pay any attention to the TV crew, cameras, or the lighting arrangements.

"She wants me to clean the toilet," she complained to herself. "For that she has to find someone else."

The veettamma next door was sitting on the veranda reading the

---

11   Mother's older sister (used here only to show respect for her age).

12   A lower garment, consisting of a length of cloth.

newspaper and heard the murmuring. She stopped reading and looked up eagerly.

The dark, skinny old woman who was cleaning the floor with a wet cloth stood up and asked, "What are you saying?"

"Oh, about our Kasthurba Gandhi."

The old woman didn't understand. But the one who was reading the newspaper did, and her face changed. It showed a kind of wonder mixed with guilt from long ago. She looked at her old servant. But the old woman didn't see that.

She was looking at the girl walking away fast in the hot sun, without an umbrella. When she disappeared from sight, the old woman squeezed the dirty water from the rag into the flowerpot.

"What a beautiful girl she was," she exclaimed. As she said that, a girl in long, flowered skirt and a gold necklace ran along the narrow footpath of a field in the old woman's vision of the past. She wondered if she should describe that picture to her mistress, but decided against it. She was too rich to consider a chain of one sovereign anything special. Nor would she care about a long, blue skirt with sunflowers.

The girl walked away angry at the whole world, not knowing about those who were on her side. That was her constant quarrel with her low birth. Even her slippers (they had marks where her heals and toes put pressure on them) and legs were fighting the world.

"Which is the Chempanthitta house?"

She stopped.

It was a woman who asked. She was about 25 years old. Along with her was a young man wearing sunglasses.

Within the black chooridar[13] and long, fitting top with glasswork her stomach was big with a baby of about eight months.

"Go this way and you will get to the main road. The last house, after you turn left."

The man wearing the sunglasses moved his lips, "Thanks!"

That is the most popular word with no meaning from within. She was tired of it.

"You crazy woman, why are you giving those poor guys the run around?"

She didn't turn around.

"Isn't this Chempanthitta house?"

A gardener who had come to cut a hibiscus branch that was coming over the wall asked the question.

---

13   Tight, long trousers worn by women.

"Let them walk. Walking is good for pregnant women."

"Oh, nice prescription! Poor things!"

He was making loud noises with the big gardener's shears, but she raised her voice above that.

"Why are you taking up for the seahorse?"

"Seahorse?"

She didn't think he watched the Discovery Channel. Ramyakutty's Discovery Channel had introduced her to seahorses jumping around in the sea. The female with a big stomach and a lean male were playing a funny game in the water. From then on whenever she saw pregnant women in chooridar, she thought of the seahorse.

But what was the point in saying these things to someone who had not watched the Discovery Channel?

When she got near him he got the smell of sweaty, oily hair and unwashed, dirty body. She didn't bathe very often. How could she? Four houses to clean, advance payment from all of them, four sets of new clothes for Onam,[14] and four wages. With this hectic life, she had no time to shower or get dressed up or anything.

"Aren't you going to the other house today? In Chaitram?"

She thought of that. That was another demon. The management there was very strict. She didn't get time to breathe. Work, work, work!

"I am not going today. My eyes are hurting."

He stared into her eyes for a while.

"It is not your eyes that are hurting." He looked her over, up, and down. She felt uneasy.

His small talk was all good, but not the way he looked at her.

"Yes, everyone in the house has some eye problem."

What she said was true, in a way. There was only one person in the house, an old woman, and she had an eye problem. But it was the usual problem with old people, she had cataracts in her eyes.

"What was all the noise today? I heard all the hue and cry, the muttering and shouting."

Without really trying, she had an opportunity to vent her anger. But she didn't want to say anything and pretended she didn't hear him.

But he forced her to listen to him, imitating her: "If they want someone to clean the toilet, they should find someone else. I am not going to do that."

"Hey, you get out, boy. Plant master."

That term also was from the school. In her old school, the students

---

14 The state festival of Kerala.

called the gardener plant master. But today, this gardener didn't appreciate the humor.

"The whole day, you have been playing with one word: 'toilet.'"

With that, she was very upset. Some words were like that. One did not get what one wanted, but got what one did not want.

"Don't misunderstand my asking. I have been thinking of it for a long time. What happened to you to be so upset?"

She tried to move away from the kindness in those words.

"That is a long story."

"OK, let's hear it. I have time."

She could talk to the whole world about anything else, but not about herself. Reluctantly, she turned her face.

"I don't know how to tell a story." Along with that refusal, half a sentence came out, "More over..."

"More over, what?"

"To tell a story you need to have better language skills. How do I get those skills?" she said with a smile. Then she wondered what he would say, if she decided to go ahead with the story.

[It was on a new moon night. Today it makes 34 years. That night, she went with the only escort she had, a small kerosene lamp, to wash the dinner dishes by the well.

In front of their house was a field that looked like a lake and stretched as far as the eye could see, like a black mirror, without lamp posts or advertisements to diminish its beauty.]

She paused, wondering if he would make fun of her or congratulate her, saying that she was good at telling stories.

Once, long ago, she was applauded by the Malayalam Pandit[15] after he had just finished reading her composition. A few months ago she saw his picture in the newspaper, on his 80th birthday. She remembered his commendation, "You know how to write."

Thinking about that, she continued the story:

[Let us call her Malathy.

She had starry eyes with arched eyebrows, chubby cheeks, and plaited hair.

When she saw the houses along the fields lit with small lamps in the windows reflected in the water, she felt like singing.

---

15   Teacher (used only for males).

Amma shouted from inside the house, "There is lightning flashing. Finish quickly and come inside." But the lightning didn't bother her. Amma was right. In the skies dark horses were ready for a war. Their hoofs turned over the black soil. Suddenly, lightning flashed like a silver whip and thunderbolts cracked with great noise. Strong winds made waves in the lake.

The lightning produced shadows from the heads of the arecanut palms that looked like hooded snakes trying to get to the opposite side. Along the fence, the grass was crushed by someone's footprints. With the next lightning she saw the golden-colored feet in brown slippers. He was walking towards her with the end of his mundu in his hand. He stopped beside her and smiled.

Her eyes stopped blinking and she stopped singing. Bashfully, she gathered the brass plates and hurried, forgetting to take the lamp. Stepping on her long skirt she fell, the brass plates clattering.

"Don't you have bones in your arms?" Amma was furious at the clatter. That was the usual question. If ever she dropped something accidentally, Amma would remind her of the number of bones in her arms.

Her breath became uneven and the words came out: "A man..."

"Where?"

Forgetting the pain in her arm, Amma took the lamp from the opening in the wall and came out to the yard.

"By the side of the well."

Amma shaded her eyes from the light of the kerosene lamp and looked about anxiously.

"What is wrong with you, girl? This is not a man, just the young one of Chathappu's water buffalo."

"What happened to the man I saw?" she wondered.

In the circle made by the orange light of the kerosene lamp there was no one. The lightning flashed like a whip and the sound of thunder continued. The lonely one-room hut could be seen clearly in the flash of lightning. By the well a brownish water-buffalo calf looked at Malathy with its mascara-lined eyes that were veiled in sadness.

When lightning struck again, Malathy lost consciousness. Her endless journey then was through dark passages and deep openings in the ground. She could hear tiny bells and half sung songs in her head.

The sad thing was when she woke up she became nameless. Gone were the days of dance and songs, with no one to support her, an orphan with no one to protect her.

Still, to her surprise, because of the two gram gold she had, an astrologer made up a garden of love for her giving the name of a lover.

That name was written on a bit of gold piece on a black string and tied around her hip where no one would see it. That lover who was hidden from everyone's eyes was supposed to be her lover in her last life also, according to the astrologer. And her mother believed him.

But people in the village made fun of her. As soon as she came in sight, they would say, "Brahmarakshas[16] is coming."

Then she would murmur to her lover that by talking about past lives he destroyed her present life.

"What was your name in the last life?" she asked. The man asleep in the gold piece was quiet.

She joked, "In this life you have a name, 'Brahmarakshas,' given by the astrologer."

Poor thing! How many beautiful names are there in the world, and he got this!

Malathy laughed.

The laughter was the end of the story.]

But no one laughed with Azhakamma. What happened to the gardener who wanted to hear the story? Where did he go?

She was surprised but felt hopeless. Was this pleasant feeling that someone loved her and would be with her in all her troubles a dreamy side of her mind that might be a sickness, as some people say?

Who knows?

---

16   The spirit of a bad Brahmin who had done evil deeds during his lifetime in this world.

GHARE BAIRE
(AT HOME AND OUTSIDE)
Gita Hiranyan

The housewife felt that by closing the metal doors of the gate on Haridas about an hour ago, she had lost the world of her favorite things.

The world she had lost was one she could not get back nor grieve over openly.

Though humiliation and a sense of loss were churning inside her like a stormy sea, the housewife did not show the faintest hint of it outwardly. She had no one who would listen to what happened and suggest a solution to the predicament. There were three people in the room along with her, but they had no idea that she had such a private world of her own. Then how could they suggest a way to regain that world?

First of all, there was her only son Asvin, eight years old. As soon as she came and sat down after closing the gate, he started his usual stunts. Today's special was because Amma[1] went out for lunch without him. He was in the forefront of those who believe that mothers are there to serve their children.

The second person was the housewife's niece—her husband's niece, to be precise. She was twenty years old and addicted to movies on TV. The housewife thought of confiding in her, but on second thought, decided against it.

She could never discuss the matter with the third person, her husband. He had gray hair and bright eyes like Indira Gandhi, but had no sensitivity. He had no idea that his wife had a world within her where he had never been. An engineer, he did not realize that even when he didn't need her, she had a body and a heart that craved for love and care. In a way, he was the reason for her tragic situation.

They were all in the dining room watching a movie on television. Only her son was not interested in the movie.

---

1 Mother.

"This Amma is stupid." No one paid any attention to the boy. They were all immersed in the movie. The son pinched his mother on her arm and said, "Stupid Amma, cruel Amma."

The niece said, "Look at her face. Isn't it shaped like a betel leaf?"

"Is it? I don't think so," the housewife said.

"She has a typical Bengalee[2] face."

Listening to her one would think that the young lady had lived among Bengalees.

"Have you seen anyone other than the Tamil and Telugu women who come during the time of pilgrimage to Sabarimala?"[3] she wanted to ask.

The son pushed his mother with all his strength and repeated the insult, "Stupid Amma."

"What is this movie?" the housewife asked.

"*Ghare Baire.*"

She was surprised to hear that. "What a strange name! What does it mean?"

The young lady ignored the question, pretending to be immersed in the movie. She always pretended to be hard of hearing whenever she didn't have an answer.

The husband said, "It means 'At Home and Outside.'"

"I wonder how it is going to end." Whether they heard it or not, no one responded to the housewife's comment.

They were concentrating on a door encrusted with light green and yellow colored glass being opened. The Bengalee bride with the face shaped like the betel leaf was taking the first step along with her husband into the courtyard.

The heroine's pointed slippers might be a sign of betrayals to come. Movies have a world full of symbols.

The housewife thought about what she had done about an hour ago, how she had closed the door and, to show that there was no going back, thrown away her gold-colored slippers.

"Look at the gorgeous bride!" the niece commented. Everyone would agree that she was elegant. Her hair was partially covered by the end of her sari with a bright red border, and the pleats tucked into the side were swinging. She was walking into her new world as the wife of a big land-lord. She was like a goddess caught in a conch in the ocean.

---

2   A person from Bengal.

3   A renowned pilgrim center on a hill top in the Western Ghats.

The housewife watched how her niece was imitating the bride by covering her head with the fine shawl.

"Amma, water."

The housewife didn't pay any attention. Her attention was focused on the man in the living room of the Bengalee bride and she ignored her son. Who was that man, a relative or a friend? The tiny light shining in his eyes, was it lust or kindness?

The housewife did not understand whatever he said. By the time she read the subtitle, the picture had changed. What a pity!

She was trying to figure out what the actor was saying by the movement of his lips when her son repeated his request, "Amma, water."

She was annoyed. The boy was always like this. He could not see her sitting quietly somewhere. She stood up, mumbling something, when she got another order, "Amma, lemon juice."

OK, lemon juice.

As she was walking to the kitchen, she wondered again what the actor must have said. Suddenly she felt that whether she knew the language or not she could follow the story.

She tried to create a dialogue of her own as she cut the lemon, and said it aloud with no one to hear her. "My love lost its natural growth like a stunted peepul[4] tree ..."

When she returned to the TV room with three glasses of lemon water the movie had advanced considerably.

On the screen a white woman with a bandaged head burst out crying. Freedom fighters had thrown something at her that struck her and caused her head to bleed. The housewife felt sorry for her.

As soon as she sat down on the sofa, her son came and put his head in her lap and started his antics. He said, "Amma is a liar. Didn't you go to Mini Aunty's house under false pretense?"

I am a liar, a bad woman. Though what the boy had said was not true, when his face touched her stomach, she felt uneasy. "Behave yourself, Kutta,"[5] she said.

"Mmmm. Amma smells good."

His nose was well shaped with a hint of redness on the edges. She was scared of it. He had a good sense of smell, like wild animals. It could recognize the smell of hot pepper being fried, iron in the fire, and ripe guava. That nose also knew the smell of human beings. The housewife

---

4   Indian fig tree.

5   Pet name for a boy.

became concerned. Would he recognize the smell of Brut, her lover's aftershave cream, still on her like an invisible wrap?

How could she overcome this small nose?

"You know," her husband heard that and looked at her. "Today I went to Haridas' house also."

"Are they here?"

"Everyone from the Gulf countries comes home in July or August, I think. When I was going to Mini's house I saw them near the junction. They were coming by car. Usha insisted that I visit them."

"Uh-huh."

"My disappointment in not seeing Mini was compensated by that visit."

"You didn't see Mini? That must be why you seemed to be brooding over something when you got back."

I am a liar, not a big liar. I am telling you only half-truths. The housewife became tearful. He thought it was because she couldn't see her friend.

"Where did Mini go?"

"She went back to Dubai yesterday, without telling me." Had Mini heard this she would have called her a liar. But what else could she say? How could she say that she went to meet her lover? She didn't want to be that truthful.

While thinking about what she had done she missed much of the movie. When her attention returned to the movie, a robbery was taking place. The new bride was opening her husband's cabinet and taking money from it. So the housewife felt that she was not alone. Still, she wanted the bride's widowed sister-in-law to check the bride's sari and find the money she had hidden there.

Silently, she congratulated the man in brown. He was a smart revolutionary who could talk a bride into stealing from her husband. The housewife realized that of the two lights shining in his eyes, one was lust and the other greed.

"You cunning man," the housewife called the actor silently, thinking of his greedy eyes. "Go slow. Despite your patriotic speeches and freedom fighting, you are shifting to the land of love and lust."

The housewife became restless. She pushed her son out of her lap and got up.

"Don't you want to see the movie?"

"I want to lie down. I have a headache."

As soon as she lay down, her son was beside her. His hair was touching her nose. It had the smell of sweat, the smell of hair that was not washed.

When he was little, his hair had the light smell of olive oil. She learned that olive oil was good for the hair and skin and asked Haridas to bring some. But the boy didn't like to be smeared with the gift from the Gulf. He disliked it from the day it was brought.

The mother recalled the day she took off the boy's clothes and rubbed him down with olive oil for two reasons—first, to show Haridas how much she appreciated the gift he had brought, and second, to show her mother-in-law, who had great praise for oil heated with hibiscus flowers, that better things are available.

Haridas, who was observing them from the dining room, put his finger on his nose and said, "Watch, an ant lion!"

"Where, where?"

"Look between your legs."

The boy was confused. Then he felt embarrassed, seeing his tiny penis in the color and shape of the ant lion. His mother laughed and the guest joined her. The boy tried to throw the olive oil bottle at him.

"Oh, please don't. When this is finished, Amma will have to go all the way to Spain for more." She said that based on the "Made in Spain" stamp on the bottle.

"That is true. It would be easier in the next life," said Haridas.

"Why so?"

"In the next life I am going to be born in Spain," Haridas said with a tinge of haughtiness.

He has already decided on the place to live next time around!

"I will be born as a novelist." That statement made her laugh heartily. She'd never seen another person so eager to be a writer.

"What will be your name in the next life: Markose, Kundera, Ital, or Calvin?"

He did not respond, but asked her not to tell anyone that the novelist had chosen her as his mate. "We will live happily enjoying sights of mountain ranges and waterfalls around the world. We don't want a kitchen. That is the only change in the script for the next life."

The power of dreams about the future! They had made this life only a rehearsal for the next one.

In the afternoons, listening to his jokes over the phone, she would laugh out loud, making her invalid mother-in-law in the next room mutter, "What is there to laugh so much? She is always laughing."

When her husband saw her doing the housework quietly, as if in a dream, he wondered why she laughed only when Haridas was there. What had happened to her?

She didn't pay any attention to the changing atmosphere at home as she daydreamed about the future. Like a child who was touched by the magic wand of a magician, she forgot the here and now and dwelled on her lover and his dream.

Deep down inside, she buried her frustration that made her a crook in this life while getting ready for the next.

Like a housewife who found pleasure in eating things on the sly when her husband or the servant was not watching, she gave in to Haridas's fondling and kisses.

She protested mildly to the idea of his coveting her body.

"What? Haven't you noticed how the squirrel vibrates? It does it with its whole body. Similarly, when you love someone, you must love him completely, body and soul." She liked the part about the squirrel's vibration and felt it was a good simile, but didn't know it was from A.K. Jayaseelan's poem. She would believe anything that Haridas said.

Therefore, today, when his mother and wife were away visiting relatives, Haridas and she decided to make their love complete physically also. Unfortunately, she didn't realize that the intensity of their love would diminish significantly once their bodies became one.

After making love she went and washed up. She realized that the diminished intensity was painful to her as she came back and sat in front of the dresser.

She watched him lying on the bed, reflected in the mirror, his feet almost white. One shouldn't think about sin at a time like this. Haridas always said that it was not wrong to give one's body to someone you love. Yet society does not approve of it. A woman loving two men is considered as something contemptuous.

She made a mark with her finger on the talcum powder that had fallen on the Formica tabletop and said, "I have a question."

"Oh!" His reflection in the mirror moved.

"You won't misunderstand me?"

"My dear girl, how many times have I told you that you don't need any of these formalities with me?"

"Can you imagine your wife Usha sitting with another man like this? What would you feel?"

"I would kill her." The reflection in the mirror may be smiling, she thought. No, it was not smiling.

She was smiling when she asked, "Sure?"

"Sure." The mirror responded with no hint of a smile.

She felt as if the earth moved under her feet, and she could clearly distinguish land and water. The next moment she began to behave as an actress. She started cursing the moments she enjoyed his caresses. Why didn't she escape from the desires of the flesh? Maybe God gave her this life as a ...

"Why are you crying?"

"I can't bear the thought of being away from you. When will we see each other again? I cannot live even for a moment without seeing you."

She knew it was the first of the countless lies she would be telling him. She was ashamed to note that he accepted her pleas with no doubts.

Still she kept telling him many painful details of separation while walking to the bus stop and waiting for the bus. Haridas had heard all these many times before, but he was listening as if hearing them for the first time.

She felt that she deserved to be killed. Still she pretended to be sad, looking at the pineapple plants and their green leaves edged with thorns.

"The next time you won't have to wait for the bus. We have decided to buy a car," he said.

"We?" she thought.

"You are a rich man. Why don't you buy a locomotive?" she said with some sarcasm. "This is dreaming of a train, not the life in Spain."

He couldn't understand why she was suddenly angry.

"We'll see."

"Buy one with four compartments."

"Why four compartments?" He couldn't figure that out.

She gave an explanation, "One for the driver, one for your wife (the chaste one, she said to herself), one for the master of the house, and one for the children."

"What about you? What compartment will you be in?"

She kept quiet, realizing that she could become a wagon that would be left behind. She thought of the advertisements for old cars in the newspapers: "as is."

"You definitely have a compartment. I cannot travel without that compartment."

Should she believe his words? She was reluctant to ask for a clarification on that.

While lying on the bed with her hand on her son, she didn't want to think of such matters.

"My love," she started to say loudly, thinking that no one was listening to her. "Sometimes I think my love lost its natural development, like a stunted peepul tree. You think of it as a decorative plant. It has leaves and branches. But it cannot give shade or breeze."

The more she thought about it, the more upset she became. This line, written by the one who is to be a Spanish poet in the next life, had more meaning to her than all the kisses with which he covered her body. She realized it only now. She also realized that in this life she was powerless to refuse this man or hate him.

A REST HOUSE FOR TRAVELERS
Sara Thomas

Malathy was lost in thought, standing with her hand on the half wall of the rest house balcony. The woods around the hotel were full of teak trees. Far away, the Periyar Lake had captured the golden-red color of twilight and was shining like a piece of silk. In the clear sky, white cranes were flying in lines. But none of these beautiful sights in the environment or the cool breeze that carried the fragrance of the wild flowers was able to catch Malathy's attention. Her only concern was how much longer she would have to stay in this wilderness. There was no way her husband would leave this place before completing his research successfully. This time his obsession was with black monkeys.

She didn't go with her husband on these trips whole-heartedly. Her dislike for a long lonely life was the only reason that prompted her to tag along. If they had a child, she could have made a special world with that child and would not have had to bear the isolation of a lonely life. Then her husband's coming and going would not have had much impact on her.

It was ten years since they married. Still she was not lucky enough to hear the pitter patter of tiny feet. Whenever she suggested consulting a doctor, he ridiculed her.

"Any stupid man can have a child. Impregnating a woman and giving birth to a child are not great acts. I have a few other goals in this life. In the middle of these you won't get me for visits to the doctor and hospital. If you are eager to take care of children, go to an orphanage and play with the children there as long as you want. That will be a social service also."

By now she had realized that she could not change these selfish attitudes. Even on the first night, the white rats he worked on were more important to him than she.

When the marriage took place, she and everyone in the village considered her very lucky. It was not a trivial thing for a professor who was educated abroad to marry an average student in his college. Her only qualification was that her mother and his older sister were good friends.

Many women envied her then. But today, if they knew the truth .... She was just his housekeeper, nothing more, except for social occasions at the college, when she was an adornment.

"Madam," it was the butler.

"Yes."

"If you tell us what you would like for dinner, we can either bring it to the room or you can come down to the dining room."

She hadn't thought about it at all. Even though she was not very hungry, she had to make arrangements for his dinner. "Just an omelet and toast with butter and jam and a glass of milk. Please bring it to the room." He did not like changing the usual menu.

The man had one more question:

"I need to know what you would like for lunch tomorrow. We cannot get any groceries here. Someone has to walk five miles to the market. Usually, the lunch menu is rice and mutton curry. If you order chicken roast, we will make it. Because there is no one else here, you will have to have the whole chicken."

She didn't pay attention to much of what he said. But the phrase "no one else" resounded in her ears.

So when he goes to the forest, she would be by herself!

"Did you say that there is no other guest here?" She couldn't hide her surprise.

"When it is not the season we get very few tourists. There is one man in the single room at the end. He came a few days ago, but rarely takes his meals here. Some days he doesn't even get out of the room. On other days he leaves in the morning and returns only at night."

Whatever he does, at least there was another human being in this eight-room rest house. But that was not enough, he should have the qualities of a human being. From what she heard, he must be an important person like her husband, or he must be a disappointed lover. She shouldn't worry about him. The bearer was standing with his small notebook and pencil, ready to take notes.

"I will tell you about tomorrow's lunch after I talk to him. Is that OK?"

As soon as the butler left, her husband came in. His face showed that he was pleased about something.

"Things worked out as I had planned. I was able to find a guide. He is a gardener who knows this area very well. Some time back he took a foreigner to a group of black monkeys. We need to climb up only a couple of miles, he says. At the most it will take an hour and a half. I am lucky; he is ready to leave by six-thirty in the morning."

They walked back to the room. She could not share his enthusiasm at all. The boredom of the day was gathering in her mind.

"When will you get back?"

"What kind of a question is that? You know the reason why I came here. If needed, I can refresh your memory—to observe and study the life of black monkeys! Meanwhile, time is not going to be problem for me. I will be back before dark. That's all I can tell you now."

"What about lunch?"

"Is that your concern? Don't worry. The chef has agreed to give sandwiches and coffee for me to take. I have arranged for your lunch to be brought to the room. You don't have to bother going down."

Don't have to bother going down, she thought with resentment. How very thoughtful! Doesn't he have anything to say about her boredom? Lucky if she doesn't lose the strength in her legs.

As if trying to entertain her, he continued to talk about black monkeys. "The behavior of the black monkeys in this part of the world is closer to human behavior. Animals usually have certain times in the year to mate and reproduce. But black monkeys are more like humans in that respect."

She had fallen asleep listening to the new discoveries about black monkeys. Half awake, she found him lost in a big fat book.

She woke long before sunrise, but pretended to be asleep. He was getting ready to leave, and was being careful not to wake her, may be to avoid more questions. He did not turn on the light but used only the flashlight to get dressed. He was dressed all in black—pants, pullover, and a monkey cap. She couldn't help smiling at the sight of him dressed like that. The monkeys wouldn't have any difficulty considering him as one of them, there was much similarity, she thought.

After lying around for a while, she rose and had a long shower. She felt energetic after having breakfast. She turned on the transistor radio sitting on the parapet on the veranda. But her mind was on many disconnected thoughts—how many hours before he comes back. Though when he does, he won't ask even one thing about how her day was—and she wouldn't expect him to. If he speaks to her at all, it will be only about black monkeys. He won't care if she is interested in the topic or not. He'll want to sit before the typewriter and type up all the notes he brought from the forest.

She heard footsteps behind her and she turned around, startled. A young man. He must be the man the bearer talked about when he said that she was not alone in the rest house. He seemed to have just awakened, for he was still in his pajamas, with his toothbrush, a mug, and a change of clothes in his hands. Single rooms had a common bathroom.

Seeing her, his face brightened. She knew that he was still looking at her with interest, as he walked away. That made her self-conscious. She combed her hair with her hand and pulled the end of her sari over her shoulder.

She heard a sound and looked in the direction he had gone, thinking that he had dropped the mug he was carrying. But he was nowhere to be seen. Where did he disappear beyond that long veranda? She looked this way and that and saw him standing on the veranda behind a pillar, looking at her. When he realized that she had seen him, there was a mischievous smile on his face. He could not be very well mannered. He dared to stare at her openly realizing that she was alone. But her anger melted away quickly. What right did she have to feel so angry? She had no business following him with her eyes. They were two individuals who like to be with people. So their actions were justifiable. But be careful, she warned herself.

She sat there enjoying the coolness of the mountain breeze. After a while, he came back the way he went. It didn't look as if he had showered. He was still in his pajamas. She pretended not to have noticed him and looked elsewhere. He came near and cleared his throat.

"There is no water," he said with a self-conscious smile. "Here you cannot get water after eight o'clock, sometimes. I overslept this morning."

She didn't say anything. She didn't want to make a hasty decision on whether she should act friendly or serious.

For a moment she stood there hesitating. He looked silly, with his unruly hair on his forehead and unshaven face. There was dry toothpaste in the corners of his mouth. He started talking timidly,

"Last night I couldn't fall asleep. So I drank all the water in the decanter, and I didn't keep any water in the bathroom either."

He had a foolish smile and she wondered what that meant. Does he expect her to give him water? As soon as she had that thought, he put out his mug, cautiously.

"If I can get a mug of water..."

She went into her room with her head down to hide her smile. For a while she hesitated. Then she came out with a mug of water. She decided it was right to think that there was nothing improper in giving water to someone who asks for it. He left after saying "Thanks" with a broad smile, and she went into her room and didn't come out. Her lunch was brought to the room. She didn't find it very difficult to while away the time. She thought about her new acquaintance. She couldn't say that they met because she didn't know who he was, nor he who she was. She tried to figure out who he could be; he couldn't be a tourist as he was there out of season. Perhaps he was a politician, businessman, or someone like her husband? Had he come there to rest after a long illness, or after being jilted by someone he loved? But the latter didn't match his demeanor.

After having afternoon tea, she decided to take a walk in the garden, as there was nothing else to do. That could give her some exercise to prevent her hands and legs from getting weak.

Without heeding the watchman's warning not to go beyond the trench around the rest-house property, she went to the rock far away. Sitting there, she could see a part of Periyar Lake. She remembered the bearer saying that sometimes elephants and wild buffalos came to drink water at the lake. Hoping to have a glimpse of that, she sat there focusing on the wilderness beyond the lake. She didn't know how long she sat there; her mind was roaming all over, aimlessly.

The crunching of dry leaves startled her. She jumped up with a tremor in her heart. Was there a wild animal that she didn't see? It took her a few minutes to realize that the man who appeared before her, parting the wild growth, was indeed the young man she had met that morning. He was clean-shaven, and his hair was combed. He had on a silk shirt and mundu.[1]

With a smile he asked, "Did I scare you?"

She didn't have a quick response. She was trying to hide the look of panic on her face.

"You must have thought it was a young elephant or something. To tell you the truth, I too was surprised. I did not expect an unusual sight like you among these bushes."

Was he flattering her? She bent her head not knowing how to react.

"Please don't misunderstand my asking. How come you are here alone in this place?"

"I am not alone. I am with my husband."

She gave him a short description of the circumstances that brought her there.

"I have heard a great deal about him. I read the article that was in the *Illustrated Weekly* last year. I am happy to have met the wife of such a famous scientist."

Although he brought his palms together in a humble gesture, she didn't miss the impish smile on his face. He might be laughing inside at the lonely life of a famous scientist's wife, she thought. She thought it was better to end the meeting soon.

But when she started to leave, he stopped her and said, "Are you dis-

---

1   A lower garment, consisting of a length of cloth.

pleased with me? If I interrupted your solitude, I am sorry. Did I offend you by saying something inappropriate?" She shook her head. When she took another step, he came closer and said, "I am really sorry. I didn't mean to offend you, I swear!"

When she looked up at his face, she realized that he meant what he said. "It is time for my husband to come back. If I am not there, he will get worried. That is why I am leaving."

It was getting dark when Jayadevan got back. After taking a shower, he had a bit to eat and sat before the typewriter.

She tried to start a conversation. "How was your day? Did things go as you expected?"

"Do I have to give the details? Yesterday I saw how interested you were in the topic when I tried to talk about black monkeys. Now I am not in the mood to talk about anything. I have a lot to do. You can go and sleep."

She wanted to tell him about the young man she met, but decided that the time was not right. She decided that she would try to sleep, with her back to the light.

That night she slept without the usual sleeping pills. She slept late and woke up only when the bearer brought breakfast. Her husband had left early in the morning. After washing up she had her breakfast and came out. The young man she had met the previous day was standing there leaning on a pillar, as if waiting for her. Seeing her he smiled broadly.

"Good morning, Mrs. Jayadev! I got up early with the help of my alarm clock so that yesterday's mishap wouldn't happen today. See, by nine o'clock I have finished all the morning routines. The question is, what to do now. Our steward Cherian told me that Dr. Jayadev has left already. What is your plan for the day, Mrs. Jayadev?"

For some reason she did not dislike his friendly overture.

"Your plans for the day, Mrs. Jayadev?"

He repeated the question and she was forced to give a response. "What plans? There are no special plans. I will listen to some music and read for a while. Other than that ... I need to while away the time."

"Then I have a suggestion."

He continued enthusiastically, "We will go for a walk around this area. You have to experience the good feeling one gets walking in the shade."

She heard the unexpected. Go for a walk with him? Not knowing what to say, she kept quiet.

"Why don't you say something? Don't you think you can trust me? Just think that I am an old friend."

She didn't respond still.

"Look, we are not two irresponsible teenagers and I am a harmless man. Come on. Be a sport. In this cold weather, unless you have some exercise, you will become arthritic."

She didn't hesitate any longer. She didn't doubt his decency. She locked her room and came downstairs with him. They passed the garden, and as they approached the forest, she felt light-hearted. The surroundings were full of new things! Swaying trees, wild bushes, wild flowers, and fruits she had not seen before! She was taking a walk after a long time. Although her legs were tired, she was cheerful and didn't feel tired at all.

He noticed that she had slowed down.

"I am sorry. I was walking too fast. It seems Mrs. Jayadev is tired. You are perspiring all over." He parted the bushes anxiously and turned to her. She was looking sweaty and pale and tried to hide her short breath with the end of her sari.

"That's OK. It has been a long time since I walked this much and I am a bit tired."

"How foolish me! How thoughtless can I be?"

Taking his shawl and spreading it for her to sit, he said, "Please sit down here for a while. We will leave after you rest for a while."

When she sat down, he took his water bottle out, gave it to her, and watched with amusement as she gulped down the water. Embarrassed, she got up quickly. What a disgrace, she thought.

"I am not tired any more. Let us get back."

"Look, if my pace gets too fast, please tell me. My lack of experience in walking with women is obvious."

He walked slowly on their return trip and enquired on and off how she was doing.

She felt that maybe she should not have gone on that walk. But when she had lunch and rested, her mind was roaming among the enchanting views of the forest and recalled her companion's humorous remarks. The walk, an unusual exercise for her, made her fall asleep, and she woke up late in the afternoon. Thinking that her husband would come early like he did the previous day, she had a quick shower, changed into fresh clothes, and came out to the veranda. She stood there and looked all around. The only people she saw were three or four Tamilians[2] squatting under a tree. She looked along the path that comes down by the rest house, expecting to see her husband.

Suddenly she thought of her new friend, and her eyes mechanically

---

2 People from Tamil Nadu, India.

went to the single room at the other end of the veranda. The bearer had said that was where the young man stayed. But that room was locked from the out side. The vitality she felt when she got up was dissipating slowly. Having nothing else to do, she went to the balcony and sat in one of the cane chairs when the butler came with a note.

"The gardener brought it in the afternoon. I came and knocked on your door, but you did not answer."

She took the note from him and opened it.

"I will be late coming home this evening. Only now the gardener said that today is full moon. I didn't think about it this morning. On full moon nights, there is something peculiar about the monkeys' behavior. I may not get another chance like this to observe that. I will have dinner even if I come late. But please don't wait up for me."

She was depressed. The loneliness of this desolate place was unbearable even during the day. At night when the forest resounds with the chirping crickets... she shuddered involuntarily.

By this time, sunlight was fading. In this mountainous region, the night came very quickly. It was just six o'clock. Darkness is beginning to surround the trees like solid pieces. The wind was getting colder. Suddenly she saw him down the road, walking with two bags, and her heart lightened. Within minutes, he was by her side, climbing the stairs with great energy. Right away he asked if her husband had not come yet. She told him about the note.

"I thought he would come at five, like yesterday. Otherwise, I wouldn't have gone out."

He said this almost to himself. She was surprised at his words, but did not ask for an explanation.

"Look, this is enough food for two or three days. About five miles down, there is Simon's provision store. One can get whatever one needs. I bought plantains, sesame seed balls, beaten rice, molasses, and buns. I can't afford to have lunch and dinner here. Let me put these in the room. I'll be back right away."

For some reason, she was not bored any longer. He came back, pulled a chair and sat beside her. She was surprised by the way she was anticipating some novelty.

"You must be tired of waiting for Mr. Jayadevan. Don't worry, I will keep you company and time will fly." He started like an old friend, as he said the previous day. She did not feel bad about it, at all. "Please don't feel bad, I would like to know Mrs. Jaydevan's name at least now."

She responded in a whisper, "Malathy."

She realized that she was meeting someone after a long time. He repeated her name as if chanting.

"Another picture comes to my mind—the jasmine plant in the 'sarp-pakkav'[3] at the ancestral home. At the time of the temple festival, it is full of flowers with their intoxicating smell!" Seeing the change in her facial expression on hearing the unexpected, he said quickly, "I am sorry, Mrs. Jayadev. Did you think I was talking nonsense? Please don't mind it. Sometimes, people make mistakes, it is human."

"Now you want to know about me. There is nothing special I have done to make a name for myself. But I have not got into any trouble. My parents call me 'Unni.' I like to be called Santosh. Isn't Santosh a good name? Mrs. Jayadev, please call me Santosh." From there, their conversation just flowed, her favorite books, music, and so on.

Jayadevan came home sooner than expected. She was still there, talking to Santosh. He was surprised to see Santosh, and said pleasantly, "So you had company, very good."

"This is Santosh. He stays in the last room, at the end of the veranda." She introduced him.

"Is that so? But I don't remember seeing you before. I know, during the day I am in the wilderness. Malathy should have introduced me."

"I have heard about you even before Mrs. Jayadevan told me about you. I read the article about you in the *Illustrated Weekly.*"

"Glad to meet you. We will talk later. I am a bit busy now."

"I know that. I was keeping company with Mrs. Jayadevan."

In his hurry to get to the room, it was doubtful that Jayadevan heard the explanation Santosh gave for his presence there.

The next day, when Jayadevan said that he would be late coming home Malathy did not worry about being alone.

She was in the room much of the day. From the time she got up, she was feeling lazy. She did not know why, but she did not want even to read or listen to music. Her mind was going through a journey of disconnected thoughts, while she lay in bed.

Before her marriage, she was a girl full of vigor and courage. Her college principal called her "smart girl." She was in the forefront for music, dancing, and even for playing pranks. Today, she was a very different person.

---

3   Snake shrine.

When did she lose her "self"? She had gone through many dark corridors under the dominance and disregard of her husband. In that darkness she had lost her "self," and now she could not find the old Malathy she respected.

After many hours in her reverie, she realized that the day was almost over. By the time she got out after taking a shower, it was almost dark.

Santosh pulled a chair for her, as if he was waiting for her, and said, "I have been waiting for a long time. I even thought of knocking on your door, but didn't think it was proper. How is it you did not come out today?"

She did not say anything. But the impatience and anxiety on his face dispelled her despondency.

The butler came as usual and turned on the lights in the balcony and veranda. Immediately Santosh got up and turned off the light that was shining on them and said, "We don't need this. We shall not be discourteous to the moon by turning on this light." He moved to the shadow of a pillar and sat on the parapet and added, "I like to sit in the darkness like this and enjoy the moonlight."

She did not have anything to say. He need not find out that the moonlight in her life was lost a long time back. For some time neither of them said anything. Each was in his or her own thoughts. The moonlight worked like a kind of magic light between them. The mountain breeze blew her hair to her face. Malathy gathered her hair and tied it.

"Don't. You should not tie up wet hair, my mother used to say it is bad for the hair. She had hair like yours, covering the whole back ..."

She had not expected to hear what he said.

Suddenly he got up and stood in front of her. "A woman is the most superior creature in the universe. Would you agree with my opinion?"

Her face reflected both sadness and disbelief.

"Woman? No, I don't have anything to say. I don't want to destroy someone's belief."

"Why do you say that? I am taking the liberty to tell you that this sight I have before me confirms my belief. You have no idea how beautiful you are, I think. No one has told you that you are beautiful?"

She realized the passion in his eyes for the first time. For some reason, it made her uneasy. Moments passed without any words.

He continued, "I understand one thing. If I don't say that now ... there is a heart longing to love and be loved hiding here."

Without waiting for permission, he was opening his heart. Malathy jumped up, agitated. "What are you saying? You were not like this until now. You came as a friend, now you have changed completely. I am leaving."

Stepping forward he blocked her way. "Pardon me. I beg of you to forgive me. I spoke out of place. With this exhilarating moonlight and your intoxicating beauty I got carried away. I am just an ordinary human being. Don't I deserve to be forgiven once?"

Santosh waited, like a culprit for the verdict, with repentance written all over his face. His tormented mind quieted down. When she saw his eyes anxiously waiting for her reaction, she bent her head down without thinking and her anger melted away.

Phew! He joined his palms together with relief. "I had faith in the goodness of your heart. Only people of good heart are able to forgive. Please sit down, Malathy. Look, I wish you would open up. Do you feel it is improper on my part to want to know you better?" he continued.

"In truth I feel that we were related in some past life. Otherwise, my mind wouldn't be so eager to know you. You may not want to believe what I say, but what I say is true."

As he continued, she lost the sense of right and wrong at some point. In opening up her heart that was closed for a long time, she was discovering herself. She was a happy-go-lucky young girl who could talk endlessly and laugh like ringing bells, who became a dreamy-eyed young woman with heart full of expectations for the future. She was tightly bound by the chains of matrimony and had hidden her true self in a shroud of detachment.

He listened intently as she talked as though the knot that kept her quiet was opened. When she finished she had the relief of a dam that had emptied the water it had held back. Far away a new horizon opened up. Later, when she thought more calmly, she did not feel guilty about opening her heart to Santosh. It was a necessity waiting for an opportunity.

The next morning she woke up and got ready with great cheer. She went to the balcony expecting to see Santosh. He was there ready with a bag on his shoulder and a flask in his hand, as if going somewhere.

"Why are you so late? Do you know how long I have been waiting? I have prepared a surprise for you, Malathy."

When he said that with obvious enthusiasm, she could not help asking what it was.

"Don't be in a hurry to find out. If I say it too soon, there is no fun in it. Come with me. I will show you."

She was a bit unsettled and wondered how she could go with him like this.

"Why is your mood changing? Look. I have everything needed for a picnic. We can do that, can't we?"

In her long, dry life with no cool shades, she had come to a crossroad. Where will it lead? Maybe for the first time in her life she would find a rest house that was cool and provided water to quench her heart's thirst. Still…

"What are you thinking of, Malathy? I'll take you to a small paradise in this wilderness. There is nothing to worry about. You are coming with me. God made this morning so beautiful just for us. Look at the sky. There are a thousand fluffy, white clouds to wish us well."

He started walking. She did not feel like objecting to his plans and followed him as if in a daze.

Passing the front door of the hotel, they crossed the road and went through the wild bushes. She was moving along the steep, narrow footpath not knowing where she was going.

After a short distance, Santosh stopped.

"Malathy, listen."

The mesmerizing sound of a brook flowing out of the rocks!

He parted the bamboo bushes and said, "Here, come into my small world!" Along the bank of the brook that flowed to a rhythm, the ground was covered by the red flowers of the gulmohar tree, mixed with the tender green leaves! For a moment Malathy was spellbound, and stood there forgetting everything.

"This is really a paradise!" Her face showed the overflow of joy within.

He spread the shawl on the flower-strewn ground for her to sit.

"You must be tired, Malathy."

"No, not in the least. Do I look tired?"

"You look like the goddess of the wilderness."

Her heartstrings were being played on, but she was not worried. The way Santosh talks!

"May I sit at your feet?" He sat close to her.

"Malathy, I am taking the liberty of saying something. For the time being we will forget ourselves—the wife of the famous scientist Jayadevan and Santosh, a writer who is struggling to make a name, do not exist from this moment. In this paradise we are two lovers, like Adam and Eve. At least now we must accept that fact. Pulling aside the mind's curtain, let us exchange our love, share our treasured experience of love."

His words were slowly breaking her mental control like a mystic spell. In the embrace of his strong arms, she had become weak and experienced moments of bliss she had never experienced before. She did not know how long she lay in the shadow of the trees, keeping her head in the crook of his arm, looking at the circles of light created through the treetops by the early morning sun, enjoying the lazy, blissful moments.

Santosh was talking and his words built a hypnotic hedge of love around her.

"I didn't do anything intentionally and I know that there is no justification for what has happened. Love is considered blind; it is also a blinding light. In that light everything else becomes dark. Our love was predestined. Two human souls destined to love each other. That we meet in this green forest was God's will." These were Santosh's words.

Malathy was unable to argue the point. She did not feel guilty nor did her conscience prick her. At a time when she was beginning to lose awareness that she was even alive, these unexpected raindrops fell on her parched life. This is God's will. Otherwise her mind that had not wavered for the last ten years . . .

For the next four days, every minute they spent together was a precious experience. In their Garden of Eden, they were like Adam and Eve. She was being loved, being recognized. Her femininity was being worshipped. When she was alone, Santosh's face full of love was a consolation. Dr. Jayadev's research had taken longer than expected, but she didn't realize that. She who used to be in a hurry to get back home seemed to have forgotten about time. The truth was that she did not realize that days were passing. On the fifth day, Jayadevan got back early. She was taking a nap after lunch.

"I have brought you good news! My work here is complete. Whatever is left can be done at home. Remember, you wanted to go to a concert? That is going to be this Sunday. You don't have to miss it. We will get there before that. We could have left today itself, but I was not able to take all the pictures I wanted because there was not enough light. Tomorrow, after taking the pictures, we can leave. This trip was highly successful. I had not expected to see black monkeys at such close quarters."

She did not hear his usual chatter about black monkeys as he continued. The news that they were returning the next day had shocked her and she was growing sad. She could not believe that she was losing the Garden of Eden so soon. What should she do? She could not even think. Only by saying everything to Santosh could her mind be calmed. Like always, Santosh would have some consoling words.

That night she didn't sleep at all. Early next morning, shortly after Jayadevan left with the camera for the wilderness, Malathy went to Santosh's room and knocked at the door. As soon as he saw her, his sleepy face brightened. "Malathy, this is a pleasant surprise! Come in, please."

"What is wrong, Malathy? What happened? You don't feel well? Is the professor suspicious of something? The watchman might have said something about us. Whatever it is, tell me, Malathy."

"He said we are going back this afternoon." Her voice was lifeless.

He was stunned. His face was drained of blood. Helplessly, he embraced her tightly.

"No, Malathy. I cannot live without you. It is impossible for me to live without you. Do you think it is possible? I can think of only one way out of this–it may be a cowardly way, but we can avoid hurting many people, especially you. We must leave this place before he returns, as soon as possible. There is a bus at eleven o'clock.

"Are you listening, Malathy? Do you doubt my sincerity? I wish to marry you, Malathy. These are not just words. As soon as we get back you can file for a divorce. I have a lawyer friend. He will do whatever is necessary. I may not be able to give you all the luxuries you have now, but I am ready to give you whatever I have. Will you be satisfied with that? I am sure you will be."

Still she did not utter a word.

He continued, "You were ready to love me even before finding out who I am. Then, how can you be quiet now? I have to tell you one thing. I tried to say this many times. But I was afraid that it would create another dimension to our love. Let me tell you who I am. We discussed my stories many times. I am your favorite writer, Santosh Kumar."

A tremor went through her body. She looked up with an expression of great shock. That face was radiant and the eyes shining like stars.

"My God! What am I hearing? Santosh..." she whispered as if she could not believe what she heard. How could she have not realized that he was her favorite writer after getting close to him the past few days? His words had cast a spell on her? He looked at her wondering eyes for a second, and then he held her close to his heart.

"Malathy, I need to confess one thing more. I was eager to win the national award for the best Malayalam novel and was roaming around for months to get an emotional theme. But my mind stayed a barren desert. I was coveting the unattainable, I know. How long I waited to see the first sprout of my creation! In the end I gave up and came here to get away from it all. Then we met unexpectedly. It was like a rain with thunder and lightning. My mind was drenched. My imagination came alive. I was eager to follow you without losing a minute. A neglected wife's depth of sadness became the basis for my creation. It was like stepping on what I was searching for, and I was ecstatic. But that was only the beginning. It didn't take long for me to realize that all my calculations were wrong. Getting close to you, when we interacted with each other and our hearts met, I was the one who acquired an empire of love. I forgot everything—who I was and why I came here. I have met many women, but never wanted to make anyone of them my own. You are the only one who captured my heart. I cannot lose you, Malathy. No, no."

He held her tight in his uncontrollable yearning. Her sobs rhymed with his heartbeats. Suddenly she was calm. She raised her head slowly. Her face was like the clear sky after a storm. He was relieved, and said, "Malathy, we must not waste time. Go get ready. I will check out and be back."

"No, Santosh." She barred his way. The determination in her words surprised him as she continued, "I have decided to go back. Let me finish what I want to say. The whole of yesterday and until a few moments ago, I could not even think of leaving the heaven that you took me to. I was so enthralled by it. But now that I know who you are I have the strength to bear losing you. You are the owner of a blessed pen and a magical mind that can soak up even the smallest movements of human hearts. I know the emotional world you create with words. Each of your creations is a stepping-stone to fame. There must be no obstacle to that. You must be free. I won't let your brilliant future be destroyed by getting entangled with an unlucky woman like me. As far as I am concerned, I don't want to change the intensity and sweetness of love I tasted in the last few days into the boring routine of married life. I am telling the truth. In unexpected moments you brought light into the chambers of my heart that were dark for years. I am sure that light will not fade even when you leave. I have experienced the happiness of a lifetime in the last few days."

Her face was smiling. He realized that she was firm in the decision she had made. His eyes were blank as if everything was wiped out in one moment. She got up slowly, raised his face with her hand, and lovingly kissed those eyes.

"Santosh, I am leaving. Wherever I may be in the world, I will read your lovely stories. Even from far away I will feel proud of your fame. I will pray for you. Wish you the best, dearest!"

Without turning back to look, she opened the door and left.

Professor Jayadevan returned before noon. Malathy was ready to go after a shower and change of clothes. He looked at her as if he was seeing her for the first time. He went nearer and looked at her from head to foot and said, "Malathy, you look beautiful! Yesterday, the gardener said that the wilderness was all dressed up after a shower in the rain. It seems that this place and our stay agreed with you. Your face has lost its paleness and looks bright."

She did not show that she heard what he said and was arranging something.

"I think you don't believe what I said. Never mind. I know you have plenty of reasons to protest. Look, in pursuing the research, I neglected you. However, these black monkeys taught me a lesson. You may find it amusing. To the male monkey nothing is more important than his mate. May I assume that it is not too late for me to have learned this lesson, Malathy?"

The sense of guilt and embarrassment in his voice was not sufficient to melt the frost of her detachment.

THE RIDDLES IN LIFE
Asha Krishnan

Uma knew that the adage "When one has too much to say, one is not able to say anything" was true. She felt that the significance of the adage was getting stronger by the minute and shaking her up. After calculating all aspects of the situation for a long period of time, she had selected some words, but why was she not able to use them at the appropriate time? This daughter could only watch helplessly as those words fell into the depth of silence and disappeared.

When she was tired of looking at the pictures on the wall, the books arranged in neat piles, and the face of the clock with the second hand that went round and round, she looked sideways at her Achhan's[1] face.

The dampness resulting from the surprise and happiness of her visit could still be seen through his eyeglasses.

Achhan's face had the unclear lines of tiredness resulting most probably from the frequent trips he had to make without any rest. It must be about eight or nine months since she had seen him face to face. During this time he had changed as never before.

Was it the change in the shape of his glasses that made his face look so different?

On his forehead there was a light shadow of the chandan[2] he had put on that morning. She remembered that it was the first time she had seen him with chandan on the forehead.

Deciding not to let the silence become more uncomfortable, she said, "Even to the last minute before starting, I wasn't sure if you would be here."

Uma had found one loophole in the chaos of packing to move away, and somehow managed to get here. In order not to jolt involuntarily before her Amma's[3] "Where to?" she had picked up her library card as her mother was watching and said, "I will be back soon." The mother

---

1   Father.

2   Sandalwood paste.

3   Mother.

knew that her daughter forgot time and place once she got into a book at the library.

She was feeling uneasy with the thought of being dishonest with her mother. As far as her mother was concerned, granting Uma's wishes was her challenge in life, though she had a few wishes that her mother could not grant. But the decision to come here to see Achhan and say goodbye was not of the child who did not oppose the likes and dislikes of her mother. Rather it was of a strong-minded girl who was determined to get back something vague in her mind that she had lost long ago. If she were to succeed, she had to pay a price—the trust the mother and daughter had built between them.

"When you are coming here for the first time, how can I not be here, Umakutty?[4]" Achhan said slowly.

Uma had always noticed that Achhan would start a conversation as if he was talking to a little girl. Sometimes he would continue like that. At other times it was only the first sentence that would have the milk-smell of child talk. But she very much liked that style of the conversation. Behind the door of time, she became a little girl with her finger in the mouth, jingling the anklets on her feet and talking baby talk. At that point, a question about her studies or exams would bring her back to the present. She was not too keen on that change.

"No, Umakutty, this is nothing short of a miracle. To tell you the truth, my child, no birthday of mine has gone by without bringing me at least one miracle. I have thought about it a great deal, but have not found an answer. Still, I feel that there is something more than coincidences."

He took off his glasses and wiped it with the corner of his mundu.[5]

"Starting with the birthday on which I got my job ... in short, I can write a book titled something like *Miracles on Birthdays.*

"Then again, it was on a birthday that I said goodbye to your mother and left home." She was thinking that he had a knack for softening blows by adding humor, as he continued, "After all that, you come to visit me for the first time on my birthday."

She hadn't realized that it was his birthday. If she had, she would not have come to say goodbye to him. Whenever she did anything on her own, without someone's help, something always went wrong. Sometimes after deciding to say or do something, she would wait too long, and opportunities would seem to slip out of her hands.

Starting when she was in the second grade, Achhan was not part of

---

4   "Kutty" is added to a child's name to show endearment.

5   A lower garment, consisting of a length of cloth.

her everyday life; he became an occasional visitor who came to see just her. At first it felt like his return from official tours. During those days, she was ignorant about many things.

But on and off she would ask, "Why is Achhan not coming?" Her mother would ignore that question and ask another, "Have you finished your homework?" or something similar. She felt that Amma had many things on her mind that she did not share with her.

One day, a back-bencher in her class named Arun asked, "Uma Menon's father left home, didn't he? I heard my mother say that."

Left home? Does that mean he won't come back?

But she couldn't bear to accept that or see his rotten-teeth smile get any bigger. So she denied it totally. She became so angry at Arun that she broke his pencil point. When she went to Amma with the same question, her mother embraced her, gave her a kiss, and said, "You have Amma. Then why do you ask that? Let us see. Whose baby is Umakutty, Achhan's or Amma's?"

Having learned to become Achhan's baby or Amma's baby according to the situation, she now had an answer ready: "Amma's baby."

"Then are you unhappy about Achhan leaving?"

"No," she had to say.

Amma brought her up to find answers on her own to the questions she had. But some questions were like riddles—their answers too.

When Achhan used to come and visit her, she went with him to the park for walks and returned with balloons in her hand that smelled of ice cream. Then she began to notice that on her return her mother didn't talk to her much. During those days Amma's silence was suffocating. As a result she began to lose her enthusiasm for going for walks with Achhan.

However, after many years, long after her student days, Achhan's absence troubled her. By then Achhan and daughter could meet only during the free time between his foreign trips and the many other demands of his professional life.

She began to feel that the visiting days were beautiful and gratifying. She used to wait for those days, but did not show any sign of that outwardly. From early on she disciplined herself as a daughter who did not hurt her mother by words or deeds, not even by a small change in her facial expression. Not to mar that picture, she became silent.

About two years ago, Achhan said to her, "All these years you lived with Amma. Can't you spend a few days with me? If you insist, Amma will not refuse you. How long can I live alone in this flat?"

The tone of helplessness and sadness in that question troubled her a great deal, but she was unable to respond.

She had learned to face such questions with no answers, but the half-hidden, embarrassing truth in them disturbed her.

Behind the wall that had been slowly built up in the mind, there was a little girl who cried quietly, longing to walk holding Achhan's finger, to listen to stories lying in his lap, and to be patted affectionately on her cheek.

But she was unable to cross the boundary of her mother's love.

Thoughts sometimes are like disobedient pets. When the master loosens control, they roam all over and cause problems. They must be held within hearing of the swish of the master's cane.

"Did you come just by yourself?" Achhan asked with some hesitation.

"How else?"

"Did Amma allow you to come here?" She realized the implications in the question, but pretended that she didn't understand.

Achhan brought some kumkum[6] and chandan in a piece of leaf along with some flowers. "This is prasadam[7] from the Devi temple here close by. Put some on."

When she was about to touch it he said, "You should never put it on sitting down. Turn to the east, I will put it on for you."

He mixed the two together and put it on her forehead, reciting:

"Sarvamagala mangalye!
Sive sarvaarthha saadhike
Saranye, thrayambake! Devi!
Narayani namo sthuthe!"[8]

"Bhagavathy,[9] shower your blessings on my child!"

Achhan put that mixture of kumkum and chandan on his forehead too; it looked like a tiny piece of the reddish sky at twilight.

She asked in a surprised voice, "Do you believe in all this?"

"We need something to hold onto in life. If you do everything trusting

---

6   Saffron powder made from the flower of Crocus Sativus, used on the forehead by women in India.

7   Remnants of the offering to God given to devotees.

8   "O Goddess, you bring prosperity, and make everything possible to your devotees. Refuge of the needy, you protect us with your powerful third eye. I bow before you!"

9   Goddess.

in God, you won't be sorry. Everything happens according to God's will. Even a blade of grass won't move without his knowledge. Still, man's ego ... No. I don't want to bore you with all this philosophy. You are at an age when you should be carefree and happy."

"Who is carefree and happy, Achha? I lost those days long ago."

Achhan seemed to have changed a lot.

Hearing something, she turned around and saw a small, white Pomeranian puppy standing ill at ease. That form slowly moved towards Achhan and stood near him, wagging its tail. Patting it on the head, Achhan said, "She is my companion now."

Its eyes, shining with surprise and helplessness, turned towards her. Achhan said its name, but Uma didn't pay attention to it.

All the selfishness and jealousy in her came out without her knowledge, and she mumbled, "I don't like these creatures."

"Why, mole?"[10] Achhan asked with a sympathetic smile. "It is a poor puppy."

"I don't even like to see these creatures. Once long ago a dog chased me."

That was a big lie. It came out of her childish thinking that in her absence Achhan's affection would be channeled to it. In a quiet way she was expressing her selfish objection to a dumb animal getting even a part of the affection that was rightfully hers.

Achhan said something to it, and the puppy turned round and round a couple of times and was about to lie down but ran in the direction Achhan pointed his finger.

"I have heard Amma tell her patients that this type of dog's hair can cause respiratory problems."

Pretending not to have heard what she said, Achhan remarked, "Poor thing! Such an obedient dog! One of my friends ...." Before he could finish the sentence, the phone rang, pushing aside the words. Achhan talked for some time in a soft tone about some serious matters: the increase in the company's expenses, how they were able to avoid a loss this month, and the downward spiral of the stock market.

Because he lived in a world of just numbers, just as he did in his business life, he could easily tear up a page from life's account when it went wrong.

---

10 Endearing term for a daughter.

She had decided to challenge him when she got a chance and to cause him some pain with some sharp words.

But...

But before this man whose advice was to leave everything to God and who lived the life of a sage, untouched by love or hatred, she forgot the sharp words.

To stop thinking about all kinds of things, she walked into his study. It was kept spotlessly clean and in good order. Not even a piece of paper was out of place. That orderliness and the light green background gave the room a kind of peacefulness. Suddenly she saw some faded toys, big and small, in a cabinet. She was mesmerized by the unexpected discovery. She stood staring at them: a doll with mascara in her eyes and a bindi[11] on her forehead, a bear beating a drum while shaking its head, a cock with a broken leg...

"All these are your old toys, Umakutty. Do you remember them?" She heard Achhan's voice at the door.

"All these are mine?"

"Whose else?"

She didn't remember any of them. It was unusual for her to think back to old times.

"In old days you wanted these toys to be bathed and dressed before you would have your bath. The doll lost its hair and became bald because of the daily bath. Those days you were a mischievous girl. One day you wanted to make your lips red like the doll's and painted them with a red pen. What trouble we had to wash off that color."

He was talking about things as if he could still see them now. Memories of bygone days have the coolness of moonlight or chandan and the clarity of ashtapadi[12] music.

"Once you had a parrot. It flew in from somewhere. We never put it in a cage. But it came to you every day. It tried to imitate the way you talked. One day we heard it calling you 'Umakutty.' It was your companion for a long time. Then one day it didn't come back. You were very sad to lose the parrot."

In a mischievous tone she commented, "Like that I lost many things halfway through life."

"Many things you didn't want to get back," Achhan said with a faraway look.

---

11 The red mark worn on the forehead by Indian women.

12 Devotional music composed by Jayadeva in praise of Lord Krishna.

"No, Achha," she said with a courage she got from somewhere. "When we lose what we don't want to get back, it is not a loss. Only when we lose something we want to keep, it becomes a loss."

Achhan's silence pained her. She felt she shouldn't have said it.

Like a little child listening to her father's story, she asked, "How did the chicken break its leg?"

"Oh, that ... one day ..."

She felt that she was drifting to far away lands in a boat of memories.

While they were having tea, she watched him. All the pleasure of his daughter coming to visit him for the first time was reflected in that face, along with the peace that comes from contentment.

Uma thought, "Oh, my God, how am I going to tell him what I came for? Where will I begin? Suppose I start by saying that I came to say good-bye before leaving this place? Or shall I start by saying that my uncles are pressuring us to move to Bangalore, although we don't want to? Actually that was the truth."

On several occasions Amma was invited as an eminent doctor to work in a famous hospital owned by a distant relative in Bangalore. She declined, giving one reason or another. Relatives, including her brothers, who were settled there tried to coax her. Finally her brother asked, "Why are you adamant about staying there? We would like to know, because we don't understand your reason. Don't forget that in case of an emergency there is no one to help you. How long are you planning to stay there, just you and your daughter?"

Recently he said, "If you are planning to stay there, just think you don't have any brothers." Finally, bowing to everyone's pressure, Amma agreed. Before her older brothers, she is still an obedient younger sister.

"Achha, I need to go ... before it gets dark."

"I thought Umakutty would stay here for a day or two."

"No. I have to go today itself. Tomorrow morning ..."

She felt as if something was stuck in her throat. The helplessness and sadness she felt increased with every word.

"We are leaving, Achha, for Bangalore. Uncles have been trying to persuade Amma. Here we are by ourselves. On and off Amma gets asthma attacks. If there is an emergency, we have nobody here. In Bangalore, all her brothers are there. Neither of us wants to go. But we have no choice."

She was looking at the squares of the floor tiles as she spoke, afraid to look up at her father's face. She couldn't bear to see tears in his eyes, if he cried. If their eyes meet and...this is the moment she feared most.

But nothing happened as she feared. Achhan had the look of a wise man. He was beyond the denials of fate. He looked as if all this was expected.

"Oh, that is good. You two have been by yourselves for too long. May everything go well! They are all doing well I hope. Please convey my greetings. It has been very long since I saw them. Your oldest uncle had a daughter who looks like you. She used to be called Chithirakutty. Long ago whenever she came she would make me sit down and teach me her nursery rhymes. She is now...?"

"In medical school."

"Oh, she will be a doctor soon! It has been many years. It seems like yesterday. Yes, everything seems like yesterday."

Achhan was not asking silly questions to change the topic. They were sincere questions. He had learned well to face everything in life. Achhan had changed a great deal!

Sunlight the shade of copper was withdrawing from the room. The western wind was humming in a majestic low tone.

"OK. Then you should start before it gets dark. Don't wait any longer. You shouldn't be late getting home," Achhan said, getting up.

Moving to the door he said, "Life throws us riddles at various times. Some of them are scary even to look at. They are beyond understanding. Others are not like that. We have to deal with whatever we get. Facing them successfully is to our credit. Is there anyone who has succeeded in solving everything? Umakutty, I am telling you this for no special reason."

Before leaving, she bent down and touched her father's feet, the traditional gesture of saying goodbye to an elder, not just as a form, but heartfelt, with great respect and sincerity.

Achhan put his hand on her forehead, closed his eyes, and blessed her. His lips were moving, keeping time to some prayer recital—a father's prayer to God to bless his daughter in every way!

As she started to leave Achhan said, "Wait a second, Mole..." He brought back the leaf with the kumkum and chandan and, handing it to her, he said, "Keep this... with reverence... Devi will bless you in every-way. She is the source of everything good."

She was walking a bit too fast. There was such an empty feeling that she didn't say anything even after being with him for so long. At the same time, some things were unbelievable. He did not upset her by asking the question for which there was no answer: when will they meet again? Nor did he make a tear-soaked request: "Mole, think of me at times." So it was OK. Everything was OK.

As she came to the bend in the main road she thought that someday, maybe many years from now, if she got a chance to go this way with Amma she would say to her, "Once long ago, the day before we left this place, I did a daring thing. So you would not find out, I covered it by lying to you. That day ... I ... went to see Achhan. I didn't tell you about it, thinking that you might get angry or hurt."

Maybe Amma would understand, and would laugh and say, "That is all right. I know this little liar very well."

By the time she reached home it had become very dark. Amma was busy calling most of her friends to say goodbye. Memories were crowding Uma's mind with no discipline or order, and she just walked around the rooms. Along came the thought that from the next day this house would not be hers ...

She realized that scattered around each room were her wishes, dreams, and disappointments of a certain time.

In the northern room the walls seemed to look at her and wonder if standing before them was the same determined little baby trying to reach the floor from the fabric crib and crying when she couldn't; the little girl who put the dolls to bed singing lullabies; the impish girl who used to take new dance steps to tunes she was humming when no one was watching. This house also would shrink into memory starting the next day.

Without paying much attention, she picked up a letter pad that was on the floor and opened it. She wanted to write a letter to Achhan sitting here at home. After reaching Bangalore also she should write, she thought. It may be a silly idea, but she should send his way a few jokes, her dreams, one or two lines from the poems she wrote on and off, a few complaints, and lots of love. The distance created by the move should be shrunk that way.

"Uma, you are here." She heard Amma from the veranda.

She closed the pen and walked towards Amma, who asked, looking into the growing darkness, "Have you said goodbye to everyone? I have no idea when we will come back here, if ever."

"Hm."

"Is that why you were so late?"

She did not want to lie, but all she could do was to make her reply sound as natural as possible. "Yes, Amma. Coming back from the library, I ran into a couple of friends. The topics went from one to another..."

Uma felt that Amma was not paying attention to what she was saying, though she was shaking her head, because she too was sad to leave this house.

Leaning on the door, looking into the darkness, Amma was carrying on a silent conversation. Suddenly she turned around and asked, "You bid goodbye to everyone, you say. But why didn't you want to see your Achhan and say goodbye to him?"

Uma had nothing to say. Memories, imagination, and truth were all getting mixed up. Another riddle that life presented?

Without saying anything she went and brought the leaf with the kumkum and chandan from her bag.

Devi is the source of all happiness!

Amma was standing there not knowing what was happening. Uma mixed a bit of kumkum and chandan, approached her mother, put a mark on her forehead, and said softly:

"Sarva mangala..."

A LOVE STORY

N. S. Madhavan

Ya devi sarvabhutheshu rathirupena samsthitha[1]

"If the elephants in Africa have ears shaped like the map of Africa..."
Ramani stopped in the middle of the sentence and looked at Karunakaran's face.

"So?" Karunakaran asked, lying next to her on the mat and resting his
hand on her chest.

"Then the ears of Indian elephants should be like the map of India."

Ramani was feeling the weight of his hand. When her breathing
became strained, he moved his hand and asked, "Where did you see Afri-
can elephants?"

"In a zoo in Mysore. In the tenth grade we went on a study tour."

"They are larger than our elephants," Karunakaran said.

"With bigger heads."

"But somewhat disproportionate. The body is not long enough for
the size of the head. The elephant's body must be like a horse's."

"They are unlucky too. They have only fourteen nails. I counted
them," Ramani said. "Isn't it unlucky for the owner if they have less than
eighteen nails? And cleft-lips at the end of the trunk."

She moved closer to Karunakaran. Ramani's fingers moved down in a
line from his long neck southward.

"Body like a horse," she said in his ear when her fingers reached his
belly button. She could cope with that room only with his touch. The
small room, with an open door to the corridor leading to the kitchen, had
only a grass mat on the floor, with a dark circle at one end from the hair
oil she used. A bamboo stick hung horizontally from the ceiling, on which
she had hung one or two items of clothing. The room had no windows.
Instead, there were small openings in the shape of clubs, spades, and
other cards.

She saw a reddish sky through the club opening. She knew that

---

1   To that Universal Goddess who dwells in all beings as sexual love.

in a little while, as usual, the earth would become quiet. During that shadowless time, every sound heard would be unmistakable. First, Amma's[2] announcement of the lit oil lamp followed by the flapping of the cranes that only Ramani could hear. By the time the cows in the cowshed–named without much thought Karampi and Ammini–stopped bellowing, darkness would have fallen. Ramani longed to be touched at that time.

"Beeru,[3] aane,"[4] Ramani said.

Karunakaran held up his right hand.

"Put it down, aane," Ramani said.

Karunakaran brought his hand down and embraced her and felt a shiver below her skinny chest cavity. As the embrace tightened, that shiver became more intense. It was her suppressed sobbing that made her tremble. Karunakaran became quiet and ran his fingers through her hair. After a while, his chest got wet as if from a drizzle. Karunakaran raised her face by the chin, like a scene in the movies. By then her eyes were sparkling, bathed in tears.

"What was that for?" Karunakaran asked.

"I am scared." Ramani said.

"Why? I am here."

"You are not here."

"I know that," Karunakaran said in a lower tone. He jumped up from the mat and looked at the night through the heart-shaped hole. Far away hundreds of fireflies lit up the bushes.

Ramani rose and stood beside him. "I am scared," she said.

"Of what?"

"Of this room."

"What is wrong with this room?"

"On this wall," she said running her fingers over it, "there are many charcoal-drawn pictures below the whitewashed area. If you look carefully during the day, you can see them."

"What pictures?"

"Crosses, the easiest pictures to draw."

"Who drew them?"

"My father's sister, Sathyamma, who used to teach at the convent school. One day she started reciting the Bible. That day she was put in this room. She is the one who drew all the crosses on the wall."

---

2   Mother.

3   Raise your trunk.

4   Addressing the elephant (aana).

"And then?"

"In this family, this is the room for the women who lose their mind."

"Is there another room in the house to lock up the men?" Karunakaran asked laughing.

"Yes, a room at the gate house. Madness in our family is like diabetes in others. Because of that everything is always ready, in case someone goes mad."

"OK. What happened to Sathy Cheriamma?[5]

"On and off when she did math, her plus sign and the sign of the cross would get mixed up." Ramani and Karunakaran laughed together. As if remembering something, Ramani stopped laughing. She held him close and said, "Again I am scared."

"Of what?"

"That I will draw."

"Crosses?"

"No, elephants."

"Elephants?"

"Tuskers, female elephants, elephants that are neither male nor female, and the temple elephants that shake their heads keeping time to the trumpeters' music and show their maleness shamelessly. Chidambaran of Ernakulam Appan, the famous Kochunarayanan, and Vaikam Chadrashekharan—I will draw them all. I will draw all the elephants in our folklore."

"How about Guruvayur Keshavan?" Karunakaran asked.

"No. I don't like those that are very famous."

"You should not draw elephants on the wall."

"No? But how can I not draw?"

If she closed her eyes, all she would see is the elephant's blackness—touchable and rough like sandpaper that one can feel. When Karunakaran kisses her on the crown of her head, her eyelids close like touch-me-not leaves, and she sees blackness. When he embraces her the blackness becomes heavier, and when their lips meet it becomes moist. Only when their tongues dance with each other does she see streaks of light wriggling like snakes. When Karunakaran's hand reaches her breast, she sees only the blackness of the elephant's forehead.

"How can I not draw elephants?" Ramani asked again.

"Thaang[6] aane," Karunakaran whispered into her ear. Without having to listen, she heard the brass lock being opened and then the long cry of

---

5   Father or mother's younger sister.

6   Listen.

the hinges. Amma was standing on the other side of the door with the lit oil lamp.

"Deepam!"[7] Amma said. The shadows created by the lamp she held in front of her made her look frightening.

"Again you are talking to yourself?" she asked.

Without responding, she looked at the mat spread on the floor. She could feel the heat coming from Karunakaran, just like the heat from the earth at the start of a rain. When she looked up she saw Achhan[8] standing behind Amma.

"Why do you talk so much to yourself, child?" he asked.

"But I never talk to myself," Ramani said.

"Other than you, who is in this room?" Achhan asked taking a step forward.

"Other than to myself, whom do I converse with?" Ramani changed the subject.

"Other human beings," Amma said.

"But nobody speaks to me."

'If you talk to others they will return the favor," Amma said.

"That is not a conversation, Amma. It is only chatter."

Achhan put his hand on the wall, laughed heartily, and said, "What you say is true. Everyone talks to oneself to have peace of mind. But when it can be heard, there is a problem. What we think about, others shouldn't hear."

"What if others hear?"

"We shouldn't let anyone know what is on our mind. Nobody speaks out their thoughts. If you open your mind to see the sky completely, it would die just like the peacock feather," Achhan said.

Amma was about to lock the door again when Achhan said, "Don't, Devi. Why do you lock her up like this?"

"Do you think I want to? I don't want to see the ugly things she does. That's all."

"We will find some other way," Achhan said.

"What other way?"

"I have arranged with a detective with special powers as an astrologer and an exorcist to find out what is wrong with her. The priest at the temple recommended him. His name is Ramar Kandar Moosath. Have you heard that name?"

"No. But hearing the name itself makes me feel relieved," Amma said.

Ramani started scratching her head with fingernails. She was feeling

---

7   Light! (Announcing the lit lamp.)

8   Father.

good and closed her eyes as she continued to scratch. Amma felt that there was something sexual there and pulled Ramani's hand away.

"It is two days since you had a shower. Why don't you go and have a shower?" Achhan said.

"Shower? Now? In this twilight when the lamp is already lit?" Amma asked.

"That's all right. The fire in the bathhouse is still burning. There is one container of hot water still."

Amma went in and warmed up some oil with small onion, basil leaves, and peppercorn. The smell of that oil reached them before she did. She put a handful of it on Ramani's head and said, "Let the head cool a bit. What thoughts are there all intertwined inside it, I wonder!"

The ashes from the burned-out soft firewood in the big stove in the bathhouse were all over the floor like snow. Ramani removed her clothes and hung them on the line, turned around, and said to Karunakaran, "Mukkiedane[9]."

When Karunakaran filled the dimpled, brass jug she said, "Beeru[10]-aane."

He splashed the water on her. She spread her hands and turned round and round, and he poured a jug of water at every turn.

"Would you give me your hand, your open hand to kiss?" Karunakaran asked.

"Why? Why just the hand?"

He poured another jug of water on her and said, "Usually girls use their hands to cover their nakedness. The kiss is for your dance with hands open."

"Not now," she said as she washed the oil off her head. "I have to tell you something. You have to be careful."

"Of what?"

"Achhan has arranged with someone to find you."

"Who is it?"

"A detective with special powers."

"A detective? All the books you take out from the library are detective stories."

"His name is Inspector Ramar Kandar Moosath."

"At least now you can stop reading Neelakandhan Paramara's books."

"I only like Neelakandhan Paramara's books. In his stories the one who commits the crime gets caught in the end. Unlike the new writers, Pottakad and Kesavadev, my Paramara recognizes right and wrong."

---

9   Get the water.

10   Splash the water.

When Ramani went back to the house in the wet towel, it was pitch dark. A single bat flying in the darkness scared her. She walked fast to the house with her head down.

All was quiet during the first part of the night. Then, jingle, jingle. The jingling of a bullock cart was heard. Turning the corner of the beaten path a cart drawn by a single animal came to a stop. They could see a huge man with long arms getting out of it. He was dressed only in a red mundu[11] *and wore a coral chain; there were some basil leaves in his hair, and he had a silver-handled cane under his arm. Looking like a golden giant, this handsome man started walking towards the house. With each step, he crushed dry leaves under his foot. The night owls stopped their calls and stared at the unfamiliar figure.*

Jingle … jingle … The rhythmic sound now came from the bag he had in his hand.

From the patio, Madhava Menon and his wife looked at the stranger.

Menon asked, "Who might it be. I don't understand."

"I am Inspector Ramar Kandar Moosath."

"Why in this dress?"

"What can I say, Menon. This is the fate of a thanthri.[12] *Sometimes I dress like a man playing with a monkey, sometimes like a stone cutter, sometimes like a college professor, and sometimes, for a wider view, as a coconut tree climber. I felt this is the best dress for this case."*

He sat down crossing his legs, took out a piece of chalk from the bag, and drew a square on the dark, shiny floor.

"This is the central courtyard," Moosath said. "First we draw the picture of the place where the crime was committed. We expert detectives call it the P.O., place of occurrence." Moosath drew smaller boxes around the central courtyard.

"Which is your room, Menon?" he asked.

He put "M" in the check that Menon pointed to.

"And this room?"

"We don't open it," Menon said. "Achu mama[13] *who fought in Basra during the Second World War used to get a monthly quota of rum from the canteen. He used to sit in that room and drink horse-brand rum."*

"Oh, it is the liquor room. So, 'L.'"

Moosath could hear pappadam[14] being fried in the kitchen. He marked

---

11　A lower garment, consisting of a length of cloth.

12　An astrologer who is also an exorcist.

13　Uncle.

14　Wafer made with black gram flour.

it "K." *Pointing to a small room, he asked, "Menon, what is this small room?"*

"That is oavmuri[15] *to use at night."*

"We will mark it 'O.'"

When he had finished identifying every room, Moosath asked, "Where is the foolish woman?"

"She is in her room. Shall I call her?" *Mrs. Menon asked.*

"Not right now," *Moosath said.*

"Get up, aane," *Ramani said looking at Karunakaran lying on the mat,* "Inspector Kandar has come to trap you."

"No one will trap me," *Karunakaran said, standing up.*

"Never?"

"Never!"

"How come?"

"I am not a thief, not a murderer, never broke into a house."

"So you won't be caught?"

"In detective novels these are the types of people who get caught in the end. What did Neelakandhan Paramara teach us? In the end wickedness will be defeated. Am I wicked?"

"You definitely are not wicked," *Ramani said, standing close to him, and added,* "Because of that no one will ever trap you. If you are trapped, who do I have?"

When Moosath put the cloth bag on the floor it made a jingling sound. He said, "We will call the police dogs to go after the one who is holding her."

Moosath opened the cloth bag and took out cowry shells and put them in ones and twos on the boxes representing the various rooms, saying, "This is my dog squad." *When the shells had stayed in the boxes for some time, searching the various parts of the house following the smell, he said,* "Came up with nothing. Now, are there things that the defendant keeps in a secret place?"

"Not that I know of," *Menon said.*

"She has kept some things very carefully in an old Navy Cut cigarette tin," *his wife said.*

"Please bring it," *Moosath said.*

"Is that necessary, inspector?" *Menon asked.* "She is an adult. She may have some private things."

Moosath said, "For women and culprits there is no privacy!"

He opened the tin and took out the things one by one, saying what

---

15   Urinal for night use.

they were as if to make a list: "One empty packet of Honey Dew ciga-rettes, five packets of choornam[16] she was supposed to have taken as medicine, four match-box pictures, one silver rupee given for Vishu,[17] *the first page of a first-grade reader."*

For some time Moosath closed his eyes and meditated. When it was over he said, "I got it."

"I don't understand," Menon said.

"What is the picture on the cigarette packet? An elephant. What about the matchbox pictures? Elephants. What is on the first page of the reader? 'A for amma' and 'Aa for aana.[18] I got it, Menon. Now we can do it."*

Moosath told them an old story: "During the time of the Cochin Maharaja who gave up the throne, Thrippunithura Temple had an elephant named Achuthan. He went crazy with rut[19] *and broke the chain that kept him tethered, running amuck. He killed the mahout who tried to chain him. There was chaos in the market place. The British authority ordered the elephant shot. But the Maharaja was reluctant to order a temple elephant killed. At that time, a young man from the north who was on his way to Ambalappuzha met the Maharaja and said, 'My name is Pachu. I am a mahout. Please give me a chance to chain the elephant.' His request was granted.*

"On the other side of an iron bridge there lived an old woman in a hut. Pachu went to her and asked for a granite pestle used for cracking the betel nut.

"The elephant Achuthan began hitting the banyan tree with its fore-head. On seeing Pachu in the middle of the bridge, it came running towards him holding its trunk parallel to the ground and shaking its head. Suddenly Pachu broke the pestle on the bridge into three pieces and the sound made the elephant stop. Pachu threw the first piece between the elephant's eyes, the second at his head, and the third at the forehead. The elephant was stunned.

"It slipped before mahout Pachu, who said in a quiet tone, 'Madak-kane.'[20] *The elephant folded its front legs and sat down like a puppy. His rut juices and tears started to mingle."*

Menon's wife placed a pot of coffee before Moosath and asked, "This and Ramani..."

"What connection? About twenty years ago during the evacuation time,

---

16   Medicine in powder form.

17   Kerala New Year.

18   Elephant.

19   Sexual urge.

20   Fold the legs.

there was another elephant that killed a young man on the same iron bridge. Have you heard that story?"

"Yes, I was studying in Madras at that time," Menon said.

That elephant's name was Veeraraghavan, about 20 to 24 years old. He began to show signs of rut for the first time. He was restless. Although it is a natural phenomenon, he had never had it before. He scraped the temple banyan tree for a long time. There was no relief for his sexual urge, and he cried in blaring anger. That cry could be heard as far as the Hill Palace. The problems of the dumb creatures!

"This and my child..." Menon asked.

Moosath continued, "Veeraraghavan also broke the chain and killed his mahout. The District Officer in Cochin ordered him shot. When the shooters lined up, a young man came forward and said, 'I am Karunakaran, son of Pachu who chained elephant Achuthan. I would like a chance to try to chain this elephant.' Because of Pachu Nair, he was allowed to try.

"Karunakaran stood in the middle of the same bridge with three pieces of granite. Veeraraghavan raised its trunk to smell for the presence of female elephants. Unable to control his rage, he ran on to the bridge. On seeing Karunakaran he stopped, and Karunakaran asked him to go back, people say. The first stone was thrown between the eyes, but before the next stone could be thrown, the elephant picked up Karunakaran with its trunk, put the tusks through him, and threw his dead body into the canal."

Moosath stood up, stretched his hand, and said, "Looking at all the evidence, circumstances, and signs, I conclude that Karunakaran's spirit is in your daughter, Ramani."[21]

"What should we do?" Menon asked.

"There is a way," Moosath responded. "I will give you a talisman with a prayer written on it. She should wear that. If he is smart he will leave, but judging from what he did it doesn't seem so. If that doesn't work, we will take him to Chottanikkara Temple and nail him to the pala[22] tree. Since he is Pachu Nair's son, Chottanikkara Amma will look kindly upon him."

"Everything will be fine with that?" Menon's wife asked.

"Everything should be. Karunakaran is a simple guy who tried to repeat history. So he may be stubborn. If Chottanikkara also doesn't work we will have a three-day pooja[23] here to get rid of him." Moosath

---

21 Italics added.

22 A tree that grows in barren land, Alstonia Scholaris.

23 Ceremonial prayers.

twirled the silver-headed stick and prayed, "Oh God, please don't make us torture him."

Karunakaran's face looked tired, as if he had been in the hot sun. Ramani said, "Inspector Moosath has found you."

"Yeah."

"What now?"

"What now?"

"You shouldn't leave me alone. You are the only one I have," Ramani said, trying to hold back her tears. "If you go away, I will be alone again."

Karunakaran was looking out at the darkness through the heart-shaped hole. He said, "Don't be afraid, girl. I won't go. I was defeated once. Who wants to be defeated twice?"

Ramani stood close to him, standing on her toes, and nibbled at his ear.

The next evening when Ramani got back from her shower, her mother tied the talisman strung on black thread around her neck, before the picture of the family deity.

"Do you feel anything?" She asked Ramani.

"Like what?"

"Like a weight has been taken off?"

"No. But I feel ticklish around my waist, as if a centipede is crawling," Ramani said.

When he saw the mother's eyes filling with tears, Achhan suppressed a smile and said in a serious tone, "Go to your room only when it is time to sleep. Now you sit here and recite the Lalithasahasranaamam."[24]

That night Ramani stood before Karunakaran wearing only the talisman. Touching it she said, "Moosath has put your arrest warrant inside this."

Ramani took his hand and made him touch the talisman. Then she stood close to him and started to rub him with her body. She pulled him down to the mat. When her body was quivering on his, she made zebra marks on his back with the nails of both hands.

Ramani put her head in her mother's lap and took a nap in the taxi on their way back from Chottanikkara. She had yellow marks on her face from kuruthy.[25] Looking at the white of her half-closed eyes, her mother started crying.

---

24   Repeating invocations to Lalitha (Durga) a thousand times.

25   Water prepared by mixing turmeric and lime.

"I think the ghost is gone," Achhan said.

"Luckily we didn't need Moosath's torture," Amma said . . .

When Ramani got to her mat to sleep, she had the feeling that she was going to be alone from then on. To shut out whatever light was there, Ramani pressed her face onto the pillow. Suddenly she felt Karunakaran's presence.

"I thought I had shut you up in the hollow of the pala tree in Chottanikkara," she said to him and got up and stood beside him.

Karunakaran didn't say anything. By then her fingers had become alive. As they went from his head to the tip of his nose and reached his lips, Karunakaran pushed her hand away. He yelled, "I am scared."

When she stepped forward with eyes shining with tears, Karunakaran ordered, "Step back!"

"What are you afraid of?" Ramani asked.

"I don't know," he said.

Holding chethy[26] flowers and a handful of tender palm leaves cut into pieces, Ramar Kandar Moosath looked at Ramani sitting in front of him with folded legs. He said, "Hey, you go away. Get out." Then he threw the flowers at her, beat her with the silver-handled cane, and took a break to recite prayers. This continued till midnight. The women who had gathered around for the ritual were crying. Far away, boatmen from the boats plying in the canal stopped on hearing Moosath's shouting.

He was furious that Karunakaran was fearless enough not to cry after all this. So he started swinging the cane so hard that his coral neck chain was twirling in the air. Drops of sweat fell from his hairy arm, shining in the light. Finally, forgetting everything, Moosath jumped up and cried, "You rascal, bloody fool, get out. Out, out."

He was about to kick Ramani when Achhan objected, "That is enough for today, Moosath."

Moosath was quiet for some time. Finally he said, "OK. Give her some tender coconut milk and put her to bed."

As soon as the door closed Ramani asked, "Was it painful?" For the first time, she started crying.

Running her hand over the marks on his back, she asked again, "Do they hurt?"

"No," Karunakaran said, "but I am leaving."

"Leaving me alone?"

"Yes."

---

26 Chrysanthus.

"Are you afraid of Kandar?"

"No."

"Then?"

"I am scared," Karunakaran said in a tired voice.

"Of what?"

"Of you."

"Of me?"

"Yeah. You have rut in you."

Ramani stared at Karunakaran, but could no longer see him. When she looked out through a hole in the wall, she saw Veeraraghavan standing in the yard. When Karunakaran got on him, he raised his trunk, made the trumpet call, and started running.

After a short while, Ramani heard the gatehouse crashing.

A Dream from Israel

Sarah Thomas

Malavika learned of the taxi drivers' strike only when she came out of the airport. The sight of the airline bus ready to go gave her a bit of comfort. But she had no idea where Hotel Samrat was. That was the hotel in which *News India* had booked a room for her. She was sure there were other reporters on the flight. An international film festival would attract reporters from every corner of the world. But junior reporters like her would have gone to Trivandrum three or four days ahead rather than wait for the opening day.

This trip was an unexpected lucky break for her. Ajai Kulkarni had been assigned for this. He is a senior editor of the newspaper who has handled the Cinema section for years. He has a personality that endears him to anyone who meets him, a great conversational style, and is an expert in getting the scoop. He is qualified for this assignment in every way. Unfortunately, he came down with chicken pox the day before he was to leave. Kulkarni recommended Malavika, in spite of her junior status, and Raja Sahib, the owner of the paper, approved it without raising any objections. The whole thing was a miracle. As far as she was concerned, this assignment was nothing but luck. The only problem is the strike. No big deal. She can handle that.

The bus was waiting. "Palayam," she heard someone say. Though she is a Malayalee[1] and knows the language, having grown up in Bombay and her parents being from Trichur, she didn't know the city at all. She was panting when she got out with luggage on her shoulders, back and hands.

"Have a sip. You look exhausted." Only then did she see the young man standing with a bottle of mineral water in his out stretched hand. It may be because there had been nothing much to do on the plane, but she had noticed him sitting in the seat in front of her, to the right. With the walkman headset in his ears, he was keeping time to the music with his hands, legs, and head from the time he boarded the plane till he landed, and the curls in his hair, tied up with a red silk ribbon, were fluttering.

---

1 One who speaks Malayalam, a person from Kerala.

To be honest, it was his hair that attracted her attention. It had the color of hot copper and, when light fell on it, glowed as if ready to burst into flames.

Malavika looked at his face, calm with an innocent look. His friendly smile showed an even row of teeth. He was young, at least four or five years younger than she. She liked him. For some reason she remembered that she had always wanted a younger brother. With no hesitation, she drank the water and returned the empty bottle with a big "thank you." He laughed heartily.

"A 'thank you' is not enough. I need a favor. I am here for the first time. If you would tell me where this hotel is—"

"I don't know this place either. But I am going to the same hotel. We will find out."

Before she could finish, he had taken her big bag on his shoulder. By the time they reached the hotel after many enquiries, they had started the beginnings of a friendship.

"I am Malavika—Malavika Madhusudan. *News India's* representative. You know that the international film festival is going on here. I am here to cover that."

Like all beginners, she was excited about her newly-acquired status. Sure, it is something one can proudly inform others, a newspaper representative covering an international film festival!

His reaction was stronger than she expected.

"Really? I didn't think so. It is my luck to have met a newspaper rep right at the beginning. I too am here for the festival, not just a spectator." He stopped abruptly as if he shouldn't say anything more.

While they were waiting in the lounge for the room-boy to bring the keys, Malavika's curious eyes fell on him. "He is handsome!" she thought. "He said he is not just a spectator. Then could he be a celebrity who became famous at such an early age? Then it is my luck, bringing the possibilities of a scoop. But how could he be so modest?"

She stopped the flow of thoughts and said, "You didn't introduce yourself. Now, let me see if I can guess."

Seeing his surprised face, she became excited.

"Hm! You must be an actor or a dancer—that is my guess."

"Sorry, you are wrong. I am not anything like that. I am just Yakub, a cinema lover, from Israel."

Malavika was a bit disappointed that her guess was wrong.

She took special care in dressing up for the inaugural session. When she got to the lounge Yakub was already there. He seemed ready for travel with a small bag in his hand. Seeing her he gave a broad smile and approached her.

"Look, your name is difficult for me to pronounce. If you say it one more time—"

She thought of teasing him, but changed her mind.

"That's OK. I have an easier name for you to call me."

She thought of the name a younger brother she had never had would have called her, the name the children in Bombay called her: "Deedi,[2] is that difficult to say?"

"No, not at all."

"You seem ready to go somewhere."

"I am going to Cochin. It has been my wish from the time I was a little boy. My ancestors lived there. I can say it is the main reason for my visit." He didn't prolong his conversation, as the auto-rickshaw he had asked for had come.

The next day she saw him in the evening at the restaurant. She was discussing the day's program in detail with some junior reporters she had met. Yakub pulled a chair and sat by her as soon as he got there, but kept quiet during the heated discussion. Though he felt that her excitement in meeting him the previous day had diminished, he realized that it was not the time to ask for a reason. As foreign representatives, they all had a great deal to say about the day's events and the open discussion scheduled for the next day.

Back in her room, Malavika was tired, but didn't care to go to sleep. She was thinking of the questions she should ask the famous Israeli director David Ezra, pleased that she was able to arrange an interview with him. He was known as a short-tempered Jew. He might get disturbed by her questions about Jewish customs. That was all right because that was the thrill of being a reporter. The thought brought a smile to her face.

Suddenly, someone knocked on the door. At this time of the night to knock on the door without using the phone to call first—some people are not considerate. Somewhat displeased, she opened the door. Her impatience disappeared on seeing Yakub standing there. But his looks disturbed her. His face was taut, seemingly from some inner conflict, and his eyes were red.

"May I come in? I ask for your indulgence for coming in so late. I had to come."

To lighten his mood, she smiled and said, "Look, no reason or excuse is necessary. Please come in and sit down."

---

2   Elder sister.

When he sat down she enquired about his trip.

"Something that happened on the trip is troubling you. Isn't that true? If you tell me what it is ... please don't hesitate."

He didn't respond to that. It was as if she had found an opening to his crowded mind.

"Didn't you say that you will interview David Ezra tomorrow?"

She was a bit annoyed that he doubted it.

"So what? You thought I was boasting? You can't believe it?"

"Yes, yes, I do believe that. I have heard that reporters can get many things done that others think are impossible. That is why I came to you at this time. I need a big favor—you may think it is crazy. But for me it is my life's mission. I carefully keep a dream in my mind, a dream that is divine, innocent, and beautiful, pure as dew drops, tender like new young leaves and warm like the morning sun—a priceless love story—an unusual story that goes beyond the boundaries of time, place, culture and religion. It is the rainbow shining on love's horizon. I have given it some shape ever since my childhood, through many sleepless nights and countless corrections with a lot of pain and suffering."

He stopped suddenly as if he was going crazy. He held both of Malavika's hands and said softly:

"Deedi, you must do me a favor. You must get this hand-written manuscript into the hands of that great creative genius. A reporter can do that. My heart is full and my feeling is that I have come close to my life's goal. I didn't expect to get a break like this. If he puts his mind to it he can show how this world full of lust, anger, and vindictiveness can shift to one of love and harmony. You know how a movie can influence people. It is the only medium that can influence the whole of humanity to discuss an idea. I wish I could have done it. I gave up that impossible dream long ago. All my efforts in that far away land failed miserably. Deedi, please say 'yes.' Give me your word that you will do it."

She could not answer him immediately. After interviewing a famous director, hand him the dream of a nobody? She was not sure if he deserved her admiration or disregard for carrying around an impossible dream in his mind. But somehow she could not ignore his heart's yearning. What else could she tell her younger brother, who thinks she can get him the moon? So she took the bundle of paper from him and said, "I will try. In all honesty, that's all I can say."

At the end of the interview, Malavika tried to give the bundle of papers to David Ezra, describing it the best way she could. When he heard it was by an Israeli writer, he stopped what he had started to say and was silent for a moment. His eyes were on Malavika while he was thinking of something, but he didn't say anything. That was all. Nothing else happened. He had to meet other reporters for interviews. Whatever was on his mind during that moment of silence was gone. His attention was on the next interviewer.

Malavika had tried to get him interested, saying that only he could figure out the story written in Hebrew. But she got the usual excuses—with the many activities connected with the film festival, and getting the needed paperwork done for the next film, how could he think of another theme? That was that.

That night Yakub was waiting for Malavika on the veranda next to her room.

"What? What happened? What did he say? Any hope for me?" She couldn't disappoint that face shining with anticipation.

"Wait a minute. You can't hurry these things. You can't hope for a miracle. Everyone is busy with his own work—meeting reporters, discussions, explanations about each one's entry, etc. I want you to realize that possibly other directors who are here could get interested in your dream. It depends on luck. For the language and the place not to become a problem, I have a practical suggestion: tell me about your dream in detail. I will write it up in English and present it and distribute copies. Most of the people who are here know English. If you are lucky, one of them will get hooked on the story."

"Deedi, you are brilliant. I will tell you the story in detail. The best I can do in English." His face blossomed at the thought.

To get ready he closed his eyes and was silent for a long time. When he started to say the story his mind was in another world.

"Look Deedi, the fragrant flowers of paarijaatham[3] may not be anything special to you. But to me it is different. Though I have never seen it, I know it. From the time I learned right from wrong, I have tried to see the flowers in my mind. Small white flowers that look like the first snow on olive trees, covering the leaves in bunches. Isn't that right? Like the lilies in the valley of Lebanon, they spread their attractive fragrance all over. I have enjoyed it in my mind. I know the foot of the trees that received the fallen flowers in the far-away land I have not seen. That was in the vast unclaimed area by the Synagogue in Cochin. Jewish Street in Mattanchery ends there.

"Do you know why I went to Cochin? To see that paarijaatham tree

---

3   According to Hindu mythology, the celestial wishing tree, Paarijaatham, came out of Paalaazhi, the ocean of milk, when it was churned by the gods and demons.

planted by a man whose name I don't know, as a symbol of his love for my father's younger sister, Rosa. He was a Hindu. She was a rare beauty with pure Jewish blood. But from her mouth came Malayalam words with the sound of bells. That was Rosa. Even when they laughed together there was the musical rhythm of Malayalam. I know all this from the old lady who came from Cochin to manage our house. In Israel I remember Rosa as a quiet person, hiding in a corner of the house, but her beauty in the painted picture when she blossomed into a young woman was captivating. Looking at it was pleasant and I was wonderstruck. The curls of her hair coming down the shoulders were like shiny copper. Her eyes were like two black beetles ready to fly. Her cheeks had stolen the color of rose flowers. Her lips had a smile as if she was hiding a big secret. That secret could be her love for this young Hindu man. All this could be my imagination also. But that is the picture I carry in my mind even today, though I also cannot forget the Rosa with her lusterless hair, lifeless eyes and sunken cheeks.

"I called her just Rosa. It must have been because she was a mental patient that no one objected to my calling her by name, although she was much older than I. In the fall, when the strong southeasterly winds blew, she would go up on the terrace and spread her hands to the open skies and stand there as if praying. When I followed her, bewildered, she would hug me tight and kiss me. I can still remember the salty taste of her tears. It pained me to hear others say that she did all that because she was not of sound mind. I didn't hear anyone saying why she, who didn't hurt even an ant, would suffer this way. Later on I learned that her psychiatrist husband abandoned her because she could not be a wife. I think my father got her married, thinking that would make her get better, and considered a psychiatrist a good choice. But the torments my father under went in Germany had stunted his mind and he could not understand Rosa's finer emotions.

"Those days father was in military service on the battlefields, Rosa was in her own world, and my mother who came from Europe was struggling to understand their Indian mindset. Then there was the old lady who came with the family from Cochin. I learned bits and pieces of history from her—about my forefathers who lived for centuries in the southernmost part of India in Cochin and the language that is spoken there, Malayalam. I grew up in this atmosphere. My childhood was strange. I don't have the strength, even today, to think of my mother's death. My father was not home as usual. But then, he could come home only once in a while like a guest, with no part in the unending family squabbles.

"Amma was taken to the hospital bleeding. I still remember Rosa hiding behind the curtain, terrified. She was shaking from head to foot. I was afraid that something would happen to her while Amma was away. My fear was wrongly placed. Instead of Rosa, it was Amma who died. I was awakened by the ambulance siren. Amma's body, wrapped in white sheets..."

Suddenly Yakub stopped. He was panting, beads of perspiration all over his forehead!

"Yakub, what happened? Shall I order something to drink?"

"No, Deedi, it is OK. Did I scare you? I am just an emotional being, unable to control myself when necessary. See how I went from Rosa's story to mine? Rosa didn't survive one year after Amma's death. She died in an accident–fell down from the balcony. I still feel uneasy to think that it could have been a suicide. After she died, I took her room. For some reason, I liked spending time in that room, quietly. My father had no time left for me after his service to the country."

"After leaving school you have to serve in the military for two years, don't you? I read about it somewhere. Why didn't you..."

Yakub acted as if he didn't hear that question. Maybe he was anxious to finish the story. Malavika did not repeat the question.

"I understood Rosa only after she died, from her diary and from the notes she'd written after she came back from her husband's home. Because the notes were written by a crazy woman, nobody bothered to destroy them. It was my luck that they were left in the table drawer. I learned why she went up to the balcony and raised her out-stretched hands and stayed there as if praying, from those notes and from the letter that was kept under the inside cover of the diary. It was written in Malayalam, but the old lady translated it for me.

"The important topic was their sacred love. Look Deedi, I do not know the name of Rosa's lover. For her he was 'Master,' the teacher my father hired to tutor her when she failed in Malayalam year after year. They fell in love at first sight. She called that experience 'a pleasurable pain.' She had added the simile 'like Isaac and Rebecca' about them. I am not sure you know that they are the blessed lovers in our holy book. Rosa and her Master's love flourished in the energy that went from his eyes to hers and hers to his, as they sat in the study room facing each other, without their knowledge, without attracting anyone's attention, through looks, words, and gestures. Later on, when Rosa returned from her violin lessons in town they would meet in the vacant yard by the synagogue, just to see each other and talk freely with no one around.

"They met there the day before Rosa's 16th birthday. That day Master had brought a seedling of the paarijaatham tree. I understand that a poem she had to learn had discussed this tree. Rosa was taken up by the story of the paarijaatham flower that spreads its fragrance throughout the land of Devas. She had learned a great deal about it by asking many questions to Master. That flowering tree was the dream of their young minds.

"Those days fragrance was very dear to Rosa. I don't know the story that is part of the Hindu mythology. You must explain that to me later. She wrote about it in her diary.

"This is not from the land of the Devas. This paarijaatham is from our own dear earth. But I believe that when it is nourished by love, the fragrance from its flowers will reach every corner of the earth." Master said that and planted the seedling in the rain-soaked ground. As far as Rosa was concerned, what Master said did become true.

"Do you know one thing? I used to wonder why the tree they considered a symbol of their love was planted in the vacant lot near the synagogue. Yesterday when I went there I understood the reason. The houses there have no front yard. They open to the street. The back yard is closed in with no sunlight coming through. Only yesterday I realized that Jewish Street in Mattanchery is like that.

"The paarijaatham in the vacant land by the synagogue was their secret. They dreamed of the tree growing, branching out, giving shade to sit under, and the buds turning to flowers, spreading their fragrance all over that place. Master wrote a beautiful poem about it. Not just one poem, but many four-liners too, and through them he gave Rosa a heavenly dream. Rosa tried and somewhat succeeded in translating them into Hebrew. I could see her heart that she herself had closed and sealed, only through these translations.

"One sad truth is that even they did not realize the closeness of their hearts and the intensity of their love. I believe that the impact of their separation would not have been so great on Rosa if that hadn't been so. Wouldn't she have at least tried to see Master for one last time to say goodbye? No, nothing like that happened. As far as Rosa was concerned, the announcement that the family was ending their life as expatriates and returning to the Promised Land–Israel–was like a thunderbolt. She literally became a 'living dead.' Muthachhan[4] did not make that decision all of a sudden. He was getting things ready in secret. From the time the Allies, through their generosity, as part of their administration of justice, or for their own long-term well being, gave a separate State of Israel to the Jews after the Second World War, he had been carrying this dream

---

4 Grandfather.

of moving to Israel. He was waiting for my father to complete his studies and get his degree from the medical college here in Trivandrum. He also wanted to sell his business without much loss. But poor Rosa and her dreamy Master did not know any of these things. The only thing they knew was to love. Neither the past nor the future came to their mind. Among the Jewish families it was not customary to consult women on serious decisions of this nature. Moreover, Rosa had lost her mother when she was a child, leaving no adult to talk to. I told you about the letter she got from Master. I have no idea how she got it. Maybe it was sent through another family that came from Cochin later. See, I have it with me. You may read it."

He opened his bag, took the letter out, and gave it to her. She carefully opened the letter that was beginning to yellow and managed to read it.

Rosa, you must not cry. From the other side of the wire fence I saw your face, swelled up from crying, as you walked to the plane. I still cannot bear that look. I even forget my throbbing, breaking heart when I think of the look of your burning heart on your face.

If you can believe in the stars as I do, take all this as the bad luck of the time we were born. Otherwise, at least we should have bid goodbye . . .

But one thing I am sure of: in this life whatever different paths we might take, the love in our hearts will never die.

Last night I had a dream. I dreamed that our paarijaatham became a huge tree, shooting up as we were watching, to the sky. It had many, many branches and they were all covered with flowers. Then something miraculous happened. The fragrance of the flowers borrowed wings from the westerly winds and flew over land, sea, mountains, and sandy deserts and reached you! Only when I woke up I realized that that fragrance was my love. It is said that dreams sometimes come true. I do believe that in the magic box of time there is such a celestial moment waiting for us.

"Master's beautiful imagination is great. Rosa must have believed it completely," Malavika said as she folded the letter.

"Yes, that is exactly what happened. Rosa lived only in the memories that Master presented her."

"OK. What happened to the paarijaatham tree? Is it still there?"

"That's what makes me sad. In a sense, it makes me happy too. There is not a sign of such a tree having grown there. Still its memory has not left that area. That is what I am happy about. Kadar Ikka, a fruit vender near the boat jetty, remembers that tree. A lean tree with many branches covered with flowers. The fragrance from the flowers, carried by the westerly winds, filled the air. During those days Jewish Street was not empty like today. The paarijaatham grew well under the care of many who thought it grew up by the synagogue by chance. Children used to collect the flowers and make garlands with them. Young people gathered there to enjoy the fragrance. Those were the days! Kadar Ikka doesn't know when the tree started to die or how it died. It has left no sign of its existence. But in his mind that fragrance is still there. That is why I said earlier that it makes me happy, too."

"Did you find out anything about Master? He might have married someone else, a girl matching his horoscope," Malavika said.

"Do you think he could forget Rosa's tear-stained face and kiss another girl? I like to think that he didn't get married. I wish to see their shining faces of love lasting forever in this world full of dark faces that emit so much hypocrisy. Kadar Ikka said one more thing: some time back another man came to his shop, a sanyasi[5] dressed in saffron clothes, looking for the paarijaatham. He didn't answer any questions, but wandered around the area the whole day and left. He hasn't been seen again."

"His horoscope must say that, I am sure," Malavika said. "Anyway, I will take the liberty to say that in my script."

"Deedi, your choice. After saying all this to you I feel as if a great weight has been lifted off my mind."

Malavika sent him back to his room after promising that she would do justice to his emotions in her script to be distributed the next day.

There was no response from movie directors, producers, or even her colleagues. Many just ridiculed her efforts without taking even a few minutes to listen to her.

As she was wondering how to break this news that would completely paralyze him, the phone rang. At the other end was Yakub's tired voice.

"Deedi, would you come over to my room?"

Then she heard the phone fall down. She waited for some time and tried to call back, but there was no dial tone. Quickly she went down the stairs to his room. She knocked on the door, but there was no response. When she opened the door and entered, Yakub was lying on the settee.

---

5 One who has renounced all worldly connections.

His face was white as a sheet of paper. She ran to him. The cushion was soaked in blood.

"Yakub, what happened to you?"

He gave a dry smile.

"Don't panic, Deedi. I knew this would happen. But, I didn't expect it so soon—the doctor had given his word—if I took the medicines regularly, and followed the directions faithfully—still..."

"Don't worry. I will call for a doctor. You will get excellent medical care here." He got hold of her hand and wouldn't leave it.

"Sit by me for a minute, Deedi," Yakub said. "You asked me if I didn't have to go for military service. I avoided answering that. I was not qualified to join the army. A person who has leukemia is not destined to live long. That was my concern. I have been on medication for the last two years after I was diagnosed with it. I wanted to get my dream to the attention of appropriate people before I died. I took the risk of coming to this film festival for that reason... Deedi, were you successful in your efforts? If I know that before I die..."

"Leave my hand... let me call the doctor! If something is not done quickly... you took a great risk in making this trip."

"Do you have a response to my question?" His fingers, tight on Malavika's wrist, were shivering. When she looked at his face, seeing the anxiety, hope, and sadness that came to his eyes, she could not disappoint him.

"Take it easy. Your dream is not wasted. It will be introduced before the whole world. Believe it. Let me go."

"Deedi, say goodbye to me..."

Malavika thought her heart would break. She felt that the unexpected gift she had received was being lost just as quickly. Tears were streaming down her cheeks. She couldn't bear the pitiful look on his face. She kissed him on his forehead.

"My brother I was not destined to have," she whispered.

"I am contented—the last thing on my mind as I die will be the memory of this loving touch."

"Don't talk nonsense. You are not going anywhere. I won't let you. All you need is a blood transfusion."

She moved to the phone, seeing him smile. She turned around only after calling the hospital and every media person she had met during the last two days. By that time Yakub's white clothes were soaked in fresh blood, and his smile was frozen.

The next day movie directors and producers got together with news reporters to discuss the unlimited possibilities of Yakub's dream. Even when the discussions got heated, Malavika was sitting quietly in a corner with her head down. She didn't see or hear anything. The only picture on her mind was a young man named Yakub, as she saw him on the marble slab in the mortuary, waiting for instructions from the embassy, as there were no relatives to receive the dead body.

The next day movie directors and producers got together with news reporters to discuss the unlimited possibilities of Yakub's dream. Even when the discussions got heated, Malavika was sitting quietly in a corner with her head down. She didn't see or hear anything. The only picture on her mind was a young man named Yakub, as she saw him on the marble slab in the mortuary, waiting for instructions from the embassy, as there were no relatives to receive the dead body.

The next day movie directors and producers got together with news reporters to discuss the unlimited possibilities of Yakub's dream. Even when the discussions got heated, Malavika was sitting quietly in a corner with her head down. She didn't see or hear anything. The only picture on her mind was a young man named Yakub, as she saw him on the marble slab in the mortuary, waiting for instructions from the embassy, as there were no relatives to receive the dead body.

ABOUT THE AUTHORS

LALITHAMBIKA ANTHARJANAM comes from a literary family, her parents and son being well-known writers. One of the early writers who brought the concerns of the Namputhiri women to light, she has received the Kerala Sahithya Academy Award (twice), the Kendra Sahithya Academy Award, the Odakuzhal Award, the Vayalar Award, and the Kalyanakrishna Menon Award. She was a member of the Governing Council of the State Social Welfare Board, a member of the State Book Selection Committee, and a member of the Sahithya Pravarthaka Sahakarana Sangham (cooperative society for writers). She died in 1987.

ASHITA has published six anthologies of short stories and has translated three of these into English. She has also written screenplays for feature films and documentaries. She received the National Award for *The Lies My Mother Told Me*.

CHANDRIKA BALAN writes under the name Chandramathy. She is a lecturer in English, for which she has a PhD. She has translated many of her Malayalam stories into English. She was executive editor at Kendra Sahithya Academy and participated in the Centenary celebrations of the Commonwealth Institute.

MARTIN ERESSERIL has a volume of short stories, a book on marital sex, and a recent Biblical novel about King David's dynasty to his credit.

GRACY published the first anthology of her short stories in 1991. She is the recipient of the Kerala Sahithya Academy Award, the Lalithambika Antharjanam Award, the Thoppil Ravi Award, and the Delhi Kadha Award.

GEETHA HIRANYAN was a lecturer in Malayalam literature. She received her first award, the Mathrubhoomi Kadha Award, while she was in college. Other awards she received included the Ankonom Award, the T. P. Kishore Award, and the Kunjupillai Award for Poetry. She died before she could defend her PhD thesis.

ASHA KRISHNAN is a lecturer in English. She won her first award as a college student in a statewide short story competition and the next in the Vanitha Short Story Competition. She won the Rajalakshmi Memorial Award for Short Story for "The Riddles in Life." Asha has published several stories in leading Malayalam magazines and presented stories on All India Radio. She is working toward a PhD in English literature.

N. S. MADHAVAN is a member of the prestigious Indian Administrative Service. He has published four collections of short fiction. He is a three-time winner of the Kadha Award, and winner of the Kerala Sahithya Academy Award and the Odakuzhal Award. One of the stories included in this collection, *When Big Trees Fall*, is being made into a movie in India.

MADHAVIKUTTY inherited her talent for writing from her mother, Poetess Balamaniamma, and father V. M. Nair, former managing director of *Mathrubhumi Daily*. She writes in Malayalam and English as Kamala Das. She is the recipient of the Asan Poetry Prize, the Kerala Sahithya Academy Award, the Kent Award, the Asan World Prize, and the Vayalar Award. She has changed her name to Kamala Suraiya.

KAROOR NEELAKANDHA Pillai is considered the number one short story writer in Malayalam. He has hundreds of short stories, three novels, and a drama to his credit. He was the founder of a cooperative society for writers. He received the Kerala Sahithya Academy award in 1960. He died in 1975. His daughter, B. Saraswathyamma, is a well-known writer.

JOHNY PLATHOTTAM became a social activist after getting his degree in physics. He has published two collections of poems and two anthologies of short stories. He included his mother's name in his pen name, "Johny Mary John," indicating his belief in gender equality, and named his son John Rose John.

SACHIDANANDAN also writes under the name Anand. He is considered a trendsetter in modern Malayalam literature. He has more than 20 books to his credit, including two philosophical works. He also writes on issues of social importance in periodicals and newspapers. He is the recipient of numerous awards, including the Vayalar Award, the Kerala Sahithya Parishad Award, the Sahrudayavedi Award, the Abudhabi Malayalam Award, the Kerala Sahithya Academy Award, and the Yespal Award. Though he has received many awards, he demonstrated extraordinary courage of conviction in rejecting two prestigious awards.

M. P. SAHIB started his career as a writer by working as a journalist for two Malayalam dailies while still in college. That led to feature articles, short stories, travel diaries, and poems. He has published two collections of short stories. He is president of the Basheer Academy.

K. SARASWATHYAMMA was one of the early writers. She got her degree in 1942, taught in a secondary school for three years, and then joined Government Service, where she taught till her retirement in 1974. She has a number of short stories to her credit and translated some of them into English. She died in 1975.

SARAH THOMAS is a prolific writer of novels and short stories. She is the recipient of the Kerala Sahithya Academy Award and the Marthoma Sahithya Puraskaram. She has also written movie scripts. She has been a member of the Kerala State Film Award Committee, Kerala Film Certification Committee, and Advisory Council of the Public Library.

MOIDU VANIMEL is currently a senior reporter for a Malayalam daily. He has published an anthology of short stories. He is the recipient of the P. Karunakaran Award and the Madhava Kurup Award given by the Kozhikode Press Club.

K. L. MOHANA VARMA is a full-time writer with 30 novels and 22 other published works (short story collections, children's books, travelogues, etc.) to his credit. He writes in Malayalam and English. He also has a satirical column on social and political affairs in several papers in Kerala. He received the Sahithya Academy award for Ohari, the story of a takeover bid, which was selected as the most popular serious work in any Indian language in 1993. Many of his books have been translated into other Indian languages and a few have been made into movies. He has held the positions of chief editor of the largest selling children's magazine, Poompatta, and the secretary of Kerala Sahithya Academy.

CPSIA information can be obtained at www.ICGtesting.com
Printed in the USA
BVOW08s1926070816

458257BV00001B/2/P